A Place In The World

Cinda Crabbe MacKinnon

Multicultural Press

ISBN: 978-0-9888483-0-6 (softcover)

Cover design by Adriane Bosworth
Cover art by Martin Johnson Heade, "Hummingbird
Perched on the Orchid," 1901

"Cielito Lindo," Quirino Mendoza y Cortés, 1882
"Ode on Solitude," Alexander Pope
"Invictus," William Ernest Henley
"Las Cerezas," Hermanos Hermoso, 1965
"Perfidia," Alberto Domínguez, 1939

Map of Colombia produced by US CIA, 1985, University of
Texas at Austin

To my husband Tomas
My supportive partner in all things

ACKNOWLEDGEMENTS

Special thanks go to my editor, Judith Faerron, for her patience, tact and skill. I would also like to acknowledge author Anastasia Hobbet for advice and readings of the manuscript, and book designer Adriane Bosworth. Others I must include are Christian Zozaya, Sheri Davenport, Nona Mock Wyman, Jan Wissmar, Maya Rappaport, Janice Johnson, Harriette Heibel, Marianne Betterley, Jerry Ball, Carolin Crabbe and the readers at A Writer's Place.

I lived in Colombia at a different time than the setting for this book, so I consulted *compañeros*, coffee growers and other sources in the course of writing this novel over several years. I welcome the opportunity to correct any failure to acknowledge a person or source.

AUTHOR'S NOTE

I was inspired by the emerald beauty of Colombia and the warmth of my Latino friends and acquaintances in writing this novel. It is a work of fiction, and any resemblance to real people is coincidental, with one exception. A remarkable woman I knew as an adolescent served as a model for Carmen, but all scenes and dialogues are strictly imaginary. Likewise the pueblo of Escondido is a figment of my imagination. Some historical or political figures mentioned are of course real, and the Black Frost of 1975 is based on a real disaster in Brazil that ironically aided the Colombian coffee market.

Colombia is a land of contrasts with snow-capped mountains, rainforests, mighty rivers, plains, hot valleys and coastlines. This geography bestows it with great beauty and an incredible biodiversity. Sadly, Colombia has a long history of strife, including civil conflict, guerrillas and drug wars. In recent years, however, security has improved significantly and a reduction of violence and kidnappings has led to the growth of business, travel and tourism. Colombia appears to be on a path to recovery.

Colombia

PART I

A WOMAN WITHOUT A COUNTRY

1971-1973

He who knows what sweets and virtues
are in the ground, the waters,
the plants, the heavens,
and how to come at these enchantments,
is the rich and royal man.

Ralph Waldo Emerson

Chapter 1
EL EXTRANJERO

Though it was early afternoon, the mist still clung to the air, as if the clouds were reluctant to lift from the hills above the coffee fields. There is a reason this is called a cloud forest.

Alicia Carvallo cradled her coffee cup in both hands, warming her fingers and inhaling the fragrant steam spiraling off the top. The pearly green mug nested perfectly in her palms.

Carmen stood washing the lunch dishes and leaned towards the kitchen window.

"Someone's coming!" she exclaimed, wiping her hands on her apron. "I'll go see who it is!"

A visitor? They so rarely got visitors. The coffee *finca* was a day's drive from Bogotá on rough roads. Alicia craned her neck to see a figure, partly obscured by the haze and the bougainvillea, tying a horse to the post of the porch. She thought it might be a local. Curious, Alicia followed Carmen and they practically collided at the doorway to the living room.

1

"*Ay!*" Alicia cried, "*Perdon!*"

"Doña Alicia, *es un extranjero...un americano!*"

"*Un americano?*" Alicia knit her brow in disbelief.

Carmen gave an affable shrug with one palm up, "*Habla poco español*...and he's dirty. *Un joven.*"

Sure enough, he was. A rugged, young man with mud-spattered jeans and boots shook out his hat and looked at Alicia in surprise as she stared back equally astonished to find a fellow Anglo-Saxon — much less a sandy-haired cowboy — on her veranda. The tired-looking horse under the jacaranda tree heaved a sigh.

"Are you *doña* Alicia?" he said, as if this amused him.

She disliked looking younger than her age. Or maybe he was just surprised to find a light auburn-haired girl with blue eyes when Carmen said she would fetch the lady of the house.

"Yes I am," she assured him with mustered dignity as she extended her hand. "Alicia Carvallo."

"Peter Shalmers."

He looked like a poor *campesino*, but in this part of the country you are hospitable to travelers, foreigners, and fellow Americans — even a cheeky one. She hesitated only a moment to invite him in.

"Are you from the States? Forgive me...I wasn't expecting an American," he said.

So maybe not impolite, she thought.

"Yes," Alicia said again, "That's what one of my passports says." She smiled, remembering she now owned a Colombian passport as well.

He leaned one hand on the dark frame of the heavy door, the other held his hat at one hip. "I'm sorry to bother you, but I could use some help. My horse is limping and it doesn't look like she'll make it into town. I wonder if you have one I could borrow?"

Carmen hovered nearby, wide-eyed.

"*Por favor, vaya llame a don Felipe o don Jorge,*" Alicia told her.

"*No están,*" Carmen replied.

Oh. Of course, the men were already back in the *cafetal* — the coffee fields. They could be out for hours.

"Well, call doña Claudia then." Alicia needed someone to help her decide what to do with this bedraggled stranger. "*Y por favor,* bring *el señor* something to drink."

Turning to the visitor, she gestured for him to enter, "Come in, out of the damp."

Peter Shalmers stepped hesitantly over the threshold and onto the red tiles. He stood next to the white wall surveying the dark molding and ceiling beams as she draped his coat on a hook. He appeared about her husband's age or maybe older than Jorge by a year or two...so probably late twenties.

"What are you doing so far off the beaten track?" Alicia asked, still taken aback.

"I'm a prospector," he said, sprawling into a leather chair. His company had him exploring for gold in the mountains. He apologized for his appearance, said he'd ridden most of the morning and walked the last few hours to spare his horse...and he'd been sick.

Probably lost weight, Alicia thought, judging by the slackness of his jeans. Americans were always venturing into the tropics and getting sick. On top of that there were no roads up the mountain and it was still the rainy season.

"How long have you been up there?" she asked, combing her fingers through her long hair.

"Two weeks. Longer than I intended."

Carmen brought them a sweating pitcher of lemonade and Alicia wondered where she had set her coffee down. She poured a glass for him which he savored with eyes closed.

"Oh," remembering her manners belatedly, Alicia pointed to the bathroom, "would you like to wash up?"

"Yeah, I would, thanks."

She heard him retching a moment later, just as her mother-in-law came in, brow wrinkled, her mouth a small, startled "O."

"We may need to put someone up..." Alicia started to tell doña Claudia as the intriguing newcomer walked out.

He managed a drawn smile, "Howdy."

Claudia inundated him with questions, ignored his request for a horse, and then said firmly, "But young man, you must rest and get cleaned up. There is no place to stay in Escondido and you are not well."

Alicia took him to the spare bedroom, next to the one she shared with Jorge, and handed him a towel.

"You're in luck: the water might be warm." The water tank was heated by the sun, so she never showered in the morning when it was cool.

"You're very kind to put up a stranger," he murmured, looking now very tired and relieved, as if he'd given in at last to the state he was in.

4

"Ah...we're very hospitable!" she grinned. In truth the Carvallos got lonely and the rare visitor added a bit of excitement to their isolated lives.

She went to find Peter some of Jorge's dry clothes. When she returned, doña Claudia was trying to help him out of his jacket. He pulled back, both hands up, protesting, "I'm fine, really. Please!" but he smiled ruefully.

Carmen brought him some *sopa de pollo* and crackers on a tray.

He was already asleep when the men got back later in the afternoon. Alicia heard Carmen's excited voice out by the jeep and caught words..."dirty and bearded...lost, maybe *un accidente*."

Felipe and Jorge Carvallo came in and listened thoughtfully as Claudia and Alicia filled them in on the details.

No, no accident. Just a crazy American who doesn't know the cloud forest.

Jorge had a charming way of cocking his head, paying close attention as you spoke. He looked at his watch.

"Too late now. I'll fetch the doctor in the morning."

———

Jorge got up before Alicia, as he often did. He kissed her forehead softly, letting her lie there with her eyes closed. A minute later she heard the front door close behind him and the gravel crunch as he walked to the jeep.

"Hey! Hey, excuse me. *Por favor señor*, can I get a ride?" It was a loud determined voice, the new male in the household. Definitely not a Colombian. They rarely yelled.

Alicia went to the window and was startled to see the prospector—bare-chested and barefooted—accosting her puzzled husband, who grinned, put out his hand, and stated simply, "Jorge Carvallo."

The Carvallos agreed to drive Peter into town on the condition that Jorge would take him to the doctor, and then he was to return and stay for a day or two.

"At least until you're stronger," insisted doña Claudia.

"Yes, yes," her husband, don Felipe—ever the genial host—agreed. "Plenty of room, food, and drink. You rest and later we show you the finca, and Alicia can tell you *las maravillas* of the Colombian jungle!" Don Felipe's English was heavily accented and often sprinkled with Spanish.

Jorge slapped the American on the back and nodded in agreement.

Peter laughed, "You talked me into it...I'd like to spend another night."

"Is settled then," don Felipe beamed.

Dr. Benevides diagnosed "non-specific gastroenteritis," in other words, some kind of tropical bug.

"Traveling like you do young man, who knows what you may have picked up," the doctor mused. He prescribed antibiotics, bland food and bed rest as needed.

Doña Claudia added her own remedy: homemade yogurt and bananas. Don Felipe added beer, saying it

6

was full of vitamins and calories. "They gives it to peoples in *el hospitál* to gain weight," he explained.

Peter put up with the yogurt-banana regimen for lunch, but preferred Felipe's beer supplements. Alicia tried to imagine her own family taking care of someone they didn't know.

Meanwhile Paco, their long-time foreman, took care of the horse. He claimed the mare was faking the limp anyway. "She was just tired of walking in the rain with a man on her back."

Peter had rented the horse from a neighbor and Paco took her home, trailing his own shaggy pony.

———

True to their word, the Carvallos kept their guest entertained. The following day, when it was obvious that Peter was recuperating swiftly, they showed him around the finca and taught him about coffee.

"Colombia is the second largest coffee producer in the world...second only to Brazil," Jorge told him.

They walked between rows fragrant with coffee flowers. Alicia trailed along, followed silently by the finca's yellow watchdog.

"The more flowers, the more fruits," don Felipe said. "We calls them *cerezas*."

"Cherries," interjected Jorge. Felipe nodded, and pointed to a dark green seed. "The bean is inside. When they turn red, they are almost ready for harvest."

"Will you pick them soon then? Is it harvest season?" Peter asked.

"No season, really," don Felipe smiled, brushing his salt and pepper mustache in place. "We pick the cherries several times a year, at least two times between *diciembre y abril*, and also whenever they seems ready. Usually 'round *agosto*. But the cherries ripen continually, at the same time they start the new seeds."

Felipe's pronounced "pick" like "peek," and "several" sounded like "sebral." Alicia could see Peter struggling to follow her father-in-law's accent.

"We harvest more in the dry season. They have more ripe fruits then," Felipe said. "Is not rare to have flowers, green cherries and ripe ones all the same time. Is for that reason that the coffee is gathered always by hand...for not to damage the new fruits."

"The days are, more or less, the same length all year," Alicia added, "So there's a constant growing season."

Peter pondered this and startled everyone by asking, "What about tree rings then?"

It was Jorge who realized what he was talking about. "Ah yes, tree rings count the years in temperate climates, but I don't think we have them. Alicia, do you know?" And looking aside to Peter with a grin, "She is our biology major."

"No," Alicia confirmed, "Tropical trees don't usually have annual rings, because we don't have seasons. But some trees record wetter and dryer years."

"Did the first stock come from the jungle?" Peter asked, returning to the subject of coffee cultivation.

"Ah no!" don Felipe beamed, raising an index finger and then lowering it at Peter. "That's what many peoples think, but the coffee is not native to South America. It comes *originalmente* from Africa...and Arabia some peoples say, but probably..." he paused to ask Jorge how to say "Ethiopia."

"Look Peter," don Felipe added putting his hand on Peter's shoulder. "See the trees there in the center of the cafetal? Long time ago, when our Carvallo grandfathers cleared the land for planting, they did it a little by little, like *los indios* did."

Felipe spread his arms to take in the landscape. He told them a few fruit trees were left standing on each small plot and an occasional large tree was left for shade or because it was simply too big to take out. The cafetal thus had the pleasing effect of blending into the surrounding cloud forest. Of course the natural vegetation was constantly encroaching at the edges. "But sometimes this is where the most healthy and abundant crop is produced."

"Allowing the native trees and plants to remain probably makes Carvallo coffee more resistant to disease and infestation than the larger operations," Alicia speculated.

Don Felipe smiled at her tolerantly. "No, I think is because we take very good care of the land, and Finca Las Nubes is in the perfect location...it's too hot down in *el valle* and too cloudy and cool farther up *la montaña.*"

She didn't bother to point out that many banana plantations succumb to blight and insects when the balance of plants and animals was destroyed for a large mono-culture covering many hectares. Her opinion, after all, was from a female — and a young one at that. It was enough that they let her come with them, while Claudia stayed on the veranda.

It started to sprinkle so they headed back along the dirt track.

Peter asked, "What does the name mean...*Las Nubes?*"

"The Clouds," Jorge answered, waving at the sky, "Papi called it that because we are at the edge of the cloud forest."

It had been just Finca Carvallo for decades, before the young Felipe had put the new name up on the gate years ago, but the locals and the coffee buyers were just starting to use Las Nubes. As he grew older, however, don Felipe was reluctant to try new things or make changes. For example, he always sold to the same buyer and Jorge thought they were being fleeced.

"But it would be an insult to Rogelio Camacho if I sold to someone else," his father had protested.

Coffee was a boom-bust industry and the finca, like many others, was fighting to remain solvent.

"It's business Papi, the finca just broke even last year. We can't do that again. Let me talk to him," Jorge had urged when they first arrived. "Our workers will suffer as well."

The buyer did act offended when Jorge explained that they had to sell elsewhere to get more per kilo, but in the end he agreed to meet the higher price.

Don Felipe was elated, "Well, *hijo*," he'd said, clapping his arm around Jorge's shoulder. "All your business education is paying off if we turn a profit after all!"

These were rough years, but Carvallo coffee was prized even by lofty Colombian standards.

It was the height of the wet season and it rained every afternoon and sometimes most of the day. Alicia took Peter around again the next morning. The rain had stopped, although the grass was saturated and the paths muddy.

"Are those your mud boots?" he asked, pointing at her once-white tennis shoes, now drenched a rich deep brown.

"Well, I had some old shoes I used, but first they mildewed, and then when they dried out they were uncomfortable."

"Tough as an old piece of rawhide, huh?" He grinned.

At least she could wash tennis shoes occasionally.

"You need some good boots to live here. You should have some."

Could...should, Alicia thought. Boots were not a priority when she would soon need maternity clothes. And where was she to buy *that* way out here?

"They are not easy to find here," she said dismissively, but maybe she could get a pair of rubber boots like Paco wore.

"So, you're to tell me about the rainforest," he said. It was part question, part command.

"Actually I'm not an expert, there are so many species."

"Reckon no one knows that much."

"Especially about the canopy, because you can't get up there to study it very easily. But that's where it's really teeming with life."

Alicia told him about the diversity. Half of all of the flora and fauna in the world live in jungles — which occupy only a small fraction of the surface area. No one ever asked questions about her favorite subject and her enthusiasm poured out.

"In temperate climates you find associations of plants, like oaks and bay trees, and there may be dozens of allied plants, or even hundreds, but a diligent amateur can get a handle on it and identify them all."

"That's a fact," he agreed. "You might run into an oak or pine tree every fifty feet hiking in New Mexico, but here it seems you don't run into the same species twice. Either that or I don't recognize it." He grinned.

"No...you're right...there are millions of different species, so there are fewer of each individual."

He nodded, reflecting on the information. Alicia had not quite figured him out. He seemed bold, but kind...certainly not shy. Sociable, yet on the quiet side...an interesting combination of traits. He looked a lot better since shaving and bathing — attractive even, as Carmen pointed out that morning.

She sniffed an orange blossom as they walked back to the house. The fragrance was intoxicating.

"Hey, who's this?" Peter asked, seeing two little pet monkeys tied to long aluminum chains near a bubbling fountain. The male stood on two legs scratching his chest as they approached, checking to see if they were bringing food. He was almost two feet high in this pose. The monkeys lived in the beautiful courtyard surrounded by colorful vegetation, but they were a sad pair.

"This is José…careful he bites! They got him first, but he was so lonely that don Felipe brought him a mate. That's Juanita over there." Alicia pointed to the smaller monkey.

"Is he happier now?" Peter asked.

"I don't know, but Juanita is miserable. José is mean to her. He screams and chases her, even bites her."

The female came over and crouched near them putting up her hand, perhaps for food, perhaps as a greeting. José hissed at her. He looked vicious when he bared his teeth, much as a family watchdog can turn into a menacing monster with the same stance.

"I think they're homesick. They're from different places," Alicia said. "José is from the Amazon and Juanita is local."

"What about you, Alicia?" He surprised her. "Did you grow up here?"

"Are you comparing me to the monkeys?" she teased.

"No," his grin was partially hidden by a sandy mustache. "But curious. You said yesterday you have an American passport, but you're…part of the family?"

"I'm Jorge's wife…we live here. The others are just visiting."

"Ah! You're married! I thought you might be their daughter, but….well that explains it." He paused, "You married young. How old are you?"

There was that forward side of him leaping out, startling her, she thought, but answered lightly, "Married, twenty-two, and expecting." Somehow she felt this validated the matter.

Peter nodded in sober surprise, then smiled, "Married, huh?" He squinted one eye at her teasingly, as if it were a good joke. Alicia couldn't help but enjoy his comic faces, although in someone else it might have been offensive. It was hard to be put off by his sense of humor because he seemed so good-natured.

They were distracted by the cry of the small female monkey as the male pounced on her cruelly. It was painful to watch.

"Hey!" Peter yelled, waving his arms. Both monkeys scurried off with José chattering irritably. Peter shook his head, then grinned and dropped his jaw jokingly as an idea came to him. "Let's move her chain to give her a few feet to escape this domestic violence."

The male was furious when he could no longer pummel his mate. He jumped up and down, screaming at Juanita and pulling her chain, but she just lay down and let him tug. At least now she could get away from physical contact.

Why didn't I think of that? Alicia wondered.

"So finish your story...how long have you lived here?" Peter asked.

"At Las Nubes? Not very long. But in Colombia since I was a schoolgirl. My father worked for USAID...the Agency for International Development."

"Ah. So you were global nomads?"

14

"Yes!" she laughed. That was exactly right, they had moved every few years. "Until we came to Colombia when I was in seventh grade."

"Are your parents still here?"

"No, they left a few years ago...right after I started college."

They had lived in Colombia longer than anywhere else, and Alicia felt comfortable here. She had never lived in the States except for college.

"Then you came back and married your high school sweetheart?"

"Not exactly, but something like that. I thought I had a job."

Chapter 2
LA FAMILIA

A young man with wavy brown hair caught Alicia's eye over a sea of people at an off-campus party near the University of Virginia. He stood with one hand in his pants pocket, smiled and raised his glass. She smiled and nodded back. Protocol decreed that she avert her gaze, but she was aware of him watching her. Out of the corner of her eye she saw him walk over to Suzy, their hostess, and say something as he bowed over her. Suzy was in mid-sentence, but he smiled at her companions and took her elbow.

Suzy raised a hand and drawled, "Jeez-Louise, Jorge." He laughed and whispered in her ear.

Cupping the bend of her arm, Jorge escorted her around conversations and two dancing couples. He grinned at Alicia as if they were old friends who had not seen each other for a long while.

"Hello." He extended a warm hand. "Suzy? Introduce us," he said, without taking his eyes off Alicia.

"You seem to be doing very well on your own," Suzy said dryly. "Alicia, this is Jorge. He's a graduate student from the business school."

"Ah-LEE-see-ah," he said, pronouncing each syllable the way Latin Americans did—as all of her friends in Colombia did, and the way she preferred to the nasal, slurred North American pronunciation, "Al-isha."

He said his own name, Jorge Carvallo...something. She wasn't sure she caught the second surname, which would be his mother's last name. It sounded like Curtis. An English name? Alicia found herself distracted because he still held her hand in his—his palms as smooth as hers. She half expected him to kiss it.

"I'd tell you to be careful, but you should know what Latinos are like," Suzy said, winking at Alicia as she turned to go.

"Suzy tells me you speak Spanish."

"Uh, yes...I do. I...," regaining her composure she finished, "I lived in South America, until I came to college."

"Ah-ha. Colombia, *no*?" He knew something about her already. "We're practically kindred spirits you know—that's my country. That's why I wanted to meet you. Did you like it?" He tilted his head to the side, giving her his undivided attention.

"Yes I did, it's very beautiful." she smiled back, "I love the mountains. And the people."

"I'm glad." His smile was soft, but his gaze was intense.

"I cried when I left for college, and again when my parents left Bogotá and I realized I might never go back there again." Alicia surprised herself by telling him this, dropping her natural reserve. There was more than that of course, the feeling of being without a home. "This is the first time I've ever lived in the States."

He laughed. "You are as much of a foreigner as I am."

"Funny that we're meeting here, and not in Colombia."

"Ah, when you were in my country, I was here in yours, but here we both are." Jorge turned an open hand up.

He spoke English barely tinged with his Spanish background — Alicia had to listen carefully to hear it — but also with surprising Virginian vowels.

"You hardly have an accent," she told him.

"My American grandfather would be pleased to hear that...if he were still alive."

Jorge could adopt a southern inflection just as easily as a Spanish accent. Alicia realized she did this herself sometimes, depending on who she was talking to. It came from slipping between multiple ethnicities and adapting like a chameleon. Here was someone who knew the world beyond his own country, a man she was pretty sure would not ask her to watch American football — a game she did not understand.

"How did you come by an American grandfather?" Alicia asked.

"He worked on the Panama Canal. Married a *latina*."

Interesting, she thought, nodding as she twisted a tress of her thick hair.

"Would you like to dance?" he asked.

She hesitated because only one couple was dancing now but he reached for her hand, not waiting for an answer. He was so confident, Alicia thought, unlike herself. She smiled, not out of politeness, but because she could not keep from smiling if she had wanted to.

His movements were strong and rhythmic — of course, he was a *Latino*. She'd missed dancing with a good partner. He turned her, making her laugh, and then held her so close she thought she might get lipstick on his shirt. But she didn't mind, she didn't mind at all.

"You're beautiful," he whispered. She knew she wasn't really, or someone else would have told her by now, but it didn't matter. She only cared that this beguiling, captivating man was attracted to her.

They laughed and talked for hours before he drove her home well after midnight. Alicia fell in love with his charisma and warm personality, and that chocolaty-wavy hair.

They were culturally complementary, whereas she often felt uneasy with American men and their matter-of-fact, expectant and unromantic ways. Jorge was completely irresistible right from the start.

A year later, and less than a week after graduating, Alicia caught a flight from Washington, D.C., to Bogotá. She couldn't believe her luck. She would spend the summer working as a research assistant in tropical biology. Jorge had persuaded his father to use his connections to get her the job in Colombia. It was how things were done in South America. You had to know someone.

The plane skimmed over the emerald peaks of the Andes then crossed the Magdalena River valley. Her forehead riveted to the jet window, she took in the mountains and valleys that lay below like a huge piece of crumpled green velvet. Waterfalls cascading from the steep slopes were like streaks of vertical, cottony froth.

They flew over coffee *fincas* and towns with tongue-twisting names like *Facatativá*, *Fusagasugá* and *Zipaquirá*, where an old salt mine had been turned into an underground cathedral. The names, which delighted the lips as well as the ear, were not Spanish but Indian, mostly Chibchan.

Bogotá emerged, glistening from a recent rain that gave the buildings a fresh, whitewashed appearance. The capital was located on a high, green plateau, elevated almost 9,000 feet. Alicia knew this bit of geography, but now saw it clearly and marveled at the feat it had been for the *conquistadores* — a repugnant term, the "conquerors" — to march from the coast, through the jungle and up the steep slopes to reach the plateau. Monserrate came into sight; she'd once ridden the cable car up to the mountaintop chapel and the magnificent view. For someone without a place to be from, she felt like she was coming home.

Alicia spotted Jorge waiting for her in the terminal of the huge Aeropuerto El Dorado. He was leaning against a post with both hands in his pockets. She loved these stances of his. They hastened to each other grinning and she dropped her tote bag as Jorge crushed her to him and kissed her. They pulled back to look at one another and would have held each other longer, but his relatives crowded around them. Jorge's entire family must have come to greet her. Two full carloads: his parents, brother Pepe, his wife Marta, their three children, and an elderly grandmother.

But she had yet to meet the rest of his extensive family. The Carvallo clan included a slew of aunts and uncles, cousins and other relations Alicia would have to keep straight. She felt welcome, though somewhat overwhelmed, and stuttered over greetings as everyone chattered at once.

"*Bienvenida a la familia!*" Jorge's father, don Felipe, greeted her with a hearty embrace. Welcome to the family.

She looked up at Jorge, startled, but he just beamed and grabbed her bags. He'd told them Alicia was his fiancée. While a future probability, they'd manufactured the engagement story mostly to ease the minds of *her* parents while she lived with Jorge's family. But then in Spanish, the word for girlfriend, fiancée and bride are all the same — *novia*.

"*Gracias,*" she stammered.

"*Yo te recuerdo,*" Marta said as they brushed each other's cheeks. Pepe's wife had gone to the same small international high school as Alicia. She certainly remembered her — Marta was the Senior

21

Class Queen, a gentle beauty a year ahead of her. She was one of the Colombian students sent to the bilingual Anglo-American high school to learn English. Students without an English background often limped along. The American and European teachers gave them C's, but didn't have time to provide the linguistic attention they needed. They made up for it in classes taught in Spanish, where the foreigners lagged behind. But like many others, Marta barely learned enough English to carry on a conversation.

They piled into the cars. Alicia and Jorge held hands and exchanged surreptitious glances in the back of the car driven by don Felipe. They drove towards Bogotá, past the ancient Chibchan statues she remembered fondly. Squat, pre-Columbian stone figures with broad flat noses and wide mouths, usually showing large teeth that lent them either a fierce or comical appearance.

"I'm back! I'm back," a happy voice inside reveled. She caught don Felipe's eye in the rearview mirror when there was a brief pause in the conversation.

"Thank you for helping me get the job with *profesor* Talavera at the University."

"*¿Qué? Ah...sí, sí,*" he replied vaguely, with a wave of his hand. "We will have to introduce you, but first a *fiesta!* You must meet everyone. Now tell us — you have lived all over the world?"

"Well, a few countries." Her family lived in Iran, Greece, and Honduras before Colombia. They'd moved around and the children picked up languages from their nannies — *chinas*, as they were known in

Latin America. "But Jorge says you like Colombia best...no?

"Colombia is my favorite place...I feel like it is my home." Alicia tilted her head and smiled in recognition of the truth in this. In 1963, when her family arrived in Bogotá, Colombia was considered a precarious post. There had been a revolution a decade before and bandits roamed the roads at night. Nonetheless, Bogotá was an interesting and cultured city for the embassy crowd.

"My father applied for a second tour of duty and USAID approved, so we lived here longer than anywhere else."

Jorge squeezed her hand, "I've missed you," he whispered in her hair.

He'd left just two weeks ahead of her, but she beamed and whispered back, "Me too."

In the city they turned up a hill and passed a tiny Indian woman laboring up the grade under an enormous bundle of kindling.

"*Pobrecita, eh?*" Poor thing, Jorge murmured, noting the expression on Alicia's face.

The Carvallo home was an old colonial house in central Bogotá. A massive wall surrounded it, with broken glass cemented onto the top to keep out intruders. A splendid red trumpet vine graced the front gate.

Jorge's parents gave her the room next to theirs, on the opposite side of the house from Jorge. Don Felipe was welcoming and doña Claudia restrained, but gracious.

Doña Claudia was convivial compared to Abuelita. The grandmother was the elderly woman in

Pepe's car, a formidable dowager, spoiled by her children. She dressed in black, in deference to a husband who had died years before, and swept her wiry gray hair back into a tightly groomed bun.

"Does she speak Spanish?" Abuelita turned to her son, Felipe, as she appraised the foreigner. Alicia felt like she wasn't even there.

"*Sí, sí, lo habla bíen,*" he told her, but she continued to address Alicia through someone else. When Alicia spoke to her directly, she turned to Pepe as if she didn't understand and asked, "What does she want?"

Alicia and Jorge lounged together in a huge hammock in the back yard, staring up at the clouds in a pastel blue sky.

"Tell me about your American grandfather," she said.

Jorge turned out a palm. "His name was Mark Curtis and he was an engineer on the Canal."

So Jorge's full name was Jorge Carvallo Curtis. It was the norm to use both the father's and then the mother's surnames. A woman continued to introduce herself with her maiden name when she married, followed by her husband's name, as in Claudia Curtis *de* Carvallo. Alicia had thought it was a nice custom until it dawned on her that the "*de*" meaning "of," actually meant "belonging to."

"You know when the building of the canal was inherited from the French, Panama was still part of Colombia, no?" he asked.

"I guess most foreigners don't know the story, but I went to school here, remember?"

He disregarded her remark and went on. "Theodore Roosevelt and his advisors decided it would be much easier to build the canal if they didn't have to negotiate with Colombia. A revolution was instigated...it became a tradition of American intervention and orchestration of Latin American politics."

Alicia's parents did not view it that way, but she could see the Latino side.

"Abuelita is from an old Colombian family. They were indignant over American expansionism and the loss of Panama." Jorge laughed as he told her the next part of the story. "There was a Carvallo family schism when my *papi* wanted to marry *Mami*...a Panamanian-American."

"Because of her father's association with the canal?" Alicia asked.

"Actually, papi never told them...*that* is a secret to this day as far as Abuelita is concerned!"

Abuelita and her husband had never approved of Claudia and now her grandson had brought another American into the household.

———

Jorge crept into her bedroom that night as soon as his parents closed their door. A smile lit his face as he strode across the floor and buried his face in her neck.

"Finally," he murmured.

She sighed contentedly.

"I love your hair," he said, wrapping a curl around his fingers. "Blond."

"It's closer to brown," she said against his shoulder, remembering that here, as in many Latin American countries, light brown or reddish qualified as blond. Everyone loved a blond — especially where there were so few. In the States, all the girls craved long straight hair. Her curly, locks were not in style, but if Jorge liked them that was fine. That was good.

He pulled her towards the bed, "Ay Alicia..."

"We have to be quiet! This bed creaks!" Alicia stifled a laugh, aware of his parents in the next room.

Without a word Jorge yanked the mattress to the floor and lifted his eyebrows with a mischievous look. She dropped any argument and melted into him. His warm skin, the exact color of *café con leche*, contrasted harmoniously with her own. Their limbs intertwined like lianas — the wild vines of the emerald forests.

Afterwards they slept the blissful sleep of lovers, but Alicia woke him in the middle of the night.

"Get out now," she whispered." Go to your own room."

"No-o," he protested, more asleep than awake, and held her snugly.

"Yes! I love you, but you have to!" She nudged him out of bed and then out the door with one last sleepy kiss.

Then she rummaged through her bag for her birth control pills. When their love affair started last year she'd managed to get pills on campus. She was methodical about taking them. How could anyone forget when they were so important? Popping a blue pill in her mouth, she crawled back under the warm covers and slumbered contentedly.

Alicia dragged the mattress back in place and waited until she was sure Jorge had gone down to breakfast before leaving her room so she wouldn't feel shy on her own with his parents or — heaven forbid — Abuelita.

He looked up with a co-conspirator's smile as she came in. She blushed. They ate *pan dulce* with demitasses of *tinto*. Meaning "ink," the word aptly describes the black color of the espresso.

Don Felipe leaned his arms on the table. "So, what are your plans today?" he asked in his hearty voice.

Alicia brightened. "Well..." she started.

"Would you like to go to the market with me in a little while?" Jorge's mother asked her.

Alicia had hoped to contact the biology department about the job, but stifled her reluctance and smiled as she replied, "That would be nice."

She could hardly refuse Claudia's invitation and Jorge looked pleased. She would call the university later.

Doña Claudia's hair was streaked with silver and she was becoming portly. She looked like a well-dressed Colombian matron, except maybe a bit tall by Colombian standards. Only Claudia's hazel-green eyes attested to her father's North American heritage.

"You can see more of Bogotá that way."

Alicia was somewhat surprised that doña Claudia knew how to drive. Many Colombian women did not, relying on their husbands, sons, the bus system or, if they were wealthy, a chauffeur.

Forty-five minutes later the men gathered in the hall to send them off.

"Will you find the number for Professor Talavera while I'm gone?" Alicia whispered to Jorge.

"Have a good time!" he said.

Did he hear her? They were all smiling, laughing, saying goodbye.

Chapter 3
HARSH REALITY

Claudia rolled down the windows and her reserve melted away as she peeled down the hill, swerving when she glanced over to give Alicia a rare smile. The cool breeze ruffled her silvered coif. The clouds still clung to the mountains, but were lifting from the plateau.

"I like to drive. Sometimes I drive all morning," doña Claudia said. Alicia surmised this was her way of escaping Abuelita. Claudia ran errands in the morning and played golf or bridge in the afternoon.

When they arrived in the crowded downtown, a large truck was double-parked, slightly over the center line. There was just enough room to pass, but Claudia waited patiently. A line of cars formed behind them and a horn blared.

"Sorry," Claudia said serenely to the driver's side mirror. After several minutes a policeman arrived and commanded her to move. She shook her head smiling, surprisingly nonchalant.

"*Pero señora,* you have room!" he objected.

Claudia was carefree on the open road, but apparently recognized her limitations in tight spaces.

"Sorry," she repeated pleasantly, "I can't do it."

Alicia coerced her face into a smile and fiddled with a strand of hair. The other drivers shouted and honked, but Claudia waited, seemingly oblivious to the havoc she created.

The policeman raised his palms to shoulder height and looked skyward. He paced a moment and then, standing on the running board of the truck, leaned inside the window and laid on the horn. A few minutes ticked by before the truck driver finally returned, jogging. A heated exchange ensued between the policeman, hands on hips, and the driver, arms gesticulating, before the man climbed into the cab and with a final yell, moved his vehicle. Alicia let out an inaudible sigh of relief.

At the market, doña Claudia clutched her purse under her arm and advised Alicia to do the same. Alicia trailed close behind her as dozens of scruffy children thrust cupped hands at them, begging. This was something she always found difficult. So many street urchins, and if you stop to give change to a few you are quickly mobbed.

This happened to her when she first moved to Colombia as an adolescent. Her heart had gone out to several thin youngsters dressed in soiled rags. As she dispensed coins into dirty palms, a throng of children surrounded her and became angry when she ran out of money. She'd hurried down the street in a frenzy with the ragamuffins trailing her, some tugging at her clothes and begging, others hurling abuse. Maybe this was one reason why not many well-to-do *colombianas* did their own marketing.

The market was festive — her grandmother's generation would have called it "gay," but that word was developing an entirely different connotation now. Some locals call it a *feria*, a fair, instead of a *mercado*.

Indigenous people in their traditional round, dark hats and shawls, or *ruanas*, were there to buy, sell and socialize. The onion people lined up across from the potato ladies, where Claudia and Alicia stopped to buy some small, round *papas* to roast. Live chickens, oval loaves of bread and freshly cut flowers overflowed from the stalls. Doña Claudia scooped up an armful of hydrangeas and bargained with a boy over a few pesos.

"*Sí señora*, these were freshly cut this morning."

"*No, no*, too much," she said, one hand stopping the air, as the other tried to return the blue flowers. The boy thrust them back at her and they bartered some more before they both shrugged and finally agreed on the price. Smiling, he touched the tip of his felt hat.

"*Gracias, señora*. Come back next week. I will have *rosas* for you."

"*Gracias*," Claudia smiled back.

On the way home they saw an old Indian woman trudging up the hill. Whether it was the same one they had seen yesterday or a different one Alicia could not tell, but the burden on her back was as large as she was.

To her surprise, doña Claudia stopped the shiny Cadillac with a jerk, and in her pastel dress, stockings and high-heels, opened the trunk for the woman to place the bundle, which turned out to be wood and kindling tied with a worn and dirty string. The bundle was so large Claudia didn't try to shut the trunk.

She opened the back door to help the woman in. The *indigena* wore the ubiquitous black hat and well-worn sandals made of straw or raffia. Muscular brown calves peeked out underneath a dark woven skirt. She settled on the seat, weathered hands folded on her tummy, and peered at the shiny doorknob, lock and windows. She looked tired, but her face was a crinkle of smiles. Alicia beamed in wonder at this side of Mrs. Carvallo.

They passed the turnoff to the Carvallo home and continued to the top of the steep hill before lurching to a stop. The woman stared at the door and fumbled at the latch.

Alicia popped out and opened the door saying, "Here you are." She helped retrieve the wooden burden, which no doubt would fuel a fire for cooking and warmth tonight.

"Gracias," the woman said, inclining her head gravely. She walked, bent over with her load, to Claudia's open window.

"You are kind, señora. May God repay you as I cannot."

Doña Claudia, equally gracious, replied, "God has already paid me."

"May he bless you then."

The polite exchange was a social ritual, although the woman was genuinely appreciative. It would have been impertinent to get out of the car with a mere "thanks" tossed over the shoulder.

Doña Claudia careened down the hill, retracing their path. Alicia tightened her grip on the armrest and glanced over to see if she was using the brakes at all. Nope...not until she turned the corner, tires screeching, half on the wrong side of the street.

When it came to her untamed driving, Claudia was truly a Latina. A seeming contrast to her earlier caution on the crowded street, the two examples were opposite ends of the same problem: she was a lousy driver. Alicia exhaled thankfully when she got out to open the gate. Claudia also got out and removed bits of twigs and debris from the trunk.

"Don't mention this, will you?"

Alicia thought for a moment she meant her driving, but doña Claudia added, "don Felipe and Abuelita don't like me to pick up wood in the car."

Their eyes met and Alicia gave her a genuine smile, "Don't worry, I won't."

Her initial impression of Jorge's mother had been one of reserve, and she was not wrong. The invitation that morning was a privilege.

Claudia rarely invited her again, but Alicia understood and liked her, especially away from the watchful eye of the family. At any rate, she didn't relish getting into a car with Claudia anytime soon.

They shared something, both being women without countries. Both born to American parents...both—except for college—never having lived in the States…both feeling more comfortable in Latin America.

That evening Alicia caught Jorge alone in the hall. "I need to talk to Professor Talavera about the job," she said.

"All in good time, *mi vida*. Don't rush these things." Jorge and his father were too cavalier about her job.

"I'm not rushing things, I feel like you're putting me off. Could you get me his number? I want to call at least."

He stared at her impassively a moment.

"*Eh, Jorge?*" doña Claudia called from downstairs.

"*Sí Mamá*, I'm coming."

He didn't get around to finding the number and Alicia had some trouble getting it herself in the morning. The operator gave her the main University number, but when she got through, she had to call two different departments. Finally she obtained Professor Talavera's number then wasted a day-and-a-half calling, with no answer.

Jorge was leaning against the hall, arms folded.

"Alicia. Look, don't get your heart set on this job…"

"What!" she interrupted him. "What do you think I'm doing here?"

"I hope you came to see me and meet my family, not just for some job."

It was just as well she was rendered speechless when Claudia walked by the doorway to the living room.

Twenty minutes later, Alicia dialed the biology department again and told the secretary her problem getting hold of the *profesor*. Yes, she said, he was in this week.

"Does he have office hours?"

"*Qué?*" she responded, as if Alicia had said something odd. The woman had a harsh voice for a receptionist. Nasal. Was there a different term besides "*horas de oficina?*"

"When can I catch him?"

"Best after class, I imagine. Or maybe before," she said in a tone so grating that Alicia held the phone away from her ear. How was this strident voice chosen to answer the calls?

"Could you tell me when his classes are?"

The woman heaved a heavy sigh, "Hold please. I have another call to answer."

———

Alicia decided to take a bus across town, and camped out at the door to the professor's office for almost two hours. She was leaning against the doorjamb when Professor Talavera arrived, keys in hand. He was a short, stocky man with a dark, slightly pocked-marked complexion.

"*Buenas tardes.* I'm Alicia Collier." They shook hands and he motioned to a chair.

"*Por favor,*" he said politely. "*¿Como está?*" Not a flicker of name recognition. Folding his chubby hands over his stomach, Talavera waited attentively for her to state her business.

She explained she'd come about the job. His face was blank.

"I believe *señor* Felipe Carvallo set something up for me," Alicia said in what she hoped was a confident voice.

"I know Felipe Carvallo, of course," he said slowly, "but...what job is this?" He tilted his head questioningly. Even though recent events had prepared her for this, her heart sank.

Then he went on, "Oh...yes. He did say something to me about an American girl looking for summer work."

"I'm willing to do most anything," she said, hoping he would not ask her if she typed. Suzy had once advised her to never admit to it unless she wanted to be a typist. "But, I would love to help you with tropical research."

There was no job.

"If there was work, I would have to offer it to my graduate students first, you see?"

Alicia could kick herself. She'd spent good money to come back to Colombia under false pretenses. She should have insisted on the address and written personally, of course, instead of letting Jorge put her off.

"May I leave my resume in case something turns up?" She'd sent don Felipe a resume to pass along, and now suspected it might still be lying around the Carvallo house.

"Of course," he smiled, but his shrug indicated mere politeness.

Disappointment and rage seethed through her, mingling with the acrid diesel fumes from the buses on her long ride back to the Carvallo's. But whom could she be mad at except herself? She'd trusted

Jorge, who had taken his father's word — probably just an offhand remark, "She could get a job at the University." She could imagine it now, Felipe giving Jorge a positive impression and Jorge magnifying a positive picture for her because he wanted her to come.

Hadn't she lived in Latin America long enough to realize that nobody ever likes to say no? So they say yes...maybe...sure — wanting to help, wanting to be nice, whether it causes more trouble and confusion in the long run or not. And you are expected to be equally polite. You cannot confront someone who merely wishes they could help you. And the truth was a woman's job was not seen as important as a man's.

And then there was her own part in all this. Hadn't she had an inkling of doubt all along?

She was compelled to wait until that night to talk to Jorge alone. She'd never spoken angry words to him before.

"How could you tell me you had a job lined up for me?" The wrath and exasperation in her voice was muted by the need to keep their voices low.

"I didn't say that exactly. I said Papi could get you one...I thought he could." His shoulders lifted a moment in the slightest shrug.

"I came here for the job! You let me believe I had work at the university."

"You're disappointed. I'm sorry it didn't work out," Jorge turned out his hands at hip level. He was a model of reason and composure.

"Disappointed! I'm devastated. How can you not understand how exciting it was to have this job right out of college?"

He tried to put his arms around her. "You wanted to come back to Colombia—at least you got that," he finished lamely.

Alicia disentangled herself. She wanted to be alone, to stew. Now she would have to start from scratch, hardly a *peso* in her pocket nor a reference on her resume. Her only plan had been to gain experience in tropical biology and count on that leading somewhere. Now she had no plan.

She didn't know what to do next or even where to go. Back to Virginia? Just because her parents lived there or because she went to the university there? That was her only tie to the place. Her parents would not be thrilled if she moved in with them either. She really was a person without a country, without a place to be from or a home to go to.

Bogotá did not have employment in her field. So, should she look for something else—anything else?

"No, no. What for? We'll be back in the States in the fall," Jorge reasoned. He put his hands on her shoulders. "*Mi vida*. You can stay here all summer. My parents want us to. You don't need any money."

Alicia hated that he was so nonchalant, and she was angry with herself for not following up. She had wanted this so much she'd not questioned if the position seemed too good to be true.

Did she overestimate her capabilities? It was hard to be self-confident when her parents had never encouraged her ambitions. Her father thought education was something of an indulgence for a woman—"she was just going to get married anyway." And now she realized Jorge had merely humored her.

He had a plan at least—to go back to UV and finish his MBA. She might leave early and look for a job there. Maybe the University of Virginia would hire her. Maybe she would go to graduate school herself. But it was too late to apply for admittance for this year, much less for funding.

———

Alicia swallowed her pride with difficulty. Meanwhile the Carvallos distracted her with social events. They attended parties in Bogotá and Bucaramanga, or anywhere else they visited. Plus they went out dancing with Pepe and Marta. Live bands played every night at the Tennis Club or the Country Club, as well as discos and nightclubs. Alicia remembered this social life from high school—you didn't have to be twenty-one to get a drink.

She made an effort to get over her disappointment, a disappointment no one else seemed aware of. But it was a hard lesson in responsibility.

Alicia decided she should go back to the States. What had she been thinking? It was almost July now, but maybe she could still find some sort of summer job. She could change her ticket, although there was a penalty fee she could ill afford. She did not want to continue to live off the Carvallos even though no one seemed to mind, or notice for that matter.

On the other hand, Jorge, Marta and don Felipe urged her to stay. Alicia sensed an unspoken expectation that she should not leave before her fiancé. And the family was holding an engagement party in their honor at the Country Club—even though there had been no old fashioned proposal to say yes or no to.

Alicia and Jorge had discussed marriage as a casual eventuality only a few weeks ago. While she was contemplating her future, thinking what she was going to do for a job, considering whether to go to grad school, and how marriage fit all these combinations, their engagement swept forward with popular support. She was dazed by the celerity of these events.

Jorge, Pepe and don Felipe bought orchids for the four women—wives, mothers and sweetheart. The three Carvallo men danced with Alicia and every female member of the household, as well as female friends. But she was slightly surprised when don Felipe asked Abuelita to dance, because his elderly mother had to be helped in and out of cars, chairs and up steps by a man on each arm.

The withered old lady practically hobbled from her seat, but by the time she reached the dance floor she had transformed herself into a younger woman. Abuelita's spine straightened and she pulled herself tall as her body remembered a syncopated rhythm. Her hands clapped and her face registered the passion of the tropics. Her hips gyrated and shoulders swayed to the sensual beat. The Carvallo table applauded and Jorge and Pepe hooted "Abuelita, Abuelita!"

She acknowledged the accolades with a tilt of her head and the flare of her nostrils, and only the ghost of amusement on her face, but she kept her eyes looking down along the line of her arm to the elbow. A classic, almost flamenco pose. The matriarch, a dancer.

Alicia had missed Latin music. She felt it summon her body movements and wanted to dance to every song. The cha-cha, rumba and cumbia could all be done, or faked, with a good partner. And Colombians are all good partners — good dancers, without taking themselves too seriously. They came to have fun, to flirt. Jorge and Alicia danced and laughed together and with his friends and relatives.

Dancing was also socially sanctioned teasing, intimate in nature. It was acceptable to look at your partner in a manner that would be suggestive in other circumstances. A harmless flirtation. Even don Felipe held her closer than necessary. It didn't bother her until a handsome friend of Jorge's whispered in her ear throughout a slow tune, crushing her orchid.

When she sat down, Jorge asked irritably, "What was he saying to you? Why were you dancing so close?" And before Alicia could reply, he added, "Just don't let Miguel take advantage of you."

"Ah, Jorge has picked another flower," was how Miguel greeted her. *Another*. But then Alicia already discerned her own green dragon. Irene, Jorge's old flame, was still carrying a torch for him, judging by the adoring looks she bestowed on Jorge and the chilly glance she gave Alicia when she extended her limp hand briefly.

Irene was buxom, but trim — petite even in four-inch heels. She wore her black hair in a sophisticated French braid, her nails were frosted to perfection and her black eyebrows carefully shaped. Like most Latin women she lined her eyelids, making her wide eyes appear even larger.

"Watch out for that one," Marta advised, just as Pepe extended a hand to invite Alicia to the dance floor. She didn't need the warning.

While Alicia danced with Pepe, she observed Irene glide over to Jorge and lean over in her low-cut dress. As she watched over Pepe's shoulder, Irene moved seductively, her eyes glued to Jorge's as they danced. A moment later, he laughed at something Irene said, enjoying the attention as they waited for the next number.

They were deep in conversation as they danced again and Pepe escorted Alicia back to Marta. When the music ended Irene flashed a grin and begged Jorge to keep dancing, but he smiled and firmly led her by the elbow, under protest, back to her seat.

Chapter 4
MILES FROM NOWHERE

Alicia had been in Colombia just over two weeks when she missed her period. She waited to see what her body would tell her. She'd read somewhere that flying sometimes upsets a woman's cycle. She put off telling Jorge until after the party.

"But Alicia you couldn't be pregnant...you are on the pill. Did you miss any?"

"No, but I've never missed a period before."

"Well, aren't women late sometimes?"

"Sometimes."

But she was as regular as the phases of the moon, so she didn't change her ticket for an earlier flight. In mid-July she said, "Jorge, I have to find a doctor. I'm over a month late now." Although she knew it was hard for a doctor to tell before the third month, she needed to find out as soon as possible.

"Why are you so distraught? We are getting married anyway."

"I'm distraught because I came here for an interesting job, and we're just partying and...and now..." She was on the verge of tears and choked on her words.

"We're having a good time, no?" he asked softly.

"Of course we are having a good time! That's not the point!"

His face clouded at her tone, but she went on, "Things are just happening to me...I feel like I've lost control over my life!"

Jorge took her by the shoulders and smiled, "Alicia do you love me?"

"Yes," she nodded miserably, and let him hold her.

"Look, I don't think you are pregnant, but either way everything will be fine."

————

In August, she sat across from a doctor with a chiseled, granite face and the usual black mustache, neatly trimmed. Dr. Julian Zaramosa was "ninety percent sure" she was expecting a baby. Alicia could tell he disapproved of her.

"But what about the birth control pills?" she asked lamely.

"We don't prescribe pills to unmarried women here," he said matter-of-factly. He sat behind his massive desk, in a posture of bored self-assurance, his fingertips touching, his head leaning to the side as if she made him so weary he could barely support it.

He sighed and suggested she was probably inconsistent in taking the pills, but Alicia immediately objected. She was absolutely certain that was not the case.

"Well then, perhaps you had a stomach flu or food poisoning that interfered with absorption," he concluded.

A faint memory flared in the back of her mind — a ghastly upset stomach just after finals. She had blamed left-over Chinese food, or maybe a bad case of nerves, and not given it another thought.

"Yes," she mused, "maybe so."

Dr. Zaramosa shrugged. She resolved to find another doctor.

"We'll get married! This solves everything!" Jorge proclaimed.

"What? How? What does it solve?" she cried. He was so cavalier! She was desperate for a solution. There was so little time for any decision. Cautiously, Alicia hinted at the possibility of an abortion.

"Don't even think about it! It is illegal, it's dangerous. It is wrong! I would never allow it!" But then in a more tender tone he said, "Don't worry *cielita*, I will take care of you. You will see. I'll always take care of you." And he kissed her.

It could have been worse. He was saying exactly what every girl in trouble wanted to hear, but Alicia saw her future floating away like a cloud over the mountains, without her. What was she going to do? What would her dishonored family say?

She racked her brain for answers, but it was as if her fate was caught in some reckless, unpredictable current, spinning out of control.

The word for pregnant in Spanish is *"embarazada."* She thought that sounded subliminally appropriate.

Even though they presented their hasty wedding plans as a spontaneous decision, Alicia was embarrassed in front of Jorge's family.

Claudia said not a word, but her back seemed straighter. Alicia did not blame her if she was unhappy with the situation. She was hardly thrilled herself. Felipe appeared delighted and congratulated them jovially with big hugs. Marta was also excited — and maybe naive enough to believe the story.

"We'll be sisters," she told Alicia.

Alicia gave her a feeble smile and sighed quietly. On the bright side, she was lucky with this family. Jorge was a kind and caring man and they were in love. It would work out.

When Alicia finally got through to her parents on the phone they demanded that she come home. She avoided any reference to her expectant state, but they must have realized.

"You promised, Alicia, you promised...if we let you go...," her mother reproached.

Let her go? "I'm almost twenty-three, not eighteen," Alicia reminded her, but gently.

Her parents refused to come to the wedding. Were they thinking that if they didn't, she'd come back...that it would not be true that their daughter had to get married. This never happened in her old-fashioned family. They were mortified. She knew her mother was worried about what her relatives and friends would think.

"Let me talk to them," don Felipe said with calm assurance the following day. He paced before the phone for a minute, his lips moving, choosing the English words carefully, selecting this one, discarding that. The call didn't go through right away. Colombia had a high quality phone system compared to many Latin American countries, but still it sometimes required patience to wait out dead lines, wrong numbers, false busy signals and an operator who droned, "Would you try your call later?"

Alicia, Jorge and Felipe took turns trying again and again all morning, until they managed to make a connection. Alicia was glad it was Felipe who finally heard an American voice at the other end. He talked to both of the Colliers at length, was gentle, persuasive, understanding, but still they would not come. It was inconceivable to him.

"Of course, perhaps you want to have the wedding in the States?"

Felipe shook his head and looked at Jorge sorrowfully. After he hung up, he whispered to Jorge, palms spread out, "How can they not come to their own daughter's wedding?"

Jorge lifted his shoulders and also shook his head, "They are mad at her, I guess."

"I am so sorry," Felipe told her, as though it was somehow his fault.

He felt sorry for Alicia, as if she were an orphan. And in a way she was—future communication with her parents would be merely Christmas cards. From that day forward don Felipe treated her with tenderness, as though she were his own daughter.

Alicia was accepting. She had not been anticipating her parents' support. She knew what they were like and what was expected of her — a formal, family-approved engagement. She only felt bad that the Carvallos were footing the bill. She drained the last of her savings for a becoming, but unassuming dress.

Under the circumstances Alicia wanted a small wedding — after all there was no one on her side of the family and her few American friends could not afford the trip on short notice. She invited only a couple of high school friends. But the Carvallos composed an invitation short list of one hundred. The family members alone totaled almost seventy and the rest were friends who *had* to be invited.

She wanted to be wed on Monserrate — the 10,400-foot peak that overlooks the center of Bogotá. The logistics of getting over a hundred people up the mountain were difficult enough, not to mention booking the popular 17th century church.

It takes over an hour to climb the steps and there were too many guests to fit in the cable cars. In spite of all of this, Jorge made it happen. His family pulled strings to squeeze in the ceremony between two other weddings booked months in advance. The older guests crowded into the cable cars, the younger ones walked up the mountain path — even the women in high heels.

It was a beautiful morning, but by afternoon threatening clouds had gathered. They did not burst until the bride and groom had almost arrived at the reception, and Jorge and Alicia took that to be a propitious omen. When the downpour hammered their limousine they laughed and ran inside together under a large umbrella. It did not matter that her gown was damp and the hem mud-spattered. They danced and accepted champagne toasts to their health and long lives together.

"*Amor, salud y pesetas!*"

———————

There was yet another surprise when she asked Jorge about their return flight arrangements to the U.S.

"I've decided we are not going back to Virginia."

"We're not?" she repeated dumbstruck.

"No. I don't want to finish my MBA. I don't need it here. Papi wants me to run the coffee finca."

Another shift in plans, just like that. He could have talked to her about it, but she did not really want to go to Virginia anyway. She was learning to be flexible.

"Now I don't have to worry about the draft either," he added.

The Carvallos still fretted over Vietnam, but Alicia had not been too uneasy, even when they started drafting college students. Jorge owned a Colombian passport. He could always go home if it came to that. He did not have to participate in a war he opposed.

The Carvallos suggested that they live at the coffee finca in the mountains. Don Felipe spent a third of his time there. Sometimes his sons accompanied him and now and then his wife, but it was an all-day drive and it would be helpful to have someone there full-time.

Jorge had some doubts—it was so remote—but Felipe needed a business manager and persuaded him. Alicia suspected the very remoteness was the idea—the bride's pregnancy would soon be obvious. But she was ready to try it. A home nestled in the Andean cloud forest would be a welcome refuge after recent taxing events.

When Alicia first laid eyes on the finca she fell in love with it. It was lower in elevation and thus warmer than chilly Bogotá, but did not suffer the torrid heat of the lowlands. Las Nubes occupied the pleasant transition zone between the cloud forests where the orchids grew, and the tropical jungle.

The house was almost as large as the Carvallo's home in the capital, but unpretentious, pastoral. A veranda partially encircled it and a profusion of vivid bougainvillea draped the railings on one side. Even the red tiled roof nurtured occasional impatiens or small ferns that managed to take root, so that the whole structure nestled into the surroundings.

Alicia could lie in a hammock on the veranda and read, or walk along the rutted paths that led through the coffee plants and into the forest. She was enchanted by the courtyard, graced with its ancient stone fountain, lush begonias and ferns and the two monkeys—although it bothered her that they were on long chains.

She was comfortable here. She could wear slacks or even shorts if she wanted and didn't have to worry about make-up or manicures. In Bogotá she was expected to be immaculately groomed and well-dressed, and pants were not well accepted. Until recently, only *putas* wore pants in public. Alicia did not have to feel like a guest here, as doña Claudia had never claimed this house. Las Nubes was merely an occasional retreat to her.

"Your mami will come more often now that you and Alicia are here," Felipe told Jorge.

"You're doing fine," was all Claudia said to her, nodding her head with a faint smile.

The first morning, Alicia picked oranges, surrounded by the fragrance of citrus blossoms. The aroma followed her as she carried the basket full of ripe fruit into the kitchen.

"*Ay*, I will pick them for you," Carmen, the maid, protested.

"I like to," Alicia explained.

Carmen shrugged. "*Bueno*, but let me prepare them." She was playing her part, but Alicia insisted and Carmen let her squeeze them into juice for the breakfast table.

Carmen was a solid woman, her thick dark hair neatly pinned in a roll at the base of her neck. She seemed to enjoy Alicia's company, for she spent much of her time alone when the Carvallos were not at the finca. In fact, she practically talked Alicia's ear off, mostly about her one-year-old, Humberto. But she was a good-humored person and Alicia did not mind at all.

Alicia kept the house filled with flowers. There was always bougainvillea, heliconia, roses and other blossoms Alicia could not name waiting to be picked.

One favorite, a creamy lily, flaunted large but delicate petals, like magnolias. The cream turned pale pink near the center and developed into bright magenta stripes in the interior. Its dark purple stamen drew her in like the pollinating bees it was designed to attract. The stamen encircled a pistil that stood erect as the pollen receptacle for the swollen ovary. She once observed insects gyrating libidinously in the pollen they would thereafter relinquish on another flower's pistil.

"You love flowers," Jorge commented, sniffing the beauty of the bouquet Alicia was arranging in a vase. They gazed at each other, their eyes communicating in the confidential way couples do, portraying more than words, more than smiles.

The day was surprisingly sunny and warm, so Alicia dressed in shorts to explore while Jorge was off working. The finca's dog followed her at a discrete distance, but when she stopped and turned around the mutt stopped too. He was a yellowish-tan color, ordinary looking except for his soft brown eyes. She squatted and the dog lowered his head cautiously.

"Who are you?" she spoke to him *sotto voce*, "Come here."

He approached her slowly, wagged his tail for an instant, and then sat down a couple of yards away. "Okay," she told him and walked on. The dog followed, but stood still whenever she paused to look at something.

"*Como se llama el perro?*" What's the dog's name? She asked the foreman.

"*Nombre? No tiene nombre, señora.* He is just *Perro,*" Paco replied smiling, rubbing his forehead before putting his hat on and going back to work.

The shiny leaves of the coffee bushes extended above her head. She sniffed at some of the low-hanging white flowers and red cherries that decorated the limbs, detecting an aroma all their own—not at all like brewed coffee, but still rich, sweet and moist.

She entered the forest and the coffee finca vanished behind her after the first twenty-five feet. Her bare legs waded through deep vegetation—not without some trepidation of spiders, insects and poisonous snakes—as her tennis shoes sank into the dark, reddish ooze.

Ropy lianas draped every tree with magically twisted vines, and tender foliage competed with other greenery for space and light in the understory. Every square foot held a new fascination: a patterned leaf, an exotic flower or a brilliantly colored insect to behold. A flamboyant, blue-green caterpillar with yellow spines zigzagged along a wet philodendron. Alicia discovered striped watermelon plant, peperomia, and monstera—sold as house plants all over the world. She even found a delicate flowering begonia that caused her jaw to drop in delight.

The cloud forest was a treat for the senses beyond the visual display—the moist scent of ripe vegetation, the sounds of birds trilling and numerous other unidentifiable noises. Was that an animal scurrying through the treetops or just the wind moving the branches far above her? Even the sound of a large, dry leaf falling tens of feet could be perplexing, sounding like an animal scratching a limb high overhead.

Many of the gigantic trees sported huge buttresses at their bases—a six-foot diameter was not uncommon. They might be mahogany, kapok or balsa trees, but with their leaves, fruits, and flowers over a hundred feet in the air even a botanist would have a hard time identifying them at ground level. She craned her neck, but beyond fifteen feet the individual branches became lost in a maze of green, making it hard to unravel which leaf belonged to which stem or branch. And the lofty canopy left everything in deep shadows.

Alicia tramped for over half an hour without getting very far. Should she carry on still deeper into the jungle? She was tempted, now that she was this muddy, but realized it might be difficult to retrace her steps if she went farther. Sobered by this thought, the lack of light suddenly disturbed her. Alicia had been so absorbed in the myriad botanic details that she had not been as prudent as she should.

She followed the sound of a stream trickling nearby. Next time she would track it into the forest and back out. Eventually she saw sunbeams shining down on the coffee plants beyond the edge of forest like a beckoning lighthouse.

Carmen was appalled to see her as Alicia took off her muck-caked shoes at the back door. She was spattered with dark mud, and sticky tendrils of green clung to her hair.

"*Ay Díos!*" Carmen cried, hands to either jaw — and took off, bosom bouncing, to fetch Jorge from inside the house. Not only was Alicia filthy, but her skin was covered with tiny red bites.

"What on earth happened to you?" Jorge exclaimed.

"Nothing," she smiled, "I just went exploring."

"It's dangerous out there, Alicia. This is not your parents' back yard in Virginia...or even Bogotá. You should have at least told someone."

"Oh, but, Jorge.... I had such fun! This is a biologist's dream." Wide-eyed, she shook her head in slow wonder. Living here helped make up for the lost job.

She had not told them where she was going because many people did not understand the allure of the jungle. They thought of it as a perilous place to be avoided or conquered rather than a marvel to be studied. But next time she would dress appropriately and be more cautious.

He shook his head for a different reason, but a ghost of a smile flickered on his face.

She examined the little red dots on her bicep. She'd not felt the tiny coffee bugs bite, nor did she itch much, but she looked like she had a mini version of measles. The coffee bugs would give her away every time she ventured very far beyond the house.

Chapter 5
THE MORE, THE MERRIER

"Whoa," said Peter, shaking his head at the monkeys. "A wife beater."

"Ignore José and he'll simmer down," Alicia said, but then added thoughtfully, "You know what they might really like?"

Peter nodded for her to continue.

"They would be much happier if they could reach the trees." Why didn't she think of this before? They only had some bushes and the metal pole with a crossbar at the top to climb on.

Peter made a face, lifting his eyebrows and tapping his temple with two fingers. Alicia laughed.

Felipe pulled at his salt-and-pepper mustache when they suggested this. He was reluctant because he wanted to be able to see them from the veranda, not have them hiding in the bushes.

"They will still come to the fountain for water," Peter said.

"OK, we will try it," don Felipe agreed and was pleased by how the monkeys perked up. They raced up the branches, swinging by their tails and running hand over hand, foot over foot.

"It's true what you say Alicia, they are meant to play in the trees."

Two small, human-like faces peered at them through the leaves and José made a noise that sounded like, *"uuh, uuh."*

"Maybe he's thanking you," Peter laughed.

———

Their guest stayed for almost week and looked much better after taking antibiotics. Peter already appeared to have put on a few pounds and was losing the gaunt look he had when he'd arrived. Meanwhile Pepe and Marta arrived for a visit.

A trip into Escondido for food turned into an adventure when the five younger adults piled into the jeep. Normally Jorge took Carmen and Alicia shopping, but now Pepe and Marta wanted to come as well to show Peter the sleepy town. Pepe drove the jeep.

The usually merry Carmen was grumpy when it appeared there wasn't room for her. It was her job and her privilege. "I'm the one who does the shopping," she protested.

"But if we take you, we won't have room for the food!" Jorge winked and smiled, charming her. He promised to get everything on the list and something for her too.

"Don't forget the *chayote*," was her final begrudging lament as they drove off. The yellow dog trotted after them past the magenta bougainvillea, down the rutted road for fifty yards before stopping and gazing at the vanishing vehicle.

Peter sat on one of the facing seats in the back, opposite Marta and Alicia, his hat dangling from the hand on his knee. Marta practiced her English on Peter and he tried out his Spanish. Alicia interpreted when they got stuck.

"Are you really a co-ow-boy?" Marta asked in a practically unintelligible accent.

"Yes ma'am," he replied for effect and when they laughed he added, "Yes, siree."

He pantomimed riding a bronco — no easy feat in a small jeep on a bumpy, winding road. The women howled and Pepe and Jorge looked back on them indulgently, but Alicia knew Jorge wanted to be part of the fun.

"No, I'm not really. But cowboy hats and boots are common attire in New Mexico."

"*Alicia, preguntale si tiene novia...o esposa,*" Marta urged her.

"She wants to know if you have a girlfriend or a wife," Alicia translated.

"*Sí,*" Peter teased, knowing he was not giving her what she wanted to know.

Marta clucked her tongue and gave him a side-long look, "*Cual?* Wife or girlfriend?"

"Neither really."

In Escondido dogs bounded along the rutted roads to greet them. They looked much like the yellow dog at the finca, the ubiquitous mongrels of rural Latin America.

Pepe pulled over near the store and they all piled out. Two women leaned out of a window giggling softly behind their hands. People in doorways gazed at them as they walked by and nodded or said, "*Buenas*" — short-speak for good morning.

The Carvallos were an item of interest whenever one of them came to town, but when Alicia first arrived with her curly ginger-colored hair she created a sensation. Children followed her, and when she bent to speak to them they touched her hair as if it were a halo.

If the sight of her entranced them, they were even more fascinated by Peter. His manner of dress was different, his hair was a sandy brown and his eyes blue. People pretended to be discrete, but couldn't help turning their heads to look and children gaped at them without pretense.

"Hey, whatta'ya staring at?" he grinned at an urchin and tweaked his nose. The child burst into giggles and began an excited dialogue with his friends as the group passed by.

Pointing to a blue bandanna in the *tienda*, Peter tried out his Spanish.

"*Cuanto?*" How much, he asked the man, his slow, accented drawl adding an "h" so it sounded like *cuAHn-toe*.

"*Como?*" the man could not understand him. Peter tended to talk softly and his mustache seemed to mute the words even more. Add that to an accent that

Escondido had never heard before and he was verbally handicapped. Undaunted he repeated the question.

"*Qué dice?*" the puzzled man shrugged, smiling at Marta who translated for them.

Their shopping completed, they loaded their parcels into the back of the jeep.

"You get in front Alicia, you are pregnant," said Marta.

"I'll sit in the back with Peter," offered Jorge, "you can both sit in the front."

When he gave Carmen the perfumed lotion he brought back from town, Jorge teased her not to wear it around men or they might lose control. She bent over her round tummy laughing at that, one hand to her mouth.

———————

That night there was music and animated conversation. They even tried to teach Peter to dance the *cumbia*. He did better than most American men, but Carmen giggled behind her hand at his attempts.

Rum and Coke was the drink of choice — as it was most evenings, for that matter. The Carvallos were hearty drinkers but Alicia was a lightweight. She was happy with one or two *tragos*, but in Colombia, more was merrier.

The men insisted on refilling her glass if she drank over half.

"No, no, a little more!" don Felipe insisted when she tried to resist.

"I'm pregnant."

"A happy mother is a happy baby," Pepe told her, smiling foolishly. Normally he was not only sensible, but the more sedate of the Carvallo men. More like his mother.

"It won't hurt," Jorge shrugged, also smiling through a haze. Claudia rolled her eyes, turning her head to the side.

After that Alicia faked it, surreptitiously draining most of her drink into a potted fern and topping off the rest with Coke. Peter saw her and she put a forefinger to her lips. He held up a palm, as if to say her secret was safe, then winked. She smiled back gratefully.

The other men had taken to singing. Don Felipe sang with a melodious baritone, but his sons were both tone deaf. That did not make them shy however. Not even Pepe. Both brothers bellowed out the words as if they had operatic tenors to share with the world. They taught Peter "Cielito Lindo." He picked up the refrain with gusto each time.

> *"Ay, ay, yay, yay, canta y no llores,*
> *porque cantando se allegran,*
> *Cielito Lindo, los corazones."*

Sing and don't cry Pretty Darling, the song advised, because singing makes the heart happy.

"You have to use your arms and your body, too," Jorge teased Peter and demonstrated, throwing his arms wide, and then wrapping him in a bear hug. The contrast between the Carvallo style of singing and his Mark Twain twang made her laugh. Peter's voice reminded her of old movies from the 50's. A lone prospector on a loaded-down mule comes into sight lustily singing "Home on the Range." Peter used his head as a punctuated metronome whether he sang "Cielito Lindo" or "Oh! Susannah"...with a big grin on his face.

The next morning Alicia and Jorge slept late and woke to peals of laughter from the courtyard. Carmen was demonstrating how Americans dance for Carolina, a young woman who occasionally helped Carmen and babysat Humberto. They watched from the window, amused. It was just as well that Peter slept through that. Carmen didn't make him out as very suave. More like an uncoordinated teenager — American to be sure — learning the Monster Mash.

A tee-shirted Jorge leaned out and said, "At least he tries. Some Americans don't dance at all."

"But, *por qué*?" asked Carolina, surprised.

Jorge was in a decidedly good humor for a man with a hangover. He shrugged, "They say they don't know how."

The women laughed again, but Carmen declared, "*Como*?...not know how? We are born knowing how. Even toddlers dance when they learn to walk."

Alicia went to get dressed and Jorge leaned with his back to the window sill. "Do you think children learn to dance or are born with the ability?" Alicia asked as she pulled on her jeans.

"Babies would surely teach themselves to stand upright and walk whether they had adults to imitate or not," Jorge mused. "Seems like if the world were composed only of children there would still be music and dancing...they would invent it."

"Yeah. So people, or at least Americans, lose it as they grow older."

Jorge just smiled, distracted from their conversation by watching her dress.

Breakfast was slightly more subdued and quite a bit later than usual. But the Carvallo sense of humor was still in evidence as they recounted the evening.

"*Oye Jorge,* you're lucky Mamá didn't catch you peeing in the shrubbery, *no?*" said Pepe.

"*Ah sí?* Who had to help who up the stairs? I'm sorry, Martita, I'm afraid my brother was not up to his husbandly duties last night."

Peter chuckled at their bantering and Marta and Pepe exchanged a secret smile, while Claudia declared, "Only peasants urinate in the garden. It kills the plants." She raised her *café tinto* to her nose, inhaling the rich aroma.

"Ah, coffee," said Peter, lifting his cup. "The hangover remedy."

"Have lots of coffee," advised doña Claudia.

The morning was unofficially declared a family recuperative holiday. They drank their coffee like their rum, savoring it slowly. They were sensual connoisseurs. After the strong coffee, don Felipe served his famous beer with lemon chaser — the sure cure for a hangover.

"Well, its Sunday," Pepe declared, putting his hands on his knees. "We must be heading back to Bogotá." He needed to get back to work at the bank, and the children had school tomorrow, but the elder Carvallos decided to stay a bit longer.

Felipe and Jorge didn't go out to inspect the finca until 11:00 A.M. They were back before 2:00 P.M. for lunch, appetites renewed, and then indulged in a much-needed siesta before returning to the fields.

———————

The five who remained at Las Nubes sat out on the veranda near a stalk of bananas hung to ripen. An insistent rain pelted musically on the zinc roof while Peter entertained them with the story of how emeralds and gold formed in the Andes.

"They are usually associated with igneous rocks...volcanoes or granitic intrusions." The silica-rich magma that formed the granitic rocks of the Andes was pretty much the same as the lava erupted from the violent Andean volcanoes, Peter told them.

"At least, the chemistry is the same. The difference between the two rock types is whether the magma cools slowly deep below the surface and allows large crystals to grow, or spews out so that it cools quickly and forms a finer-grained volcanic rock."

"Why are our volcanoes so violent? They erupt so suddenly," Alicia wanted to know.

Jorge agreed. "In Hawaii the lava just spills out giving people warning, time to escape."

"It's the high silica content in the Andes...it makes the magma extremely thick and viscous so that it plugs up the vent and then explodes like a pressure cooker," Peter explained. "In Hawaii, the lava is very fluid, so it flows easily. When it hardens, it becomes the rock called basalt."

"And why do emeralds grow so beautifully in our mountains?" Claudia asked. She owned a few to go with her greenish eyes.

Peter pondered this, sprawled on a leather-slung chair, the elbow of one arm resting on the opposite wrist as his hand stroked his jaw, as if coaxing out a response. The answer was complicated, but had to do with the left-over liquid in the magma. Alicia listened, fascinated.

"After the magma begins to crystallize, the remaining liquid melt becomes concentrated in certain elements...such as gold, silver or those that form gemstones," he paused reflectively. "This enriched fluid makes its way through fractures in the rocks, which become mineral veins. Colombia just has the right combination of rocks and chemistry."

They all knew the majority of the world's emeralds come from Colombia—and the highest quality.

"Have you geologists found any new mines?" asked don Felipe.

"No. As far as I know they are working the same deposits the Indians and conquistadors found. Arguably, the most valuable mines in the world."

"Really! Why is that?" Jorge wanted to know.

"Well, emeralds are rarer than diamonds and they could get mined out...making them the most precious gem on earth."

The rain turned to a cacophonous drum-roll on the corrugated zinc above their heads, forcing Peter to yell so that his last sentence could be heard. With their conversation drowned out, the group filed inside where the tiled roof and second story muted the downpour.

"You must go to the gold museum in Bogotá," Felipe said, wrapping a companionable arm around Peter's shoulders and tapping his chest with a knuckle.

"I've heard it is good."

"The best in the world, *mi amigo*. The best."

In the morning, the rains had let up and Jorge and his father were out on their rounds with Paco. Alicia was in the kitchen with Carmen, pouring herself a cup of coffee in her favorite pearly green mug.

"Where's the milk, Carmen?" she asked.

"*No hay leche, señora.*"

"No milk? *Por qué?*"

"*Quién sabe?*" Who knows.... "Paco didn't say why his boy could not fetch it today. Sick maybe."

"I'll go to the dairy. We need milk for coffee if nothing else."

"But the men have the jeep."

Alicia thought a moment then said, "I'll take the horse." The road was impassable near the top anyway.

"Well, who's going to saddle it?" Carmen laughed, "Not me!"

It was true. Alicia had never saddled a horse successfully. The one time she tried, the clever horse swelled his lungs and abdomen so that the saddle—and Alicia with it—slipped down his side the moment she tried to mount. And, she would have to figure out how to attach the funny wooden milk carrier. She would ask Peter for help. She ran into him at the door.

"Hey cowboy, I need someone to saddle my horse. You can come, if you feel like a ride."

"Sure. Where are we going?"

"Up the hill to the dairy...Paco's grandmother's...to get some milk."

Carmen smiled and waved to them from the back door. She looked girlish with her bare feet, the hem of her apron caught up in one hand, one knuckle between her teeth.

"Someone needs to buy that woman a pair of shoes," Peter said.

"Oh, Claudia has tried. The problem is her feet are so broad from going barefoot all her life they can't find a pair to fit her."

"Don't they make wide shoes here?"

"Nope. Even men's hardly fit her."

———

They rode their horses up the dirt road. Old impressions where tires or cart wheels had gone before were eroding into rivulets. Soon it became impossibly and impassably rutted, even for four-wheeled vehicles.

"What's that mountain peak in the distance?" Peter asked. "Is that Nevado Tolima?"

The peak was barely visible over the treetops and through the hazy sky. A perfect stratovolcanic cone with a white cap.

"No. Nevado del Tolima is on the road to Bogotá. It's taller. The one you see with the snow is Volcán Charimpó."

"Is it active?"

"I don't know," she replied.

"Probably is. I'll be working over there sometime. I read Tolima and Nevada Ruiz are something like 17,000 feet."

"Pico Colon, up north, is even higher," she said.

The mountain peak disappeared from view as they entered the cloud forest. In twenty minutes the old road narrowed to nothing more than a well-worn trail. Occasionally they had to duck down on their horses' necks to avoid a low growing limb or dripping vine.

"Watch out for snakes," Alicia called out as Peter dodged some foliage.

He was looking over his shoulder, grinning as he came out under the vine, "I am, believe me. I am!"

A few minutes later they sighted the old lady's home. It was a simple dwelling with adobe walls and a corrugated zinc roof, but she'd planted bougainvillea, impatiens and ferns which gave the modest place an air of beauty. A dozen cows with tinkling bells grazed in a meadow surrounded by the misty cloud forest.

"*Hola?*" Alicia called.

The woman came out of the barn, more like a shed really, wiping her hands on her apron. "Oh, you must be the new Carvallo bride!" she smiled widely, her face crinkling like rumpled wax paper. She wore rubber boots, and an old black felt hat partially hid her gray braids.

"Well yes...I am," Alicia replied as they dismounted. "And this is our friend, Peter Shalmers."

"Soledad de Quiros to serve you." She inclined her head with the old fashioned, but still standard introduction.

The cows roamed in the grass, which was fenced in near the trail but apparently nowhere else.

"Don't the cows wander off?" Alicia asked, pointing to an animal at the edge of the clearing.

"Only the stupid ones, and only occasionally. But I always find them. They never go very far before they start mooing for me to come rescue them." Soledad spoke with her hands on her hips, which jutted out to support her small round belly. "Your milk is inside. I was just going to put the can in the stream to keep it from going bad."

They stepped into the little cabin and found it was hardly more than a shack partitioned into two rooms, one for sleeping and the other for cooking and eating. No running water, just the pipe they noticed outside, siphoning continuously from a stream. The dwelling sported a wooden floor, however, instead of an earthen one. A bunch of cheerful flowers stuck in a jam jar adorned the crude wooden table. The spotless milk can rested on the floor.

"Let me get this," Peter said, lifting the heavy container.

Alicia noticed the muscles in his forearms swell with the effort.

Peter left the following day to go back to work. Alicia was the first to say goodbye and extended her hand. Peter took it in his own warm, rough hand and gave her a look she could not decipher. He was forever teasing. Then Peter turned to don Felipe to shake hands.

"None of that...*un abrazo,*" Felipe cried and enveloped Peter in a bear hug. Everyone hugged after that.

Peter had entertained them as much as they had entertained him...they would miss him. He invited them to visit his camp someday.

"Maybe in the dry season," Felipe exclaimed with an affectionate pat on the back.

Peter nodded. "It's a long ride by horse. Sometimes a helicopter takes me in and out...always room for one or two more."

"Oh! I want to go," Alicia burst out. She immediately realized the inappropriateness of that, coming from a woman, married or otherwise. She sensed the Carvallo's displeasure. "Could we go sometime, Jorge?" she back-pedaled demurely.

"Well maybe," he nodded, and smiled as if this was a good idea.

"It's a date then," said Peter grinning. Paco held his reins while he mounted and Peter thanked him and shook hands.

He saw Carmen standing behind the family. "Carmen!" he called out, "*Hasta luego!*" She giggled at his accent, but beamed broadly showing her gold tooth and ran to the front. "*Hasta luego, don Peetro!*" Her way of saying Peter was a cross with Pedro.

There he sat, in jeans and boots on the horse. He smiled as he turned, and tipped his hat, "Well, so long."

"Get along little dogie!" Jorge said to his retreating back.

After that Peter was almost a regular in the household. They saw him more often than Marta and Pepe, who only came for the occasional weekend. Peter dropped in once a month or so planning to spend the night, but stayed for days. Jorge and Alicia gave him a little table as a desk to draw up his maps and write letters and reports for his company. He brought a typewriter.

Chapter 6
PROSPECTING

People were afraid they would be lonely at the finca, but Alicia never was. She felt happier than ever before. The Carvallos came once or twice a month and stayed for a few days. Peter, with their encouragement, often used the finca as his office rather than drive all the way back to Bogotá.

"I'd like to pay you rent for the room you let me use," he told Jorge. But of course Jorge wouldn't hear of it.

Peter went home to New Mexico over Christmas. When he came back, looking as doña Claudia said, "as if he hasn't had a haircut in a while," he was laden with gifts. He also hand delivered a Christmas card from his family. It mentioned them both by name, thanking them for their hospitality and friendship.

"I don't know what Peter would have done without you. He was so happy to have someone to speak English to!" wrote his mother.

He brought them items that were difficult to obtain locally: chocolates, the latest records, and best of all a pair of boots with thick soles for Alicia.

"Oh, they must be expensive. I don't know how I can accept them!"

"She'll find a way though!" Jorge joshed.

Alicia was so excited, already envisioning herself sloshing about the finca, climbing to the top of the hill and boldly exploring the rainforest. She tried them on.

Peter said, "I bought them a half-size larger than Jorge told me. You can always wear an extra pair of socks if they're big."

"Thank you!" Alicia hugged him in delight and he laughed. A thick pair of socks and they would fit just fine. She almost blurted out that they were the best present she'd ever had, but then was cognizant of Jorge at her side being a good sport. She was astonished that Peter had gone to such trouble for her.

"And Carmen...look what I have for you! Extra wide shoes in your size."

"Para mí? No!" Carmen smiled, but looked at the shoes doubtfully.

"Well try them on," Alicia encouraged her.

When she did, Carmen's face broke into a delighted grin.

"I can get them on," she drew in her breath in amazement. "They fit! I didn't think they made shoes that would fit me!"

Everyone laughed, but Carmen had never in her adult life had a pair of shoes that fit properly. Alicia was impressed with Peter's choice—the extra wide low-heeled shoes could be casual or dressy.

Alicia had seen Carmen walking back from Escondido carrying a pair of ill-fitting high heels once. The next day her feet were raw with blisters. These new shoes would make the long walk a leisurely stroll by comparison.

"Ay don Peetro, gracias!"

Jorge's present turned out, rather mysteriously, to be a pipe. But he doesn't smoke a pipe, Alicia thought, confused.

"So what's with the pipe?" she asked.

The two men grinned mischievously.

"Shall I tell her or you?" Jorge blurted. They laughed and confessed that Peter had introduced Jorge to marijuana.

"I have some if you want to try it," Peter told her, his eyes full of enthusiasm.

She wanted to do everything they did, but...drugs? "No way! I'm not going to smoke that stuff when I'm pregnant!" What were they thinking?

"My sister does," Peter quipped.

"She's pregnant? I didn't think she was married."

"I hope not! But I doubt it would stop her!"

"We won't force you, Alicia," Jorge said, giving her a full grin. "But you're going to love it!"

Then they broke into raucous laughter. Alicia couldn't say their silliness bothered her. No wonder they were so much fun...they were high. The three of them were back to singing little ditties and telling jokes and the hours passed quickly.

Peter left and they didn't see him for over three weeks. Then on a sunny morning in January, Alicia heard the gravel crunch on the drive, and there was Peter in his Toyota jeep. He swung his legs out and strode towards the porch.

"Hey, you guys want to go for a helicopter ride?" he grinned.

"Jorge's gone, and he won't be back until late."

"Well, it's now or never. Do you want to go?"

Alicia's face lit up. "Yes!" she said on impulse. Jorge would not like this, much as he liked Peter. No one would approve, but she pushed the thought out of her mind. She was not going to pass up such an adventure. "When will we be back?"

He shrugged, "In the afternoon. Well before dark anyway. The pilot won't fly after dusk." Then, seeing her hesitation, he added, "I promise to have you back."

She could be back before Jorge.

———————

Alicia hadn't realized how small and insubstantial a helicopter was. A little bubble of plastic. She felt as if she was standing on the ledge of the world's tallest open elevator, watching the ground fall away. But she was soon distracted by the beauty below her. This time of year many of the trees were in bloom and the top of the canopy was dressed in pink, red and yellow blossoms. The incredible display stretched for miles.

Forty minutes later, the helicopter landed in a little clearing in the jungle.

"Where did this come from...who cleared this?" Alicia asked, yelling over the *thop, thop* of the chopper blades.

"I think it's an old Indian clearing. They must have farmed it and moved on in recent years," Peter replied. Unbuckling his seat belt, he turned to the pilot. *"Las cuatro,"* he hollered, pointing at his watch then lifting four fingers.

The pilot shook his head, *"Muy tarde...las 2:00?"* It was 10:00 A.M. now. The pilot was concerned about the weather deteriorating as the afternoon progressed.

Andean mornings were usually fine this time of year. If it was going to rain it would be in the afternoon. Peter nodded and they scurried out of the helicopter, the winds generated by the propeller blasting their hair and plastering their clothing to their bodies. It felt as if the blades might graze their scalps.

"I thought he would wait!" Alicia cried over the noise as Peter ran back for a box of supplies.

"He'll be back, don't worry."

Peter took her to a small tent near a rushing stream.

"This is where you live?" Alicia could hardly believe he stayed in this...pup tent, for it was hardly bigger than that...for weeks at a time.

"Yup. Well, it's where I sleep. I live outside unless it's raining."

There was also a small stool, a hammock and boxes of supplies covered with tarps.

"At least I don't have to worry too much about theft this far from civilization," Peter grinned.

He showed her his camp—his maps, a geologic compass called a Brunton, a hand lens he used to magnify minerals for identification. Near as she could gather, he hiked around all day collecting rock samples, drawing lines on his maps showing where to find the different rocks and taking meticulous notes in a little water-proof field book.

"Mostly if I find something interesting, it is usually weathered and not in place...it's called *float*." This meant, he explained, the rock had been moved—by water, gravity and erosion—and he then had to explore its origin, uphill or upstream, until he found the parent rock. The idea was to find a mineral associated with gold, then trace it back to a vein which could contain gold or other minerals.

"Like what other minerals?"

"Oh, quartz is the most common...sometimes pyrite."

Alicia liked listening to his laconic way of speaking. She watched Peter's face as he spoke and could see he wanted her to understand why he was so intrigued with his work. He obviously loved it...the adventure, the places he visited and the mental challenge of figuring out a puzzle.

"You're lucky you know," Alicia said, thinking of Jorge. The main reason he didn't finish his MBA she knew was because he didn't want to sit at a corporate desk in a city building day after day.

"Yeah...and they pay me to do it too," he chortled.

"Peter, what would happen if you found gold or something in the mountains behind us?"

He pulled on his lower lip thoughtfully. "Well, the company would evaluate the rate of return versus the cost. If it looked promising, it would mean a new road for you."

"I'm not sure we want a new road," Alicia said, envisioning trucks grinding gears and belching diesel fumes in front of her house.

"Maybe electricity and phone lines, jobs for the locals...."

"You're putting a positive spin on it, but what are the consequences?" She made a face to soften the question.

Peter sighed. "This is always a conflict for me. I love my work and being outdoors, but if I do a good job, there are environmental impacts."

"What if you didn't report it?"

"Come on! That would be dishonest...and eventually I'd be fired for being useless." He laughed unconvincingly.

They sat in silence for a while, then Alicia noticed something in the underbrush. With her arm still discretely in her lap, she nudged Peter and pointed with one finger.

"It could be a jaguar, you know," she said, her body tense.

They were sitting on a tarp and he moved quietly behind her, his face next to hers. "Look at the big leaves," he whispered without pointing.

Even as the adrenaline rushed through her, she was aware of Peter's closeness. She gazed at his strong arm, thinking how tan he was, just as she saw a slight disturbance in the bushes out of the corner of her eye. It could almost be the wind, but a pair of eyes—human eyes—stared out of the dense undergrowth.

"Look Peter there's another one!" She motioned ever so slightly with her head. The figures were concealed too well to tell if they were male or female, but they were Indians. "Do you think they're dangerous?" she asked, only half in jest. There were still headhunters in the Amazon, but that was far away. Peter sat with one knee flexed behind her shoulder, the other leg to her side while he supported himself with one arm on the ground. His body half-cupped hers when he bent forward, the closeness both pleasant and unnerving.

"I don't think so. I thought I felt someone watching me last week, and another time I spotted one of them."

The two cultures sat watching each other for perhaps five or ten minutes. Once Alicia relaxed she could have sat there all day. Ominous clouds gathered overhead, but if they noticed they had forgotten their inauspicious significance.

"I think one is a woman," Alicia whispered.

Peter leaned against her and when he spoke, his face brushed her ear. The figures in the bushes were completely still. Finally she called out, *"Hola!"* and gestured for them to come. The woman started at Alicia's voice and glanced over to her comrade.

"They're not going to speak Spanish, you know," Peter teased softly.

Alicia saw the woman put a hand to her mouth as if to suppress a smile, and say something to a smaller figure next to her—a child? Peter and Alicia couldn't tell. The woman turned slightly and whispered to someone else behind her. Then they realized there must be four or five Indians hidden in the bushes.

"What could we give them?" Alicia fingered the hand lens hanging around his neck.

"No way!" he chuckled. Instead he handed her the package of cookies they had munched on earlier. Alicia stood and took a tentative step towards the woman, holding out her hand. The woman backed up just as cautiously.

Alicia stopped as she realized they were all moving away, and a low, urgent male voice spoke to the others. Peter managed to shoot a quick picture just as the group turned as one and disappeared silently into the forest.

She counted six of them, some of the men wore thongs and the woman a sort of short skirt. None were very tall and Alicia realized the "child" must have been a teenager. Some of the men carried stout sticks. They had not run, they'd simply melted into the vegetation as if they were part of it. Alicia stood in silence, staring at where they'd been.

Then she looked up in surprise at the dark roiling clouds she'd failed to notice before. The moist air felt heavy and it started to rain hard.

They crawled into the tent in the driving rain. Peter lay on his side, supporting his head with an arm bent at the elbow, and made room for her. Alicia sat on his sleeping bag. She felt like this was akin to being in a man's room — or on his bed. But it was hard to sit up because the roof was low, and her back already ached from sitting in a cramped position. She rolled her shoulders and head back to relieve the tautness. After a few minutes Peter patted the space between them and said, "It's OK, I won't bite."

Alicia sank down on her back with relief, but voiced her real anxiety. "God, the chopper isn't going to make it."

Jorge would be angry if she didn't get back soon.

Peter didn't reply, but glanced at his watch. It was well past two o'clock. He rolled onto his back and they lay there not speaking, staring at the top of the tent, listening to the steady rain.

"Doesn't this thing leak when you get a downpour?"

"Oh...it's happened," he smiled, "when it rained for twenty-four hours straight once."

The rain slackened, but the humidity made the air thick. An electric tension between them made it even thicker. A woman nearly six months pregnant, lying next to a man who was not her husband. And he was such an attractive man, in a rugged sort of way.

Alicia almost laughed out loud at her Byronic illusion. Her face must have betrayed her because one side of his mustache twitched upward in a teasing smile and he said, "Is it just me or do we have an uncontrollable desire to press our lips together?"

"We can't," Alicia said, but knew such a thing would have been entirely possible – probable, if she was single.

Seven or eight months ago she could have stayed here in this clearing in the jungle for a week if she wanted to. She felt a pang of guilt and remorse at the thought. Peter rolled onto his side, propped up again on one elbow. It must be a long time since he's been with a woman, Alicia thought. Suddenly she laughed out loud and he didn't ask why, but laughed as well.

Just then they heard the helicopter. They clung to each other in the rain-turned-to-drizzle and laughed all the way to the chopper.

Jorge's brow was a thundercloud of furrows when Alicia returned in damp clothes, tendrils of hair clinging to her face. His ire made her feel guilty.

"You've been out all day with Peter, haven't you?"

"Yes, I have. Didn't Carmen tell you? He invited you too, but you were not around. He came back into Escondido for supplies and the helicopter pilot was waiting so he couldn't...." Alicia spoke quickly, but he interrupted, to her relief.

"You got to go in a helicopter? Damn! Why didn't you come find me?"

"I didn't know where you were. Did you go into town?"

They stood there looking at one another for a minute before Jorge said, "I think he's attracted to you, that's what I think...you like him, don't you?" As she moved towards the stairs, he shouted, "Don't you?!"

How did he know when she'd just discovered it herself? She turned back to him, "Of course I like him."

"Do you find him attractive?" he badgered, his jaw a hard line.

"Yes, he's attractive...but Jorge, nothing happened and nothing is going to happen." Alicia took a step toward him and put her hand on his arm. She could feel the muscles tense. "I'm expecting your child," she said softly, as much to herself as to him.

"Just remember that," he said, but not so angrily now.

"I'm sorry," she said, and she truly was. She'd had such a glorious afternoon, but didn't want to hurt him. She had almost forgotten him, almost forgotten, for a few hours, that she was married. Almost, but not quite. Alicia hadn't been wed long enough for the status change to become automatic in her mind and behavior, in spite of her pregnancy.

"I know what men are like," he called after her. Her father had said the same thing to her once.

After she bathed, Alicia caught sight of herself in the bathroom mirror as she was drying off. It seemed the little grapefruit developing within her was steadily turning into a large, ripe melon. Jorge came in and leaned on the doorpost a moment. Her skin felt stretched across her stomach and she thought how embarrassed she'd be for anyone else to see her naked like this. Jorge moved behind her and put his long arms around her. His hands looked deeply tanned on her pale skin. Alicia leaned back against him and he said quietly, "I love you. I was worried about you."

Her heart melted and she turned around and kissed him sweetly.

Chapter 7
THE TREMOR

The life inside her rolled around every few minutes, it seemed. Alicia half reclined on the bed, supported by her elbows. Jorge lay on his side, one hand on her swollen belly.

"If it's a girl let's call her Magdalena," she suggested.

"It's not going to be a girl," Jorge assured her with a teasing laugh.

But even in jest this seemed more capricious than amusing to Alicia. "This baby has a 50-50 chance of being a girl."

"Not this baby. Not Jorge Carvallo's first child," he laughed. "This man is full of male seed," he beat on his chest and then flexed his bicep as if to prove it.

"Jorge, you'll love her, boy or girl." It was half statement, half question for reassurance.

He kissed her forehead, "Of course I will and...if you have a girl, you can call her Magdalena or anything you want, and she'll be just as pretty and nice as her mother."

"There! Did you feel it?"

Jorge nodded, staring in wonder at his hand on her taut, protuberant tummy, and then lifted his beaming face to hers, "It's like a miracle, isn't it?"

She nodded back. It did seem like a miracle that the two of them had produced a small human being who would make his or her appearance in a few months. A tiny baby who would grow to adulthood. An everyday occurrence, but a veritable miracle when you thought about it, nonetheless.

Alicia was in fine health, never encumbered by the nausea that inflicts so many expectant women. Only her growing bulk hindered her as she carried a larger bundle out front week by week. She'd tired easily in the early months, but the relaxed lifestyle had restored her. Now she felt more energetic, her attitude indefatigably optimistic. The change in her body chemistry made her feel like she was on a hormonal high.

Jorge and Peter could have marijuana, Alicia didn't need any mood enhancement. She woke each morning in delight, first to the blend of sounds of the finca — the cock crowing, the dog's bark, a worker's whistle, the monkeys chattering, birds singing and all the other, indefinable sounds from the surrounding forest. And then, she became conscious of the aroma of coffee and the sweet rich scent of the land.

———

Felipe and Claudia were back for a few days. Claudia brought Alicia some cloth with small blue flowers to make a maternity smock. It became her only dress in a country where a woman in pants was a rarity. The rest of the time she wore Jorge's khaki pants, unzipped and held up by an unattractive cord which she tied to span the mound across her waist. She concealed the unsightly string and the gaping opening of the pants with one of his shirts, hanging below hip level. The smock she sewed herself on an old treadle machine which, it occurred to her, must have belonged to Abuelita. Alicia had never pictured her here before — on their turf.

As night fell, they gathered on the veranda to watch the sun sink below the horizon, and the stars emerge. The chairs leaned back at just the right angle to comfortably survey the heavens without getting a neck ache. When Claudia or Marta was present, the women would vie to see who would spot the first star. Alicia had come to admire Marta's quiet serenity and found her easy to talk to. The men seemed less interested in the stars, although Jorge played the game with her when there was no company to distract him.

"There!" Claudia called and they followed the line of her arm to a faint twinkling. Alicia silently recited a rhyme from childhood:

Star light, star bright, first star I see tonight.
I wish I may, I wish I might, have this wish I wish tonight.

She already had everything she wanted, so she wished for a healthy baby.

They sat talking softly until suddenly a shooting star streaked across the sky. Four faces stared in wonderment, their jaws dropping ever so slightly as they exclaimed, "*Ah*," "*Uy*," and "*Ay-yay- yay!*"

"They say that's a sign," Jorge murmured.

They sat quietly for awhile and then Alicia remembered to ask about the Colombian Indians. Claudia was one of the few people in the country, outside of university academics, who was interested in the Indians.

"The early Chibchas were hunter-gatherers and I think their real name was *Muiscas*, but their language was from the Chibchan family. Most of the Indians were peaceful...except for the Tolimas."

"Where do they live?" Alicia asked.

"Lived. These were pre-Columbian tribes. The Chibchas inhabited the plateau of Bogotá. The Tolimas lived southwest of Bogotá in the Magdalena Valley, and they were fierce warriors and cannibals."

Felipe, not wanting the women to have this conversation without him, contributed, "The first inhabitants of South America had to pass through Colombia in order to migrate south or east."

"You know the Kunas of Panama? The ones famous for their appliqués...their *molas*?" Claudia asked.

Alicia shook her head.

"They were originally from the Sierra Nevada of Colombia. They migrated to San Blas before the canal was built."

But Alicia really wanted to know about the tribe she'd seen with Peter. "Do you know the name of the Indian tribe that lives near the volcano?"

Claudia leaned her head back and pursed her lips as she thought. "The Quimbayas used to live in the next valley over. They were known for their gold work."

"But, did they all die out? What happened to them?"

"I guess they may still be there, Alicia, I don't know. When did you become so interested in Indian cultures?"

"Peter has seen some. They come to his camp." She did not mention she had been there herself.

Claudia sat forward in her chair and turning to her asked, "Oh! What does he say about them?"

"They are so isolated that none of them speak Spanish. They are shy and don't wear much in the way of clothes. I...don't know what else."

Claudia cocked her head to one side and smiled, "Tell him to take a picture of them. Tell him to trade with them. Maybe he can bring back some interesting items."

"I will. Do you think they could be dangerous?"

"*Quien sabe!* But if they are the descendants of the Quimbayas....they were peaceful farmers in the Cauca Valley. I think they took to the hills centuries ago, to escape the conquistadores."

The conquistadores enslaved the indigenous people of Colombia just as they did in other parts of the New World. Many native people, perhaps most of them, died from harsh lives as miners and slaves, or of diseases to which they had no immunity.

Later that evening, Claudia gave her a book to read. It began:

"There is no evidence to suggest that the man called Cristoforo Colombo — Cristobal Colon — Christopher Columbus, ever set foot in the country that bears his name....

"The legend of El Dorado started with a story that the Chibchas or Muiscas threw gold into a lake as offerings. A party of Spaniards started up the Magdalena Valley with hundreds of men in search of the Chibchan gold ... only a fraction of the force survived. They named the plateau Santa Fe de Bogotá after the town of Santa Fe in Spain...."

To while away the coming rainy days, Alicia thought she might enroll in a correspondence course in pre-Columbian history. This would suit her fine for although she missed the lectures and stimulation of academic life, she missed the sorority-fraternity scene not one *pico*. She made a few good friends at UV, but Alicia found the students cliquish for the most part. She stood out like a sore thumb freshman year in Sears catalog clothes that were fine for high school in Bogotá, but far from stylish in the States. The girls all wore those cute, matching wool sweater-skirt sets back then.

Being at least two years behind in campus fashion was the least of it. Her lack of knowledge in the music scene flabbergasted her peers. She recognized the Beatles and Bob Dylan and a select few popular tunes like "Mr. Tambourine Man," but didn't know who Buffalo Springfield or Creedance Clearwater Revival were, much less The Byrds. Nor had she felt a compulsion to know these things, although she'd realized this was considered pitiable. Not hip.

Furthermore, she was already spoiled by the "include everyone" hospitality of the equatorial countries, and Americans seemed almost unfriendly and even rude by comparison. Alicia had a theory that there are fewer oddballs and geeks in Latin America because the society embraces everyone. In high school, parties were open to everybody, bring anyone. To do otherwise, to exclude a classmate, was considered not just snobbish, but churlish.

When an American boy joined her high school class in Bogotá the group made an effort to welcome him from day one. Introverted Curtis was pale and gangly, incredibly skinny—and a whiz at math and physics. Being something of a "Poindexter," he seemed to expect to be excluded and was shy of the newfound attention. He seemed startled, even suspicious when several kids sat down with him at lunch and asked where he was from.

"Indi-ana," he stammered.

There were no bully football captains to compete with—Latin Americans are not so macho in that regard—and he was respected for his mathematical abilities, something he may have been forced to downplay in the States. Nonetheless it took weeks to get him to join in the fun. A year later a self-confident Curtis was boldly asking girls to dance. He turned out to have an attribute much prized in Colombian society: a sense of humor. The class saved him from the misery his high school years might have been in Indiana.

Alicia thought of that time—and the sense of belonging—as the happiest days of her youth.

But then she'd nothing to complain about these days, either. Her husband was affectionate and their lives revolved around each other. She had gotten over any guilt or fantasies regarding Peter—at any rate they were more romantic than threatening. Nonetheless, Alicia decided not to play with fire. She would draw the line with Peter. This is what married couples did—temptations were always there, you just had to avoid them.

The boots he gave her came in handy. She wore them whenever she walked into the surrounding cloud forest/rain forest—it was hard to know which name to give the habitat because of the gradational boundary between the two. If you traveled down slope you were surrounded by what a biologist would call rain forest. However on the western side of the cafetal the cooler, moist cloud forest enveloped you. Most of the finca seemed to be magically caught between the two in a perpetual spring. There were misty mornings, but they invariably cleared by noon. Hot and humid days were few and far between. With the winter months however, rain was more the norm.

Every few days, while Jorge was out with Paco, she would explore. Jorge became tolerant of her escapades in the jungle. Some days she accompanied the men around the finca and other days she was content to putter in the garden or hang out with Carmen. Once a week they drove into Escondido for supplies.

———

The second week of 1972, in the middle of the night, Alicia's eyes flew open. They were jarred from a sound sleep by a dull roar, followed by an impact, as if a truck had run into the house. Then the bed shook violently and the whole house trembled and groaned. Jorge leapt up.

"Alicia...stay where you are...it's an earthquake."

But she was already on her feet clutching his arm. The shaking world terrified them as they huddled under the doorway precariously. Structurally this is one of the strongest places in a house. She thought with horror that the roof and walls might collapse on them, but just as suddenly as it began, it was over and sanity returned to reality.

As they each drew in lungfuls of air Alicia realized she must have been holding her breath.

"That wasn't too bad," he told her.

"Whoa." Bad enough.

It was pitch black. The generator was off for the night and there were no lights. They could hear Carmen's frightened voice calling, *"Don Jorge!"*

"Sí? Are you OK?"

She was, and he told her to go back to bed so she wouldn't fall down in the dark, but she was too frightened. Alicia searched for matches to light the lantern on the dresser.

"Ay, Díos! Another!" Carmen thought had she felt a tremor the other day. Her hair, which she normally wore in a bun, fell in loose thick braids to her waist.

"Where is the flashlight?" Alicia asked.

Jorge sighed, "I don't know where I put it. You stay here and I'll go find one."

It was crazy for them to live in a house with no lights and not have a flashlight handy. Alicia made a mental note to buy more. She sat on the edge of the bed, one hand protectively over her swollen abdomen. Carmen held the other hand in both of hers.

"*Ay, Díos*," she said again, "Do you think there was any damage?"

"Probably not, it was a small one."

"I hope *mi bebé*, Humberto, is safe."

"I'm sure he is," Alicia reassured her. "Who is the girl that takes care of him for you?"

"My daughter, Carolina. She's almost nineteen."

Carolina occasionally dropped by with Humberto. Alicia had not realized she was Carmen's daughter. A daughter not much younger than herself! She'd figured Carmen was close to forty when they first met, but a hard life ages a woman quickly. In truth she was thirty-five—Carmen had told her so herself. That meant she'd had her daughter when she was in her mid-teens.

They could hear Jorge rummaging around, cursing as he bumped into furniture in the dark. Alicia took the lantern to the door.

"You should have the lantern," she called.

"I found a flashlight. Papi's," he said. Finally he returned and coaxed the reluctant Carmen back to her room, which adjoined the house.

"Wouldn't you like me to stay here, nearby?" she said. She would have slept at the foot of their bed, or sat there all night if he'd let her. Back in bed, Jorge and Alicia held each other. Snuggling like a couple of puppies, they fell asleep.

A few days later Peter arrived. He got out of his jeep whistling, then stretched after the long ride. Straightening his back, he strode up to the porch steps. Alicia smiled broadly at the sight of him and offered a friendly arm and a cheek, but instead he put his arm around her and kissed her right on the lips. Not passionately nor lingeringly, more like a husband's everyday affection. That was the trouble, she thought, he didn't quite cross the line where she should rebuke him, but he was toeing it. He smiled looking down at her. Enigmatic. That's what he was — and a little more than friendly.

"Quite a little bundle you're developing there," he nodded at her swelling stomach.

She was bewildered and her face took on the color of a ripe guava, but she didn't have time to respond as he ambled past her asking, "Where's Jorge?"

Jorge's jeep pulled into the driveway and Peter turned back to greet him.

"Hey, did you feel the earthquake the other night?" Jorge asked.

"Hell, it was like a giant thundering through the forest, shaking the ground and the trees!" Peter exclaimed.

"It wasn't so bad...two women jumped into *my* bed," Jorge replied grinning, arms akimbo.

Peter said the shock they had felt, the impact, was the arrival of the first wave, the pressure or "P" wave, and the shaking was caused by the undulating secondary or "S" waves that followed it.

That evening, Peter explained the latest geological theory: the heavier oceanic plate off the Pacific was sliding, being "subducted" under the continental plate with the Andes, and this caused the earth to move. "Sometimes a small earthquake is a precursor to more activity."

He used his hands to depict the two plates, with the oceanic one diving below South America. The theory was called "plate tectonics," which postulated the world consisted of a number of large plates, each floating and moving on convection currents deep within the earth. This revolution in scientific thought had polarized the geologic community until recently.

"That's why we have volcanoes in the Andes," he added, "The subducting plate eventually begins to melt at depth and the molten material rises to the surface as volcanoes."

"Reminds me of Jules Verne," said Jorge. "Remember the movie 'Journey to the Center of the Earth?'"

Peter laughed, "Well, not quite like that."

The elder Carvallos arrived unexpectedly the following afternoon.

"Were you worried about us?" Jorge asked as he helped get their things out of the jeep.

No, they were used to earthquakes. They had another agenda.

"We think Alicia should move to the city to wait for the baby," Claudia announced.

"Oh! I will, but I have almost seven weeks yet!"

"Our grandchild could come in two or three weeks just as easily as in seven weeks," Felipe agreed with Claudia in a knowing voice.

Jorge listened, tilting his head to one side, then nodded, "We were thinking she would move back next month, but..." he turned to face Alicia, extending a hand, "maybe it should be sooner."

She made a face showing her reluctance and Peter watched the exchange bemused.

Alicia planned on going to Bogotá two weeks before her due date to find a crib and all the items one must gather up for a newborn. "Umm, three weeks, I'll come in three weeks," and seeing their exchange of negative glances, she offered, "OK, maybe two weeks."

The baby will probably come late, she thought, and I'll be stuck in Bogotá for months. That evening, in the privacy of their room she told Jorge, "I don't want to be away from you so long, I'll go crazy in your parents' house."

"*Ay, mi amor,* I am planning to go with you."

"But...what about the finca?"

"It can take care of itself for awhile. I'll come back once a week or so."

"And we won't be able to return right after, either...we should wait two or three weeks!" Or more she thought, but didn't bother to say so.

"The rains will be starting anyway and we'll be cooped up here inside with little to do. In Bogotá we'll have a social life again," he smiled.

"Jorge."

"*Sí, mí vida?*"

"I need an allowance." She changed the subject.

"What for?"

"So every time I need money, I don't have to ask you."

"What do you need money for at the finca?"

"Well, besides weekly food, I might want to buy something...for example, for your birthday."

He smiled broadly, "I'll try to remember not to ask you why next January."

"No. I need some money of my own." It took more persuading before he finally agreed to a bi-monthly sum. Looking away, Alicia rolled her eyes good-naturedly that she had to jump through hoops to win this concession.

———————

The baby was born in the wee hours of the morning, two weeks after the conversation with the Carvallos. Like many mothers-to-be, Alicia had a bag packed and ready to go at a moment's notice. As they prepared for bed that night, she developed severe stomach pains. It was too soon for labor, so she waited them out and Jorge went to sleep. She tried going to the bathroom to see if that would make her feel better. Then she lay down on the throw rug and brought her knees to her chest to ease the cramping.

Jorge woke up and gazed at her rolling on the floor.

"*Hijo...!* Alicia do you think you're going to have the baby early?"

"I don't think so. They say it's much worse than this. Oh God!" she moaned.

"Maybe we should wake my mother."

For the Carvallos were back again—already. They'd arrived that very afternoon, to ensure Alicia made it back to Bogotá. She hesitated to wake doña

Claudia, but she was getting worried. Her abdomen was hard as a rock. When he came back she said, "Maybe we should go."

If she was full term she might have been brave enough to have the baby at home rather than drive to Bogotá in the middle of the night, but with over four weeks left to go she was nervous.

"Yes of course, you don't want to take any chances!" Claudia was behind him in her nightdress. She wore a hair net to preserve her hairdo.

"Oh hell...I don't want to drive all the way to Bogotá in the middle of the night if I don't have to!" Jorge said. He slumped on the bed. He wasn't good at having his sleep disturbed.

"Well, you have to," Claudia said briskly, then asked, "Can you count contractions, Alicia?"

"No, they don't seem to be very regular. It could be just stomach cramps."

"Get dressed, *mi'ja,*" Claudia said, using the familiar contraction for *mi hija*...my daughter.

Claudia and Felipe walked them out to the jeep. Alicia appreciated their calm assurance as she trembled in the night air — was it *that* cold?

Her mother-in-law clutched a shawl about her shoulders. Alicia did not see her troubled face as she called out, "You'll make it. First babies take forever!"

"Drive carefully," Felipe admonished, standing with his hands in the pockets of his robe.

The treacherous road was as much a concern as Alicia and the baby. They never drove the route at night. Besides the ruts and tight curves, there were crazy drivers and — God forbid — *bandidos.*

"Don't worry Papi. At least I can see the headlights coming around the corners at night."

Colombian drivers are not known for driving cautiously or even staying in their lane. Fortunately, Jorge was a very good driver. They drove about an hour on the winding, bumpy dirt road, the young mother-to-be groaning with every jolt. She now knew for sure this was not mere stomach cramps.

"*Ay*, Alicia how are you doing? Do you want me to go slower or faster?"

"I'd say faster, but this road is too dangerous."

"At least we don't have to worry about the traffic. We'll be on the paved road in less than an hour. I can go a little faster."

Luckily, it was not raining and had not rained all day. The unpaved roads were much worse in the rainy season. The moist air changed as they descended deep into the valley, becoming thick and warm.

Years later, Alicia would marvel how this trip of hours and hours was only about a hundred miles, if you traced a straight line on the map. But to get to Bogotá from the finca you had to drive down the rutted dirt roads and hairpin curves to the Magdalena Valley, cross the bridge over the great river where the paved road began and then wind back and forth up the narrow road that climbed thousands of feet. And if you got behind a plodding truck or bus, passing was next to impossible.

The mountains and vegetation formed a formidable hurdle to travel, but also a protective barrier. A screen from the rest of the world.

Shortly after they began their ascent Jorge pulled over, left the engine running and ran to the side of the road.

"What are you doing?" Alicia cried in exasperation, although she knew, because she could hear a waterfall. Everyone stopped at the small waterfall because a shrine to the Virgin had been erected years ago, after a bus had fallen into the chasm below. The road claimed at least half-a-dozen lives a year, not including the occasional disappearance of someone who was killed or kidnapped by guerrillas or bandits, and never heard from again. Travelers stopped and prayed for a safe journey. The stop had become a family ritual for the Carvallos.

She saw Jorge's face briefly illuminated as he stooped and lit a votive candle. He trotted back grinning, "I left her a few pesos. Have to pay our respects, no matter how big the rush!"

At the next small jolt in the road Alicia felt hot liquid saturate her thighs, the back of her dress and the seat of the jeep. "Oh God!" she exclaimed, her fingers flying to her lips.

Jorge looked at her sharply, questioningly.

"My waters broke."

"So what does that mean?" he demanded.

"It means we don't have a lot of time."

Alicia bit her lip. Neither one of them was prepared to deliver a baby in a jeep...much less a premature baby. "We could go back to the *clinica* in Ibague," Jorge suggested. They'd passed the town just fifteen minutes before, but could now see the lights of Bogotá.

"No, Jorge, I want Dr. Samper...but *hurry*!" she wailed. He drove with all his skill, as fast as he dared.

Chapter 8
BIRTH

They made it to the hospital in record time—five hours and twenty minutes.

"She's fully dilated, give her Demerol," a young intern ordered, "...and take her in straight away."

A nurse asked, "Do you want me to shave her?"

"No time."

"I'm premature, maybe I shouldn't have medication. Oh!—" a pain interrupted Alicia. "I don't think I need anything yet," she gasped, in spite of the pains. She *would* need something if they got any worse.

"Don't be brave," the doctor smiled calmly, raising his eyebrows in a conspiratorial expression, "You'll love this!"

Groaning, Alicia was wheeled right in to the delivery room. Whenever she cried out, someone applied a gas mask to her face and knocked her out cold. Dr. Samper, never made it to the hospital. There simply was not enough time.

"You need to push harder now," Dr. Ortega, the resident, told her when she came to.

Alicia made a drowsy effort in her dreamlike state, but she felt powerless. Thirty-five minutes later, baby George was delivered from her with forceps. Jorge and Alicia were unaware this was only Dr. Ortega's second delivery. She was relieved that the baby was safe and healthy—and she'd even produced the boy the family wanted.

Dr. Ortega woke Jorge—always a solid sleeper—to inform him of the birth of his son.

"*Y mí esposa?*"

"Fine! You can see her in a minute."

At the nursery Jorge asked to see his son, but was told to come back later. Then he found Alicia and held her hand.

"You OK?" he asked with a wan smile.

"Yes, but they wouldn't let me hold the baby. Please ask them to bring him in," she entreated.

"Alicia it's 4:30 in the morning. Let's get some sleep. I'm beat!"

Stunned, she almost said, What about me?

———————

Alicia lay in the semidarkness, recovering as much from narcotics as from childbirth. She calculated she'd labored just over seven hours—well under average—and hardly any of that time in the hospital.

It wasn't what she'd imagined at all. It was more as if they had extracted the baby and she was merely an extraneous vessel. A container to be pried open. When she complained to Jorge, he said, "Listen to the doctors, they know what they are doing."

But instinct made her feel otherwise. She was supposed to be holding her baby; to be happy, not angry and frustrated. She resolved to go home as soon as possible — get out of this hospital where they stuck you with needles and did what they would to you and your baby, in spite of your protests.

Later, her mother-in-law said, "Well, if you had been in Bogotá, Dr. Samper would have been here to take care of you."

Aha...so there's the "I told you so," Alicia thought. She resisted the impulse to tell Claudia that Bogotá was not her home.

As she lay waiting for the sun to rise, Alicia listened to the sounds in the hospital and imagined their life with a newborn. She pictured herself nursing him in the hammock, Jorge holding him by the fountain.

She twirled a strand of hair through her fingers and decided to plan the garden in her head, to pass the time. She'd already added papaya trees to the fruit trees. A man at the nursery in Fusagasugá told her to plant two — a male and a female — but warned her they did not do well in Bogotá and might not grow at the elevation of the finca. But the papayas flourished regardless — invigorated by the climate. Las Nubes was even warm enough for citrus and banana trees to thrive. When they returned she would expand the vegetable garden. She would plant lettuce, peppers and tomatoes. Perhaps peas and green beans too.

Eventually they brought her breakfast, but not her baby, and she fidgeted with the cold scrambled eggs until someone took them away. She was about to burst with impatience and boredom when Peter showed up at the door with a grin and a bouquet of flowers. Alicia opened her arms in delight, yet found herself suppressing an odd impulse to cry.

"How did you know I was here?" she cried.

"You husband woke me up before five o'clock this morning to tell me," he laughed.

It wasn't even eight o'clock yet. Well of course, Jorge, but she'd expected him to go right home to bed. On impulse he drove to Peter's and woke him up, sure that Peter would want to know right away. Jorge would probably sleep past noon himself.

"I'm so glad to see you! I'm going crazy here!"

"Well, where's Little Jorge?"

"George," she corrected. "We decided on the English version to avoid confusion."

A nurse popped her head in the doorway, *"Buenos días,"* she said kindly. "So, it looks like the baby will make it. *No?"*

Alarmed, Alicia sat straight up in bed and exclaimed *"Qué?!"* A pain tore between her legs and she drew in her breath sharply. Peter looked at her questioningly.

"Oh, I thought you knew. I shouldn't have said anything!" the nurse blurted and ran off.

"I'll go find out what's going on," he said, leaving the bouquet on the bed as he hurried out in pursuit of the nurse.

"Hey!" she heard him call out after the swiftly retreating nurse. Alicia smiled despite her anxiety. He was so American. Peter hardly spoke Spanish, but didn't let that hold him back.

She waited impatiently and even tried, gingerly, to swing her legs over the side of the bed. A pain stabbed her as she lowered her feet. She had not expected an episiotomy with a relatively easy labor and premature baby. Moving carefully, she used both arms to help nudge her legs back under the covers, and strove to regain a comfortable posture.

Alicia heard Peter's raised voice down the hall. What was he saying? She heard fragments. "...Better find someone who is in charge... *now*... and you...." He sounded stern. Polite, but authoritative, in charge.

He entered the room exhaling hot air, but immediately grinned seeing her worried face.

"Everything's OK. The doctor is coming to explain."

He sat on the bed and laid a gentle hand on her forearm. After all her frustration and fear, his kindness caused tears to gather in her eyes and threaten to spill over her cheeks.

"It's going to be OK," he reiterated in his low voice. "The baby had some breathing difficulties and they put him in an incubator, but he's OK now."

Soon a doctor appeared at the door, walked over to shake Peter's hand and introduced himself before turning to Alicia.

"*Señora...*," he looked at the chart in his hand, "...Carvallo. Your baby is fine and healthy. There is no need to worry. The pediatrician saw him only an hour ago and Dr. Samper will check you this morning."

"But what happened? Why didn't someone tell me?"

"We didn't want to worry you. You need your rest. The baby had one lung that didn't inflate properly, so we put him on a respirator. But there was never any serious danger and he is breathing normally now," he said with a tight smile and supercilious tone he probably used to reassure young, witless women.

Peter exchanged a glance with Alicia as if holding his tongue, but then changed his mind and pointed out, "I think she would worry less if she was kept informed."

In the doorway the doctor bowed his head with almost exaggerated courtesy and said, "From now on your wife will be informed of every problem."

When he was out of hearing range Peter intoned, "Well, Wife, how did I do as a new father and husband?"

They burst out laughing. Alicia had never felt so grateful or as fond of anyone as she did at that moment. "You're wonderful, Peter. Thank you."

After he left she picked up the bouquet. It was a lovely arrangement of pink lilies, baby's breath and forget-me-nots. She was glad he had not chosen the ubiquitous carnations or gladiolus florists sell—they reminded her of funerals.

Something woke Felipe Carvallo at Las Nubes at dawn. A rumbling? He lay there listening for the sound. An earthquake? It was perfectly quiet now except for Claudia's gentle breathing and the cock crowing in the stillness. He thought about Jorge and Alicia, hoped they were safe. He smiled. Did he have a grandchild yet? Getting out of bed, he dressed silently.

There was something odd about the sun's faint glow beginning to creep through the slats of the shutters. He stood rooted for a moment and then unlatched one. They'd enjoyed many a papaya-colored sunset over the Andes from this window, but a sunrise was not possible from a window which faced west, not east. Cumulus clouds partially shrouded the large mountain in the distance, but its summit emitted an eerie red-orange glow. Just then he heard a soft boom from far away.

"*El volcán*," he whispered.

Those weren't clouds at all. Incandescent gas and dust particles spewed from Volcán Charimpó and drifted into the atmosphere, floating northeast with the wind. The rest of the sky was a clear, perfect blue.

"Claudia, wake up," he called to his wife. "Come look at this."

Claudia stared at the spectacle, uncomprehending in her sleepy state. Bursts of vapor created one tumbling cloud pile after another, building to a height as great as the mountain itself.

Down in the kitchen they talked over steaming cups of black coffee.

"Do you think it will affect the finca, Felipe?"

"*Quien sabe?*" But then he added, "*Creo que no,* it is a long way."

"But if there is ash? It could be a nuisance," Claudia pointed out.

"It won't bother us, *mi vida.* It may stop tomorrow," he replied smiling and patted her hand.

"Well, I guess we shall have beautiful sunsets until it does."

They packed the jeep to return to Bogotá and the volcano was temporarily forgotten. They had a new grandchild to meet.

The dust clouds in the atmosphere blew eastwards, causing spectacular colored twilights not only in Colombia and Venezuela, but around the globe, as the sun's rays reflected off the fine particles, and scattered the spectrum of light.

———

Almost six weeks passed before Alicia could return to Las Nubes with the baby. For her the time was interminable, especially the first eight days after she left the hospital. The saddest day of her life was when she went "home" to the Carvallo house without the baby. Little George stayed in an incubator for a week and this meant she could not breast feed.

Alicia's chest had always been modestly endowed, but now she admired her full—if painful—breasts. They would not be voluptuous for long, nor would she have the satisfaction and relief of a suckling infant. But, she thought, the important thing was that he appeared to be thriving.

Jorge went back to Las Nubes almost weekly and stayed only for a day or two, but it took the better part of a day to drive each way. At most, they saw each other three or four days a week.

He didn't mind the bustle of Bogotá. The crazy traffic and noise that seemed cacophonous to her was part of the excitement of the city to him. Every time a bus or truck drove by the house late at night the noise of grinding gears and a diesel engine straining up the hill woke her.

Alicia visited the hospital every day and wanted to stay for hours. When Jorge was in town they went together. The first time, she'd wept—George looked so tiny and cried so pathetically on the other side of the glass. She longed to comfort him.

"I feel so helpless," she said, leaning her head against Jorge's shoulder. But he seemed oblivious to her, lost in his own thoughts. Perhaps he's just dealing with his own sadness, she thought. When he was at the finca, she relied on Claudia for a ride and felt she should only stay a short time, although her mother-in-law was patient.

The pain in her breasts subsided after five or six days, as did the fullness. Either Marta or Claudia dragged Alicia to bridge parties, showers for brides and mothers-to-be. She didn't really know most of the women, although she had met some of them briefly at her own wedding.

She somewhat begrudged shopping for these events and often found them tiresome. She also resented having to ask Jorge or don Felipe for money to buy gifts. But the relatives threw a baby shower for Alicia too. It was better than twiddling her thumbs she supposed, and people meant well, although she longed to get back to their life at Las Nubes.

At least Marta was supportive. "It will be better once the baby comes home. Any mother would be restless. I would be."

"That's just it! I feel like a caged lioness. I want to fight someone for my cub!"

Marta laughed, but she was right. They all fussed over George when he finally left the hospital after ten days. Alicia didn't mind getting up to feed him at least twice a night. He was still catching up on his weight and needed nourishment every few hours.

He weighed 5 pounds and 8 ounces at birth—not bad for a preemie, but still underweight. She thought he looked a little like a skinned rabbit when she first saw him. Now he seemed bigger every week and was getting downright robust. Once when Alicia came to feed him, he was screaming at the top of his lungs and she laughed because Marta said, "Look he's shaking his fist at you. He's saying 'hurry up woman!' "

One weekend Jorge did not return to Bogotá from Las Nubes as planned. The Carvallos told her not to fret as Saturday came and went.

"Maybe he had too much to do this time," Claudia suggested.

Maybe he had car trouble, Alicia thought. She didn't even want to think about bandits and guerrillas on the roads. What could have happened?

"I wished I had gone with him," Felipe whispered to Claudia.

"Then we might be worried about both of you," she said.

"I wonder if the volcano is acting up." It had quieted down shortly after its first outburst, just as he'd predicted, but last week when he'd gone there with Jorge there had been a fireworks display two nights running. The newspaper, *El Tiempo,* said it was visible from as far away as Medellín. The sunsets were noticeably beautiful in Bogotá whenever the clouds lifted in the evenings.

Sunday and Monday passed as quietly as Saturday and now Alicia was truly concerned. There were no phone lines to the finca, but surely Jorge could go into town to call. Unless...unless, what?

"He could have trouble getting a connection," don Felipe said. "I'll call the store in Escondido to see if there is any news."

The owner, Antonio González, said, *"Sí,* don Felipe, I saw don Jorge in his jeep...I think it was Sunday, *o tal vez sabado."* The man promised to get a message to Paco and they could call back tomorrow for news.

"Ah Jorge!" Claudia shook her head as if she thought her son irresponsible to worry them this way, but was wordless beyond that.

"Bueno, it's only been five days. Sometimes I had to stay longer than I thought," responded don Felipe.

"Yes, but during a harvest or..." Claudia broke off as Felipe gave her a significant look that said, *don't make Alicia worry.*

"I'd go see what's going on, but we need a jeep. Our car might not make the fords."

Pepe and Marta had taken the other jeep to visit family in Giradot.

"*Dios guarde!* Don't even think of taking the Cadillac!"

"Perhaps we could borrow a jeep. I could call Peter's office," Alicia said.

"Don't worry," don Felipe patted her arm, "*Mañana, mañana.* Let's give him another day. We know he was fine Sunday."

The phone rang late Tuesday afternoon and Claudia answered. Alicia trotted to the phone cradling George, and waited nervously to see if it was Jorge. She could hear the relief in Claudia's voice and knew it was him even before she nodded, waving a hand impatiently, then bent over with a finger in her free ear, straining to hear the connection.

"We've been worried about you! Yes, she's right here. The baby's fine, growing fat. *Ah huh, ah-ha.* OK."

"Wait! I want to speak to him!" Alicia called out, just as Claudia returned the phone to its cradle.

"I'm sorry Alicia, we didn't have a very good connection. He said he would rather speak to you tomorrow when he gets back."

"But what happened, what did he say?"

Claudia hesitated, her face changing from impassive to uncomfortable, "Just that he was busy....I think Peter was there," she sighed.

Alicia wanted to punch him when he finally arrived, all smiles and hugs, at dusk on Wednesday — but she couldn't very well in front of his doting family.

"What were you doing?" she demanded.

He appraised her before answering, "There were things to do," he shrugged, evidently feeling no need to explain himself.

Three generations of Carvallos drove back to the finca in great spirits—Jorge, Alicia and little George in the lead, Felipe and Claudia following in the second jeep. It was Claudia's first trip to the finca since George was born. Felipe had gone with Jorge once during that time, but now that the young couple was going back his parents accompanied them. Alicia wished they had taken more of an interest in the coffee recently, so that Jorge could have spent more time with her and George instead of his exhausting weekly drives to and from Las Nubes.

In the mountain mists, they stopped at the shrine. They tucked their arms under their *ruanas*—the woolen ponchos once common everywhere but vanishing in the cosmopolitan areas. Indians wore them along with their ubiquitous black felt hats, but upper-class Colombians were shunning the *ruana* for European coats. All the Carvallos still wore them— they lasted for years and were serviceable and comfortable in the countryside.

Claudia held back the red woolen fringe on hers as she leaned toward the small flames to light her own candle. Felipe fished in his pocket for change and plunked it in the little metal box.

The shrine was safety insurance and the stop broke up the trip, but the real attraction was the waterfall. It was not spectacular like the mighty Tequendama Falls south of Bogotá, but the mountain water was clear and clean—while the polluted Rio Bogotá could often smell foul. The shrine made a decent picnic spot when it wasn't raining or cold, and they almost always had it to themselves.

The falls began over twenty-five feet above their heads, gushed into a large culvert under the road and cascaded out other side another twenty feet to the rocks below. Then the torrent rushed, tumbled or fell short distances for the remaining seventy feet to the roiling bottom of the chasm.

Alicia loved to stand behind the falls in the dry season and peer through the sheet of raging water. Jorge tried it, but the rainy season had started and there was too much water hurtling over the falls to allow anyone to get very close without being drenched by the spray. He grinned, pulling his dampened shirt from his skin as he stepped back on the road.

"Let's get going," Felipe called.

Clouds billowed overhead, gathering for an afternoon storm. The dirt section of the road remained ahead and it could be dicey in the rain. Sprinkles splattered the windshield, then the rain fell in a torrent for thirty minutes before it turned gentle and warm as they climbed toward the road that led to Escondido. The potholes were bad, but there were no washed out sections and the jeeps had no trouble with the ford.

A small landslide had tumbled onto the road, however, forcing them to stop. Jorge peered through the rain-spattered windshield to determine the best way over the obstruction. Putting the jeep into four-wheel drive, he traversed a path over the mound of dirt, skirting a small boulder on the left. Felipe followed his tracks. Having accomplished that, Jorge began to sing at the top of his lungs, serenading Alicia gaily.

Que las cerezas estan maduros esto lo se...

"The ripe *cerezas* are your cherry lips, *Cielita*," he leaned to nuzzle her chin and continued, exaggerating the romantic lines.

...que tu eres joven y muy bonita, tambíen lo se...

"That's you...young and very pretty. And here's one for you Georgy Porgy, about baby chickens."

Los pollitos dicen, pío, pío pío, cuando tienen hambre, cuando tienen frío.....

The nursery rhyme is as famous throughout Latin America as "Mary Had A Little Lamb" in the English-speaking world.

"You have an amazing repertoire," Alicia laughed.

"When Papi drives with me, we sing the whole way," he told her.

"What! Over five and-a-half hours?" she exclaimed. "Well almost. Sometimes we take turns. Sometimes we try to think of a song the other doesn't know. Do you know this one?" Jorge switched to "Perfidia" a somber ballad of restless love.

Woman, if you can speak to God, ask him if I have ever stopped loving you...
I've looked for you... and can't find you.
Why do I need your kisses, when your lips no longer seek mine?

He sang it melodramatically with George's little eyes, just learning to focus, watching his father in wonder.

Y tú, y tú, y tú,...who knows where you roam
Who knows what adventures you'll have,
so far from my side.

Chapter 9
THE ACCIDENT

Carmen stood flat-footed on her bare feet, her small stomach thrust forward. She was saving the shoes Peter had bought her.

Carmen's children—Carolina and little Humberto—were also there to greet the returning family. They were both attractive like their mother, without really looking like her. The toddler had huge eyes framed by dark lashes and both he and Carolina had masses of dark curls like their mother, who kept her tresses pinned up.

Carmen raved over baby George and introduced him to Humberto. She tried to sound out his name and laughed at how difficult it was.

"I may have to call him *Jorgito* or *Chichí*," she said-—*Chichí* being the Spanish nickname for "baby."

"José escaped," Jorge told his father as he saw him walk out to the fountain later that day.

"How? That monkey cost me 400 pesos...! *Agh!*"

"Sorry Papi, Carmen just found the collar lying on the ground, as if he'd slipped out of it."

Alicia listened silently. She'd contemplated letting Juanita, the female, go and leaving her collar to be found just like that. Now José was free, but it would be too suspicious for both monkeys to "escape." At least Juanita's existence would improve.

They easily, automatically, settled back into life at the finca. Alicia was relieved when the Carvallos returned to Bogotá. She was fond of them, but she and Jorge had had no privacy for almost three months now. What a pleasure to wake up and have the house to themselves. Just the three of them — and Carmen. Carmen was not just a housekeeper, she was a mother herself and thus an advisor and aide.

Jorge didn't rush out early this morning. Instead he luxuriated in bed, watching George take his bottle. The baby cooed earnestly with his rosebud mouth and Jorge exclaimed, like every other parent, "He's just so cute!"

Despite his inauspicious beginning the baby seemed to be developing precociously. At three months, he devoured his bottle with such voracity that Alicia tried him on a couple of teaspoons of oatmeal, which promptly re-emerged from his other end in what Carmen proclaimed was a healthy consistency and robust quantity.

One morning while she helped Carmen squeeze oranges for juice she asked, "Why don't you have Humberto come stay awhile?"

Carmen shrugged, "*Uy*, I'd like to, but it doesn't seem right since I'm working."

She paused, glancing sideways at Alicia, holding her breath. She cut the succulent flesh of a ripe orange, leaving the half-globes on the worn, smooth wood of the table. Alicia pressed and squeezed each half on the green glass bowl with the ribbed dome in the center. The golden-orange liquid ran out, plentiful and full of pulp.

Alicia said, "Well he could probably stay here with you most of the time."

Carmen's face shone, "*Ay*, doña Alicia! That would make me so happy!"

Alicia wished she'd thought of it before. Gazing at the oranges she said, "I should make marmalade with the rinds. We're out."

"I'll make sure he doesn't get in the way! Do you think don Jorge will mind? I'll send him home whenever doña Claudia comes."

Alicia smiled, "No, he won't mind."

Jorge probably wouldn't mind if there were half a dozen kids in the house. In fact he turned out to be wonderful with both his own son and Carmen's. Not that he changed diapers or anything like that; he simply enjoyed being with them to the delight of the two babies.

As she turned to leave the kitchen Alicia paused and leaned against the door jamb, "How do you think that monkey got loose?"

Carmen shrugged good-naturedly, "*Quíen sabe?* I hope don Felipe does not think me careless. He was secure when I fed them the night before."

"When was that?" Alicia pressed, but casually.

Carmen pursed her lips and gazed at the ceiling, humming as if she'd hardly heard the question, "Ah....the day before the men left to go back to Bogotá. Yes."

The men. "Oh, when Peter was here?" Peter could have discussed this with her.

"*Sí, sí.*"

George lay sleeping in his mother's arms as she slowly swayed to and fro in the rocking chair. He would soon be four months old. Marta and Pepe had come yesterday and Peter arrived to find them all on the veranda. The clouds were rolling in, the air heavy with moisture.

"How has the volcano been?" he asked, settling down with a glass of *chicha* — home-brewed fermented punch.

"Oh it puffs occasionally," Alicia told him, "And gives us a pretty sunset when it isn't raining."

They watched Jorge and Pepe teach Humberto and Pepe's little boy, Marcos, to kick a soccer ball. Peter shook his head, smiling, and Alicia, thinking she read his thoughts said, "Whatever negative stereotypes Latin men are given, they do not get enough credit as fathers."

"I wasn't even thinking of the Latin lover image," Peter commented, "I was thinking how everyone imagines this part of the world as dangerous and dominated by guerrillas and drug thugs."

"I guess that is true, but family ties are very important here. In spite of rough politics and occasional violence, Colombians have gentility as well as passion," she nodded.

The guerrillas and their world were a separate reality, a distant thought to this familial, bucolic scene.

Jorge took Humberto by the hand and toddled him back to the porch, "That's enough for now. It is starting to rain." Then to Alicia, "Do you want me to hold the baby for awhile?"

"No he's sleeping. I don't want him to wake up."

Marcos stretched out his chubby arms to Marta to be picked up. She spoke sweetly to him, "I already have your brother in my lap," and looked helplessly at her husband.

"Venga amor," Pepe took off his son's wet shoes and hoisted him into the chair with him. Marcos settled comfortably against Pepe's chest and arm, his little legs dangling.

Jorge planted a kiss on his own son's sleeping face and turned to see Humberto's arms out-stretched in pick-me-up expectancy.

They all laughed just as Carmen came out with *bocas* — snacks — for them to eat. *"Humberto, no moleste don Jorge."* But she laughed too as she passed around a plate of *bunuelos* — fritters — and *hormigas Escondidoanas.*

"Ah, you must try these Peter. *Hormigas Escondidoanas*, named not after our little pueblo, but the big town of Escondido." Jorge chuckled and hauled Humberto up into the hammock with him where, pretending effort, he showed him how he could "remove" his thumb and put it on again.

"*Tan bueno que es don Jorge,*" murmured Carmen.

"What are these?" Peter asked, as he reached for the crispy *bocas*.

"Fried ants," grinned Pepe, "Jorge's favorites."

Peter did a double-take, grinned back and chewed on, "Crunchy."

"You could have warned him!" Alicia said, but everyone laughed, including Peter.

"That would've spoiled the fun!" said Jorge.

"Christ, I'm the only one without a baby in my lap!" cried Peter.

"We'll get you one, next time we'll bring Nena and loan her to you!" Marta teased. Nena, their oldest child, was in Bogotá with her grandparents.

"What are the three of you talking about?" Jorge asked.

"*La vida tropical,*" Marta joked. Life in the tropics.

"Pretty good life, no?" Jorge grinned at Peter, who nodded.

———

Alicia had sowed seeds in her vegetable garden the week she returned to Las Nubes, and already they were feasting on lettuce, peppers and tomatoes. The green beans were not yet ready to eat but she was pleased with the progress they made, winding their way up the beanpoles and putting out little pods.

The melons were plump and fragrant. It seemed it was just cool enough for broccoli and even peas. She was amazed at the flavor of her produce. There is nothing so tasty and crunchy as a carrot pulled right from the ground, scrubbed to a shiny orange and munched immediately.

The plants grew rapidly in the fertile volcanic soil and warm temperatures, but the insects, and sometimes other predators, took their toll. She learned to plant more than they needed in order to share a portion of her crop with the critters. She used no fertilizers or chemicals in this her first garden, as she learned that certain plants, like onions and marigolds, repelled insects.

Paco walked by and asked, "Aren't you going to plant more potatoes?"

She shook her head, "They take up too much space." She decided they were cheap to buy and not worth the effort.

The farm's golden mutt lay next to George's stroller, watching her hoe. She turned the tenacious weeds over in the dark soil, picked a slug off of a well-chewed lettuce leaf and then decided the leaf had to go as well—it was barely a lacework pattern supported by its ribs. Lettuce was hard to grow in the tropics, strawberries nearly impossible.

"I think the bugs get as many tomatoes and lettuce as we do," she told the no-name dog.

He wagged his tail and panted, encouraging her. Alicia straightened and arched her spine to stretch, one hand on the back of her waist.

It was time he had a name. "Old Yeller," she named him, after the dog in the children's book.

She turned their kitchen scraps into compost, significantly reducing the amount of garbage to be disposed of. It astonished her how quickly it turned to a dark organic soil in this warm, moist climate. She began adding paper as well. They did not have stacks of newspapers, and as long as the quantity was small compared to the kitchen refuse, there was no problem.

Every week one of Paco's men took the rest of the garbage and placed it in a hole in a far corner of the property. Even though the family had for years reused all of their bags and glass jars, their private landfill was starting to take up far too much space.

George was six months old and on the verge of crawling. It was time to return to Bogotá for his check-up. Alicia changed out of her shorts for the drive. She had taken to wearing shorts on the warmest days—Jorge didn't think they were quite appropriate around their male workers or even his parents, but he had given in. His theory was: let her have her way over the little things, he would have the last word over the bigger decisions.

They had planned to take off early in the afternoon, but first they waited for George to finish his nap, then they decided to have an early supper rather than be hungry on the road. Now Alicia and Jorge sat on the front porch, as usual after their meal. They could not be rushed, they lived the sedate pace of South American life, a gracious life. They might be late for an appointment and were always "late" for social invitations—but then, it would be odd, if not rude, to arrive on time.

"We'd better get going or you'll be driving most of the way in the dark again."

"I reckon," he smiled. Reckon. He'd picked that up from Peter.

"I hate to leave," Alicia sighed as they got into the jeep.

The light seemed particularly golden, the air moist and sweet. In retrospect it might be said their unwillingness to leave, to relinquish the moment, was a premonition. But for now, bliss and beauty surrounded the finca. The passionflower vine was in full bloom.

"Well, we haven't been back for months and now it's time for George's check-up with Dr. Gamboa. Isn't that right Georgie?" Marta took her brood to Dr. Gamboa and had recommended him.

Jorge held George high before placing him on her lap. "Our son will be crawling before we come home."

They drove out the driveway past the bougainvillea. The yellow dog trotted alongside beyond the graceful jacaranda trees fragrant with blossoms, and watched them disappear. As they drove through Escondido, two small brown boys in faded ragged pants raced alongside the jeep shouting, *"Adios don Jorge!"*

Jorge grinned and waved as he drove by the town square with its giant *ceiba* tree. No one knew how old the tree was, but the elders claimed it was old when *they* were children. It must have been around for well over a hundred years.

"Que le vaya bien!" someone else called out.

"My goodness," Alicia commented, "Everyone seems to know us...or you!"

"Well they've seen me all of my life. We hire half the town to pick coffee."

They drove in silence for an hour along the winding dirt road. It was still light out. The green hills were bathed in warm colors—the golden-amber lights that appear right before dusk. Once they met another car and a little later a bus. The bus careened around the corner, veering beyond the edge of its lane, making it difficult for the two vehicles to pass.

"Whew," she breathed, "they drive like idiots."

Jorge smiled, she always said that. "Shall we sing?"

"I'm tired. You sing." She found her throat dry from the fine dust that filtered up from the road through every crevice. It was *veranillo*—little summer—the short break in the rains that usually occurred in July. It had lasted three weeks this year with only occasional gentle showers, so the roads were more dusty than muddy.

He sang a few rambunctious drinking songs and then settled down to serenading his small family in his off-key tenor. He would take his wife's hand whimsically when he got to a romantic line, but then quickly return both hands to the wheel to maneuver a curve.

They looped around the hills and as the light faded, Jorge turned on the headlights. His theory—that it was safer on these roads at night because you could see the headlights before the vehicle—seemed logical when they passed another jeep on the next curve. Its lights, beaming around the corner, gave warning of its approach.

"That's the third car this evening. I'm surprised there are so many on the road," he noted.

"Look at the moon," Alicia whispered. It had come up over the hills in full glory as the red sun set behind them. It was a beautiful evening with chirping *animalitos* they could not identify, crickets perhaps. Amazing how the mere scraping together of tiny wings could produce such a racket. The moon disappeared into the purple shadows and then re-emerged to turn the road into a ribbon of moonlight. It reminded her of a song Felipe liked to sing: *Solo la luna me acompañaba* – the moon was my only companion.

"*Que lindo!*" Jorge proclaimed.

He heard the oncoming vehicle before he saw it. It had no headlights to warn them as it careened around the curve and into their path. Jorge moved his right foot instantly to the brake and his left to the clutch as he swerved with practiced skill to the outer edge of the road. In that split second he realized he had to either meet them head-on or drive over the precipice. The jeep fishtailed and screeched to a stop. For a long instant, they watch horrified as the car skidded towards them before metal met metal in a jarring crash that sounded like an explosion.

Alicia slumped in the seat, dazed. Half in shock, she expected Jorge to reach out, to ask if they were okay. As if from a distance, she heard George screaming. Miraculously, he was still in her arms. Vaguely she heard male voices in the road, swearing but laughing. "*Puta!*" someone swore drunkenly.

And then all sound muffled as her own heartbeat pounded in her ears and icy tendrils of fear rippled through her. Jorge was silent and still, draped over the steering wheel. She stared at him in bewilderment, his bloody face turned toward her. She struggled out of her seat belt to switch on the overhead light.

Two figures stood next to the driver's window. A third was getting out of the other mangled vehicle.

"Uuh, este más bien está muerto!" That one's dead, one of them slurred.

"Oh dear God!" Alicia cried, hardly able to breathe.

She frantically felt for Jorge's pulse.

"Eh, está muerto?"

"Shut up!" she yelled in English and set the three drunks to whispering as she laid her head on Jorge's chest listening for a heartbeat. She felt rather than heard it pump and was doubly relived when she also felt his chest rise faintly as he breathed.

He was alive but unconscious. He had not been wearing a seat belt. The windscreen was smashed into a spider web where his head had hit. They had not been going very fast—you could not drive very fast on a dirt road with hairpin turns and potholes. They could have been killed all the same. A head-on collision.

She quickly evaluated which of the three men was at least not staggering, and gave him the wailing bundle that was George. They all stared into the driver's side. Alicia could smell the reek of rum in the air surrounding her.

"Help me stretch him out," she ordered in Spanish.

"*Sí señora!*" they replied in unison. They seem to have sobered slightly.

They pushed the front seat back as far as it would go, then shoved and tugged until Jorge lay awkwardly across its length, his legs hanging out the passenger door. He moaned as the men lifted and dragged him, and her heart leapt at this sign of life.

Then she noticed one leg turned at a funny angle. She felt the large bump of broken bone pushing against the flesh of his calf. He shouldn't have been moved at all, but there would be no ambulance on this country road. She thought about splinting his leg, but knew she needed to get him to a hospital as quickly as possible and that might take another couple of hours. She rolled down the window and leaned the broken leg out of it. Then she carefully closed the door, bending the other leg against it.

The baby was still howling at the top of his lungs. Alicia took him from the man and laid him on his father's chest—praying that Jorge didn't have internal injuries as well—as it was the only place she could see George. Alicia sucked in her breath as she realized the baby blanket had blood on it. She ran her fingers over his little body lightly, quickly, and found no evidence of broken bones. He seemed to be quieting. The blood must have belonged to the man who had held him. She couldn't worry about them now.

She eased into the driver's seat, placing Jorge's head in her lap. His face frightened her, even in the dim interior light she could see it was drained of color. The seat was back too far for her, but it was the only way his head would fit between her and the steering wheel. George protested as Alicia fit him into the depression between the seat back and his father's body. The engine started, but for a sickening moment the vehicle rolled back an inch as a wheel spun in the soft mud and gravel at the edge of the overhang. She attacked the brake frantically, but then mercifully the crumpled jeep leapt forward as she shifted into first gear.

"You shouldn't be driving...turn on your lights!" she yelled as she veered around the other vehicle. Alicia was hardly aware of what she was doing, but she drove the jeep by rote, as if on automatic pilot.

After they crossed the Magdalena River, three-quarters of the way to Bogota, she thought she heard him moan. She pulled over and turned on the light.

"Jorge! Jorge! Oh God!" she cried as if she had just fathomed the seriousness of their plight. Hearing the distress in his mother's voice George began to cry again. She slapped Jorge's face lightly and his eyelids flickered. She tried it again.

"Please wake up!"

"Nooo," he moaned in protest to the slaps. She tried to rouse him once more and his eyes flickered open briefly, he shook his head weakly. She knew the longer he remained unconscious the more serious his condition. There was nothing for her to do but drive on. She caressed his cheek, pressed her lips firmly together and started on the road once more. George continued to shriek.

"Be quiet," she told him, her jaw set, her tone dead serious. Amazingly the child stopped crying, as if rendered speechless, unaccustomed to such a cold tone from anyone.

Barely able to see the road through the smashed windshield, she drove with the window open so she could peek out as needed, but it was not so cold now they were down the mountain. She leaned out to see a truck blocking the road in front of her. Half a dozen men, some with guns. She registered this hazily. God! Was it possible to have two disasters in the space of one evening?

As she rolled to a stop, a gruff man with long hair and ammunition slung across one shoulder pointed a gun at her and ordered her out. Instead, she clung to the steering wheel and began to cry, to explain, "*Accidente... hospital...!*" She heard her voice rise hysterically and made no effort to control it.

The bewildered man called out to his companions. Someone bought a flashlight and shined it on the disheveled woman, the wailing baby, the bloody unconscious man on her lap, the broken windshield and crumpled fender.

"She's telling the truth." They discussed the situation. "Let's let them go," the bewildered man suggested.

"Should we help them?" another asked.

"No! Just a bunch of rich people." Someone else said they could drive them. "No, no! Too dangerous, we could be caught!"

"We should keep her... *americana...!*"

"No, please!" Alicia said through her tears. "I can drive...please, please just let us go," She used all her wiles. Begging. Crying pathetically. Acknowledging they had the power.

Finally someone organized the removal of the truck blocking the road.

"Buena suerte, señorita," someone offered in a serious tone. She started to correct them and realized how ludicrous that was.

"Good luck," the others parroted. Some swore. Another laughed.

Señorita, she snorted to herself in spite of this nightmare. Couldn't they see she had a husband and child? She thought maybe she *was* having a nightmare and hoped she would wake up soon in her own bed at Las Nubes with Jorge sleeping peacefully by her side.

The road continued to unwind slowly before her like a huge ball of yarn unraveling endlessly. Somehow she clung to the wheel and managed to stay in her lane. Mercifully, George went to sleep, lulled by the motion of the car. They were climbing now, up to the chilly plateau where Bogotá lay. Jorge muttered and moaned now and again, causing her heart to pound with hope, and fear. Reaching behind the seat she felt a *ruana* and managed to put it over him and George.

"Wake up darling, we're almost there."

She might have been talking to herself. She had only a vague idea where they were and no sense of when they would arrive.

"I just want to sleep," Jorge said, his voice slurred and groggy.

She shook his shoulder gently, "No, Jorge, please...wake up!" He groaned.

She forced herself to focus on the road, feeling like they were in limbo and she was driving the shattered jeep into eternity. At last the lights of Bogotá emerged, twinkling.

Chapter 10
ADJUSTMENTS

A nurse took the baby from her. Finally, after hours of hell, hands were reaching out to help them. Someone patted her and smoothed the hair out of her eyes. She let them. The voices were tender, consoling, but efficient.

She slumped into a chair next to Jorge's bed, staring at his smooth, olive-skinned hands with their long fingers. She took one limp hand in her own. It seemed as if he might be dead, but then she heard him speaking weakly, more than he'd spoken throughout the ordeal, although somewhat garbled.

Now a doctor was gently asking her questions and she heard herself reply mechanically, as if she were a robot. They examined her bruises and allowed her to stay in the room with her husband.

"Are you sure you want to be in the same room? You need your rest too."

She assured them she did, even though they said someone would check Jorge every twenty minutes throughout the night. A nurse promised her the baby would be well cared for, and gave her a sedative. By the time they left, he was asleep again and she wanted to wake him to hear him speak to her, to see his swollen face smile. She wanted to stretch out on the narrow bed with him and press their bodies together, safe and close.

She lay on a padded cot and listened to unfamiliar noises—hospital bustle, voices, occasional rumbling from the street. Not at all the soothing sounds she was used to at home when they fell asleep. But hearing Jorge snore softly, sleep overcame her, creeping over her exhausted mind and body.

During the night Jorge had a seizure while they were shining a light in his eyes to gauge his pupil reaction. Alicia, who usually awoke at the slightest noise, slept right through the lights and commotion. The sedative, combined with exhaustion, rendered her practically comatose.

In the morning, a specialist examined Jorge, "You have a concussion, but you appear to be on the mend." He would have to stay twenty-four hours for observation and rest. He could speak, eat...and, were his leg not broken, walk. Only his recent memory seemed impaired; he'd no recollection of the accident. He surprised Alicia by telling her he did, however vaguely, remember part of the drive to the hospital.

"I thought about telling you I was OK, but I wanted you to worry about me...a little," he gave her a weak smile. "I didn't realize it was serious....or how long it was."

"What? You rat!"

"I was sleepy and my head was killing me. I guess I slept most of the way? I thought about pretending not to recognize you this morning just to see what you would do," he grinned.

Alicia made an exasperated face, but forgave him, glad that he could still be playful, even under dire circumstances. She should have been annoyed, but was just glad to be able to look into his chocolate eyes again. And she didn't really believe he was conscious much after the accident. He didn't remember the men who had held them up.

"Were they *bandidos*? *Revolucionarios*? Drug smugglers? What did they want?"

"I didn't ask them."

"My brave little wife! You must have been scared. They could have been the FARC."

The *Fuerzas Armadas Revolucionarias de Colombia* were the country's most infamous guerrillas — Marxists, who had started out as the "People's Army" seven or eight years ago and gone bad.

"Yes," she thought, amazed. She'd been dazed and so frantic for Jorge that she had felt more angry and desperate than scared. Her unexpected reaction had saved them. Maybe if it had not been for the accident they would have been killed, kidnapped or at minimum robbed, and left stranded on foot and penniless in the middle of the night with their baby. Another disappearance, mugging or robbery on Colombian roads. "I didn't even think to offer them my purse!"

"Maybe they were FARC. They must not have thought we would make very good soldiers!" Jorge kidded. *"Bandidos* would have asked for your money."

The guerrillas kidnapped civilians and pressed them into their military operations — even children. The right-wing paramilitary, FARC's enemies, were rumored to do this too. All of the numerous guerrilla factions were bandits as far as Alicia was concerned.

They had to stay in Bogotá for two weeks until the Head Doctor, as Felipe called the neurologist, allowed Jorge to leave. In addition, the orthopedist wanted to check on his leg before he left town. He was in a cast to the knee — which they would have to drive all the way back to Bogotá to have removed in a month or so — and on crutches. Jorge was a terrible patient, irate and impatient to walk.

"Hey! Could someone bring me my coffee? I can't wait on myself here," he shouted in choleric tones at Alicia, the Carvallo's maid, Rosa, or anyone within hearing distance.

Mostly he did not like to be left alone unless he was sleeping, in which state he spent an inordinate amount of time. Only George could make him smile.

The week before they planned to drive back to Las Nubes, the family sat around the table after lunch as usual. Pepe got up, followed by Marta. They vanished upstairs to grab a quick siesta before he had to return to work. Rosa was clearing the dishes when Abuelita announced, "I would like to go back to Las Nubes for a visit."

They all turned to her in surprise. She had not made the drive to the finca in years and she wasn't getting any younger. She'd turned 78 in August.

"The road is worse than ever, Mamá, and so dusty," Claudia said.

Abuelita ignored her, "I miss it. I want to see it again before I die. Do you ever have visitors?" she asked dreamily.

Jorge blinked and told her about Peter.

"So what does this *americano* want at the finca?" her tone changed.

"He's a friend, Abuelita," Jorge replied gazing at his coffee.

"He's looking for gold," Felipe added.

"Let's hope he doesn't find it."

Alicia and Claudia sat listening quietly. Sometimes it was hard to get a word in edgewise, although Abuelita never had the problem—tapping her glass with her spoon if necessary.

"Now why would you say that, Mamá?" Felipe said. "He's a nice young man, it would be good for him and bring work and money to the country."

"Ha!...Hmmpf!" she snorted.

Jorge left the table with a dark look and after a while Felipe and Claudia walked into the hall, talking. Alicia stood up with George in her arms and Abuelita started struggling up on her cane, but sank back down again.

"*Niña*," she heard the old woman say.

Alicia looked up startled, to see if the word "child" was actually addressed to her. The dowager had never spoken to her directly before. "*Sí, Abuelita*, can I help you?"

She started around the table, but the old woman put up a veined hand and then motioned for her to sit back down. Alicia obeyed and waited, her back erect.

"He's a pretty child," she indicated George who was struggling to be free. Alicia sat him down on the floor and he promptly rolled over on his stomach and began the serious business of learning to crawl. First he balanced himself and "swam" with all four limbs in the air. Then he managed to get his knees under himself and pumped back and forth on his chubby little arms, expressing some glee at his accomplishment. After all, he'd no one to imitate here. Except for the difficulty of balance, learning to walk would be easier.

"*Sí señora,*" Alicia stammered slightly, wanting to watch George, but paying attention.

"You like living at Las Nubes."

"*Sí señora. Me gusta mucho,*" she felt like she was at an interview.

"I was a young bride myself when we lived there. We were very content...*muy contentos.*" She nodded and her crinkled face broke into the semblance of a smile. She was suddenly unintimidating, almost kindly. It was her eyes—they brightened for a moment as her mind took her back many decades to recapture the happiness in her youth. Alicia could suddenly envision a young woman in a long dress roaming the gardens, waiting for her husband to come home.

"Now tell me, what do you like about it?"

Alicia replied, "Oh...the trees, the birds...the way of life."

The old woman nodded again, "How are the jacaranda trees?"

"Oh! They are lovely," Alicia said and also told her about the fruit trees and all the flowers.

"Claudia never took to it, a pity," Abuelita clucked her tongue and then regarded the younger woman for a moment. "You don't look like a diplomat's daughter. You seem more, ahhhh.... purposeful."

Alicia didn't know what reply was required of her. She started to say she wasn't a diplomat's daughter, but Abuelita continued in a more serious vein, "The foreigners can be dangerous. They change things they know nothing about. If they find gold, they will pave the road and build more roads through the trees. It will make everyone happy at first and then Las Nubes and Escondido...could turn into Medellin and Cali."

"I can't imagine..." Alicia started, but was distracted when, out of the corner of her eye, she saw George reach for a napkin which had fallen on the floor, moving an arm forward an inch followed by the other knee and his torso. He collapsed with a triumphant baby noise making his mother smile.

"No, no one can imagine," Abuelita went on curtly, wagging a gnarled finger. "You have to live a long time to see that development...is not always a good thing." She nodded sagely, then smiled at her great-grandson.

The rains washed Peter out of the hills and he arrived at Las Nubes to find Jorge and Alicia gone.

"Ay, don Peetro, I'm so worried about the *familia,*" Carmen told him. "They have been gone for two weeks. They never go for so long."

She'd no inkling about the accident. She would have had to walk into town to see if they had left her a message.

Peter settled into his room, inked his maps and typed up his notes. Carmen was delighted to have someone to look after. He took her and Humberto into Escondido the following drizzly day for supplies.

"Why don't you take the day off and I'll come back for you tomorrow? I can mind the finca," he flicked his hand out to make her understand she could go.

"*Uuhn....doña Alicia....*"

"Won't mind a bit," he finished the sentence for her—as best he could in Spanish. "I'll take responsibility," he said tapping his chest.

With a face betraying excitement, she rattled off a string of sentences; he only gleaned "*mi hombre,*" but that gave him the picture.

"OK," he grinned, "I'll pick you up *mañana. Comprende?*"

"*Sí, sí! Comprendo!*"

Carmen used the rear-view mirror to comb her hair and put on some lipstick before skipping off for her unanticipated rendezvous. Peter smiled after her, thinking mischievously that he'd given her more than just an unexpected day off.

The house was silent when he returned. He had never been at the finca when it was not full of people.

He was quite used to being alone, however. Liked it even.

On the way to his room he passed Jorge and Alicia's door. He back-tracked a step and stood in the doorway a moment before entering the room. Peter sat on the bed, stared at a pillow and picked it up idly. On impulse he held it to his face and inhaled her scent.

What am I doing? He shook his head and smiled warily.

He put the pillow back and picked up her notebook, flipping through the pages. An ordinary black and white notebook, the kind the school children used. Her handwriting was not the usual feminine script, it was functional, not flowery, yet there was a certain grace to it. It seemed to fit her.

Her drawings were very good and showed meticulous attention to detail. Flowers were described, petals and stamen were counted, colors and other features labeled. Leaves were shown and labeled *pinnate, palmate*, etc., so they could easily be identified — or at least classified — by a botanist. There were interesting seedpods, insects, ferns. A funny looking flower caught his eye. It was odd but somehow familiar, perhaps a houseplant he'd seen before. The long leaves overlapped to form a thick rosette base and a single flower jutted out of the top.

Alicia had labeled each part of the plant and written:

May, 9, 1972
Bromeliad — (Aechmaea rhodocyanea?). Fallen from above.

Silvery banded, up to 22" long.
Watertight reservoir.
Hot pink bracts (each 1") with tiny blue flowers.

A line labeled what Peter erroneously judged to be a petal of a single huge flower — it was actually composed of many small bracts and flowers.

Snapping the notebook shut, he put the distraction aside and went back to his room. He opened the window to clear the mustiness from the room. The air was damp, but fresh and cool.

Peter enjoyed inspecting the fruits of his labor almost as much as the fieldwork. Putting it all together, making sense of rock samples, geochemical signatures and hundreds of years of prospects and old mines dating back to the early Spaniards. Like a detective organizing clues, solving a puzzle.

He worked backwards. First, he came across a mineral or an old prospect, which might merely be allied with gold or platinum. His job was to scout out possibilities for further exploration. If he was clever and very lucky, he might find a deposit. So far he'd found only mineral associations and collected hundreds of rock chips and stream sediment samples. He hoped to find more vein materials where precious metals were most apt to be concentrated.

He began cleaning and prioritizing the samples for packing. He would ship the best to the lab for analysis. He picked up a specimen and examined it again — for the second or third time — with his hand lens. What looked like an ordinary rock to most people revealed minerals identifiable by crystal shape, form, hardness and other properties under the lens. Was that a tiny piece of gold, or just a bit of mica stained with iron oxide?

There was a petrographic microscope in the company offices in Bogotá and sometimes he went to the trouble of cutting the rock into a paper-thin slice and using the scope to accurately identify and quantify the minerals present. If he found minerals associated with gold, platinum, or other precious minerals worth mining, he would go back for a more detailed inspection of the area.

The next day when he went to pick up Carmen, her daughter Carolina with her as well as her son.

Carolina eyed him, smiling, cocking her chin, confident in her youth, "*Hola Peeter.*" Not *don* Peter as Carmen usually addressed him.

Carolina took the front seat. He grinned back at her, "*Hola, qué tal?*"

———

It took the repair shop in Bogotá an inordinate number of days to fix the jeep's windshield and hammer out the dents. *Mañana,* they were told day after day. Finally, over two weeks after Felipe dropped the vehicle off—and a week after it was promised—the old jeep was ready. Its front fender was straightened, but the metal still bumpy and the fresh paint did not quite match the old worn color of the rest of the body.

Alicia was relieved they could at last return to Las Nubes and their normal life.

They arrived late in the afternoon in a downpour. Alicia ran for the house, carrying George.

"Paco!" Jorge bellowed from his crutches as he negotiated the steps, "Come help with the bags!" He had left the jeep door hanging open and was soaking wet.

Carmen ran out to help Paco, hefting bags up the steps to the veranda where the tin roof drummed its usual din to the rhythm of the cloudburst.

After they had changed into dry clothes Carmen told them, "*Don Peetro estuvo aqui.*"

"When? For how long?" Alicia asked as she shifted George on her hip. Peter had stayed several days and just left — which meant he wouldn't be back for a while.

"I made him *americano* food," Carmen grinned, showing her gold tooth. She meant spaghetti, which Alicia had taught her to make.

Alicia had not prepared many meals before getting married, but Carmen was impressed that she knew how to bake bread and cookies from scratch and could make "exotic" foreign foods like spaghetti and chop suey. Carmen, on the other hand, was an experienced cook who knew how to season an ordinary dish to coax out extraordinary flavors.

She taught Alicia to make *casado* — a standard meat, potato and vegetable dish — and stretch it into leftovers for *mañana* and soup the third day. *Casado* translated as "married." It was one of those basic dishes a married woman was expected to know how to prepare.

"Go away! Let me sleep." Alicia had to wake Jorge every day or he would sleep all morning. It was difficult to get him out of bed.

"It's after eight o'clock." Sometimes it was nine o'clock, but otherwise these were the words they exchanged every morning. She'd tried to get him to readjust to their old schedule — up with the sun and early to bed. It didn't make sense to leave the generator on long after dinner, or burn kerosene lamps all hours of the night. But he often slept during the day and stayed up late.

Alicia was up first and usually waited so they could breakfast together. Jorge hated being on crutches, but could not manage without them, especially the stairs.

"Maybe I should make the couch into a bed for you downstairs," she suggested.

But he did not like that idea. She helped him dress and was by his side most of the time. She drove the jeep for him and learned something new about the finca every day.

Their water supply relied on rainfall, which was usually copious. The rain ran off the red tiles sloped on top of the house and into the gutters. From there it funneled into a large, screened cistern. The gutters had to be kept clean, both to prevent them from clogging and for hygienic reasons.

"Make sure Paco checks them," he told her.

She drove Carmen to Escondido for groceries and supplies and left Jorge at home to rest. Carmen was good company and Alicia enjoyed the drive. In the village there was always someone cheerfully willing to carry their bags in exchange for a modest tip. This was helpful because, with the two children, they usually had at least one arm engaged.

Jorge complained if they took too long because he got bored. While he let her go around the finca with Paco, he would say, "Don't be gone so long this time."

She would have enjoyed her new responsibilities, except Jorge seemed like a different person. He was subdued, less interested in his wife, their son, and the finca. Alicia figured he was just a poor patient, anxious to get out of his cast.

But even little Humberto noticed, *"Que pasa con don Jorge?"* he asked his mother.

"He's sick," Carmen told him. "We must play quietly and be very nice to him." Humberto nodded somberly, his eyes wide beneath dark lashes.

There was something else. The week they returned, Jorge had another seizure. It was over in a second, but he was supporting George on his good knee when his upper torso twisted violently, flinging the child to the floor.

Alicia picked up their startled, but unharmed, son reassuring him with her touch.

"You OK?" she asked Jorge. He blinked, his face impassive, as she stared at him, frightened.

"Que...que pasó?" he asked. The look on her face clearly conveyed something had gone wrong.

"You don't know?" Alicia cocked her head.

"No," he answered in a slow, uncertain tone. He realized he must have dropped George because one minute he was holding him and now the child was in Alicia's arms, sniffling.

She told him and they sat and talked about it awhile. Jorge was obviously confused about his loss of consciousness, but said, "I don't think I had an actual *seizure*."

"You need to go back to Bogotá and see the doctor. This could be serious."

"No!" he said in a way that told her it was useless to argue. "Don't tell me what to do," he added in curt Spanish.

They had always spoken to each other in English when they were alone, but he'd begun addressing her more frequently in Spanish.

"Look, Alicia. I had a little episode before. It's no big deal."

Jorge actually feared something was seriously wrong, but couldn't admit it to Alicia—it was too frightening and she would just nag him and frustrate him even more. He was functioning fine; he just didn't quite feel like himself. It was as if he were watching someone else portray Jorge Carvallo—an actor he didn't agree with and had little control over.

The children seemed far noisier than before and Alicia irritated him with her worried eyes. His parents were even worse, yet he had the feeling he would not have found them so annoying a month or two ago; that maybe he wasn't being entirely fair—or worse, rational.

Her eyes were wide. "Does the doctor know?"

He nodded. The doctor had given him medication in case the episodes continued. Phenobarbital. He would start taking it. Maybe he'd had other episodes without realizing it. If he lost consciousness for just a second or two but didn't hurt himself, how would he know?

Alicia wanted to hold him, but he would not permit it. He disengaged her clinging arms, struggled to his feet and hobbled outside, seeking the relative peace of solitude. He could walk without crutches now, but gritty ceniza found its way down the heavy cast and it was driving him crazy. He needed to get the damn thing off. Maybe he could do it himself. Didn't they just saw it off?

Only their lovemaking conveyed the intimacy they once enjoyed. That night, lying in each other's arms with Alicia's head on his shoulder, everything seemed all right again.

But she needed to broach the subject. "You seem so far away these last few weeks — so preoccupied...or something." Her hand traced a curve across the smooth caramel skin of his breast.

He stiffened then sighed, hesitating before saying, "I don't know...I've been thinking...it just seems like I went to school, got married, started working and now we have a baby. It just happened so fast. I wish I'd had more time to have fun."

Stunned and indignant, Alicia had no idea what to say. She lay very still, almost afraid to move.

After a long pause he continued, "I've been thinking...I'd like to take off for a while. Maybe buy a motorcycle and tour South America for three or four months, you know?"

She felt her chest constrict. No, she thought, I do *not* know...but decided it was best not to argue at this point. Just wait. See if this Che Guevara fantasy passed once he was more himself. Jorge could be impulsive, but he was not irresponsible. When his parents came in a week or so they would reason with him.

"Well, it was just an idea," he blinked, his eyes perplexingly wet. "I've always wanted to drive the Pan American Highway."

Don Felipe decided to buy a new jeep after the accident and put it in Jorge's name. "They will be pleased to have a new one."

"Put it in Alicia's name," Claudia suggested. A novel idea. Claudia's name was not on their cars or other assets. Felipe frowned, "I could I suppose, *pero por qué?*"

"She deserves it—taking care of Jorge and running the finca too. Let her pick the color."

"No!" That would require a shopping trip with the women, too much effort. But he had to hand it to Alicia, she shouldered responsibility capably. "They only come in tan or green—maybe gray."

"Tan, I think, or the gray. Not that dull jeep-green," said Claudia.

Felipe smiled tolerantly. His family was full of modern ideas.

But he bought the new jeep and drove Abuelita to Las Nubes for a visit. It was the first time she'd driven through the mountain passes in almost eight years. Pepe followed in Felipe's vehicle with Marta.

"*Que bello es Colombia!*" Abuelita exclaimed. "Nothing has changed! Only the trees are bigger."

Alicia ran out when she heard the jeeps pull into the gravel drive. "Marta! What a good surprise!" she cried and embraced her warmly. She needed a friend to talk to.

There was the new jeep, but Abuelita was the real surprise. She was a different person at the finca. An old spark from her younger years still smoldered. She wanted freshly baked bread and swore the coffee tasted better at Las Nubes than in Bogotá.

"It's not processed here Abuela, it is the same coffee we drink in the city," Pepe, the realist, told her.

"It tastes better," she insisted.

Alicia half agreed with her. Coffee and food seemed more enjoyable here—the very air was a pleasure to inhale.

Abuelita rarely got out of her chair in Bogotá, but she strolled the wet grounds on Alicia's arm, or her son's, taking an interest in the vegetable garden, and flowers.

"Ah, you've done a good job taking care of the place. *Ay!* Look at that orchid! What a beauty!"

Abuelita was so happy and energetic Alicia feared she might decide to move in with them. Despite their tenuous new alliance, she did not want to live in the same house with the old woman. Neither did Jorge.

He was content to let Alicia take his father and Pepe around the finca. Pepe and Alicia were both heading towards the driver's door of the new jeep when she put a hand on his arm.

"May I drive?"

He looked at her wordlessly a moment then managed, "But...I'm here," he said, rather ineffectually.

Alicia was actually a decent driver. Practice had made her capable of maneuvering in tight spots, mud and rocks, but neither Pepe nor Felipe could believe it.

"Ah, let her drive the new jeep!" Felipe said, as if humoring child. Then to Alicia, bent over the wheel, "Do you know how to double clutch?"

"Yes, it's just like the old one, no?" she said, refraining from adding that she did this every day.

Before they headed back, Alicia broached the subject most often on her mind these days, "I'm very worried about Jorge."

"Ah! He'll be fine!" Pepe said.

"No, I mean, since the accident he's not himself. He's very grouchy."

"Well, anyone would be with their leg in a cast. Maybe he still has pain," Felipe offered dismissively.

"It is almost as if his personality has changed."

"We'll try to come more often," he replied patting her knee.

That wasn't the point, really, but she let it go.

When they returned, they heard an irritated exchange as they entered the house.

"*Sin vergüenza*...shame on you...letting your woman do all the work," Abuelita railed. "You're just coddling that leg!"

Jorge limped off, fuming silently. Alicia caught Pepe's eye, but Felipe ignored the commotion.

Later Alicia brought up the same subject with Claudia, but she didn't want hear it either. It drove her crazy that everyone thought he was perfectly normal. They viewed the problem as his broken leg. Alicia was worried about his head. They made no distinction between physical and psychological. A mental problem or brain injury was not acceptable.

Only Marta was sympathetic, but she said the same thing, "Give him time."

Time didn't seem to help much though. The air was rife with calamity that year.

PART II

SLEEPING GIANTS

1973-1977

Chapter 11
VOLCÁN CHARIMPÓ

It happened in the midst of the dry season. They heard what sounded like thunder rumbling in the night. It was strangely quiet when they awoke that morning—a quiet soon broken by excited voices. Downstairs Carmen and Paco were speaking to each other in fast, animated tones. The room was dark and Jorge considered going back to sleep, but looking at his watch he told Alicia, *"Ya son las 7:15."*

They were usually up by now—or at least she was. It didn't sound like rain but it must be cloudy—the sun should have risen an hour ago. He rolled over and closed his eyes as Alicia propped herself up on her elbows.

There was a soft rap at the door. *"Doña Alicia,"* Carmen called. Alicia got up quickly—Carmen never disturbed them.

"Venga vea! Come see! *El volcán!"*

They trotted down the hall and looked through the big glass window at a strange landscape. Everything was gray, as if they had landed on the moon...as if gray snow had fallen over night. Every structure, every plant was shrouded by a thin layer of volcanic ash and dust—*ceniza*. The rumblings they had heard were volcanic explosions in the distance. The ceniza rained out of heavy, yellowish clouds.

By the time they dressed and went out to inspect the finca, the ash was hardly falling, but small drifts accumulated next to the west side of the house. Carmen was busy sweeping the porch so they took George with them. Jorge held him while Alicia drove. The eruption cloud was dark and ominous in the direction of the volcano. It obscured the mountains and everything beyond the nearby hills. Every coffee plant was dusted with gray.

Jorge shook a branch and they watched ash the consistency of fine sand fall off in a heap.

"*Aghh!*" he exclaimed shaking his head. "We can't clean every bush!"

"It shouldn't hurt the fruit," Alicia said, thinking *if* it stops. "Ash is supposed to be good for the soil."

"*Aghh! Sí*, in fifty years! Or a hundred!" he jabbed his hands on his hips and swung around, craning his neck skyward. "You're supposed to be the scientist—what about photosynthesis?"

"It will rain soon and clean off the leaves."

And that's just what happened. It started to drizzle that afternoon, but the next day there was a downpour that lasted into the night.

When Alicia woke the next morning, the sun was shining through the window. She ran outside barefoot to find every exposed surface washed clean, every leaf fresh with dew.

Jorge watched her from the window, still wearing her nightgown, and smiled vaguely, shaking his head at his young bride—he still thought of her that way, although they had been married for almost a year and a half. She was four years younger than him. When they met Alicia had not yet turned twenty-one and four years seemed a significant difference. Was she twenty-three now or twenty-four?

Her hands were wrapped around her bare arms for warmth, her face turned to the heavens with a faint smile. She reminded him of a rhyme:

> *"Monday's child is fair of face,*
> *Tuesday's child is full of grace...*
> *but the child born on Sunday*
> *is blithe and bonny, good and gay."*

Sometimes her lighthearted spirit was almost annoying when he felt as gray as the ceniza and she contrasted gratingly with his mood. At other times, like now—when she appeared to be embracing the world—it was enough to save him from the doldrums. He knew this was what they needed...to stay optimistic and start anew.

———————

Unfortunately Volcán Charimpó was merely toying with them. Like a fickle lover, it had promised them a return to Eden and then reverted to its destructive behavior. The very next afternoon a new rumbling signaled another eruption.

The cycle continued, weeks of dark skies and depressing ash-fall, followed by cleansing showers. The situation was not improving Jorge's mood. Even Alicia felt oppressed, with darkness and ceniza everywhere. The landscape, once painted in a palette of greens dotted with the bright hues of flowers and fruits, had turned monochromatic.

It was the plants that bothered her most, every flower had faded under a dusting of gray. The funnels of the calla lilies filled with dark ash and sand until the weight bent or broke their stems. Likewise leaves and other blossoms were weighted down. An outdoors bursting with light, and lushness of life and sound had taken on the dull stillness of an old black and white photograph.

Juanita, the monkey, was constantly eating the grit because she would drop her fruit and pick it up later coated gray. Alicia tried to keep the area clean, but it was a losing battle.

Even Carmen's indefatigable optimism was flagging.

"I clean and clean...and still there is ceniza in every crevice, on every surface! *Uy, yay, ay!*"

And the children were beginning to be grumpy because their mothers kept them confined indoors on bad days. Humberto, who normally had the run of the courtyard, resented this restriction of his turf. George, who crawled around after him, was equally frustrated.

But today there was some relief. It had been windy overnight and the day was dawning clear. Jorge slept and George was just beginning to stir as Alicia rose and showered. She slipped into George's room silently, still combing out her damp hair. He was smiling sweetly and at his most appealing. Glad to see her.

"Ma-ma."

"Good morning, Little One."

He rubbed his cherub's face with a small fist as she gathered him from his crib and into her arms. They went outside, George still mellow and sleepy, his little body warm from his crib.

It seemed the earth had just awoken and showered too, even though it was no longer the rainy season. A pink sky in the east revealed one of those rare days of clear skies and glory. The soil was still gray, albeit a darker, healthier-looking gray since it was damp. The plants had been refreshed by the showers and were dewy. Alicia kissed the top of her son's head.

She decided to give herself a treat. Turning around she walked briskly back to the house and put George down in the kitchen. He balanced on his mother's index fingers as she leaned over him and grinned at the sight of Carmen.

"Will you take him?" Alicia asked.

"*Uy! Buenos días, venga mi amor,*" Carmen stretched her arms out to him.

He went willingly—Carmen's warm bosom as good as his mother's. He hardly distinguished between the two nurturers. George let go of Alicia's hands and with a look of concentration, tried to take a toddling step to Carmen. Both women lunged to reach out for him before he toppled and laughed as he giggled in glee.

"He is almost walking!"

"Almost!" Alicia said, wide-eyed with delight, "Tell don Jorge I've gone for a walk, OK?"

"Before breakfast?"

"*Sí.*"

The sooner she got off the more time she would have to herself. Jorge might sleep for a couple of hours yet with no one to wake him.

As she walked down the corridor she glimpsed something shiny on the hall table. She stopped to take a closer look and saw it was a ring. Jorge's wedding ring. Why had he left it here where the children might find it? She picked it up and tried it on. It fit over her own. She never took hers off—even to shower. Alicia put it down, moving it to the back of the table where it would be safer from little fingers.

Out on the back porch she put on the boots Peter had given her—how had she ever managed without boots?

She headed south and east this time, downhill into the wet rain forest. She followed one of several creeks on the property and then took a small fork, a rivulet really, one that barely flowed except after a good rain. Sticking to streams was her custom, the best way to avoid getting lost.

The smell of the forest was moist and heavy. Miraculously very little ceniza remained on the plants. Much of it was filtered out by the upper story of leaves, but the trees must have been cleansed of their load by the rain, for here and there were small piles of ash that had apparently slid off leaves in little clumps.

A butterfly, perched on a leaf, was attempting to open wings laden with moisture. It must have just emerged from a cocoon. New to the world it flexed its wings, opening them ever so slightly. Its life would span a mere two, perhaps three, weeks.

Over three inches tall, it displayed delicate legs, proboscis and antennae. The shiny black wings were dotted with purple spots, blending to an iridescent turquoise. The color, she had learned, was due to tiny overlapping scales on the wings. She watched for several minutes as the butterfly ever so slowly fanned its wings open, displaying its glory like a peacock. She was tempted to blow on it to help the wings open wider, but knew that might actually cause it harm.

Instead she took out her notebook and began to write. Alicia treated her outings as if they were part of a biological research project and took meticulous notes. She was essentially doing thesis work, without limiting it to one topic, and without the guidance of a university mentor. She couldn't possibly detail everything, even if she stayed at the same spot all morning, so she allowed herself the pleasure of being selective. Describing, drawing whatever curios of nature appealed to her most.

She was a fair sketcher but had never considered herself much of an artist. She drew best somewhat subconsciously, keeping her eye on the object and letting her pencil transfer the image blindly, without looking at the paper. She did this now, never taking her eyes from the butterfly. She knew from experience the more she concentrated at trying to make it right, jumping back from object to paper, the more likely she was to distort the proportions and details.

After five or ten minutes she was pleasantly astonished to see the drawing—it wasn't bad. In fact it was lovely, as if someone else had drawn it. Someone who knew how to capture the scale and every true trait of the winged beauty. As she focused more on attention to detail and accuracy than to the drawing itself, she was improving, something she would never have thought possible. Smiling she wrote her name next to the date, *January 15, 1973,* owning her creation.

The creature had finally unfolded its wings, but they were still too damp to fly. It would be a while yet before anything near the forest floor was dry. The butterfly would have to be more patient than she could be.

"Good luck," she told it, hoping it would not be spotted by a hungry bird or other predator.

It was after ten o'clock. She should get back. Retracing her steps along the little rivulet, she stopped to observe a fat scarab beetle. She'd sketched one like this before. She flipped through her notebook back to an entry early last year.

Beetle >2 cm by 1.5 cm. Iridescent coloring, includes blue-green and purple. Lifespan approx. 50(?) days.

Alicia knew that some of the flora and fauna she encountered were probably unnamed and perhaps unknown to anyone but herself. There are so many unidentified species of insects that she had few qualms about deciding to name the beetle. However, she was not very familiar with insect classification. She chewed on the pencil trying to remember the genus name for scarab beetles...*Canthon?* At last she scribbled *"Beetle: (Canthon?) iridescensia."*

She upgraded her previous drawing of the creature, noting the antennae were barbed, the middle two legs more crooked than the other four and the feet sharp little weapons. He was moving along at a good pace and soon disappeared.

As she lifted her gaze preparing to stand, she spied an orchid plant with not just one blossom but two, nestled among the leaves of a philodendron. One flower was spotted and past its prime, but the other was a fresh and dewy specimen whose petals were just opening. Ah! And there was a third promising bud. The flowers were a pale lilac and the central trumpet had yellow markings against a purple that became deeper and darker in the center.

But what, she wondered, were these flowers doing here? Orchids usually grow in the canopy — not in the understory. Somehow these beauties had fallen from the treetops and landed in the cushioning arms of the philodendron. Perhaps some animal had ripped the plant out, or dislodged it, jumping from branch to branch. At the base of the plant the fat pseudobulb and aerial roots were still attached to a bit of bark. She could take it home and it should survive. Curling her index finger against her thumb, Alicia flipped a few ants and another insect off. A seedpod was also forming. She'd read the seeds are tiny — almost powdery.

Orchids are intriguing with their extraordinary shapes and elegant colors. They have three petals and also three sepals, which look just like petals. The most beautiful and colorful petal is shaped into a cup or a trumpet where the pollen waits seductively for a pollinator. They survive by cross-pollination and rely on their gorgeous looks, competing to attract various pollinators from butterflies and hummingbirds to bats, with an extraordinary exhibition of lures ranging from coloration, figure, pattern and scent.

Some orchids impersonate insects, evolving the form, hairs and design of a female fly or bee to attract the male. Completely fooled, the male insect climbs onto the flower and goes through the motions of copulation with acrobatic poses that guarantee he exits laden with pollen.

Alicia stared into the complicated beauty of the funnel. The colored pattern had wooed a small unsuspecting insect into its center. It was now covered in a viscous liquid produced by the orchid's sexual organs.

The top of the long, convoluted tunnel was shaped like a trap door and the insect was trying to extricate itself, picking up pollen as it navigated the sticky maze. Alicia walked on, admiring the flowers' delicacy and demure cunning, and tripped before she made herself pay attention to large roots and a host of other obstacles she could fall over.

It had been a wondrous morning—the beetle, the butterfly, and now an orchid had practically fallen in her lap. It could have fallen a few feet further and she never would have seen it. It could have been snagged in the tangle of overhead branches and lianas. It should have by rights been damaged in its descent—

what are the odds that such a delicate flower could survive a drop of... what? Sixty feet? Perhaps more. And yet, against all odds, an intact orchid plant— rather than just the blossom, which would die in a matter of days, a week at the most—lay in her hand. She wondered if she had discovered a new species.

She might as well name it...she was pretty certain *Cattelya* was the genus name for this orchid. What was its outstanding characteristic to give as a species name? She looked up at the canopy as if for inspiration while she thought, and a smile flicked across her face. She could name it for herself, *Cattelya aliciana,* no one need ever know this bit of vanity.

She tucked her notebook into the back of her jeans and began to walk quickly. Jorge would not be pleased that she'd left him all morning. She'd been lost in the world of the rain forest and had not thought of him or George, much less the finca, until now. It was eleven o'clock as she left the canopy of trees at the edge of the coffee plantings and picked up her pace. Walking was easy here between the rows and there were fewer distractions.

Noticing that there were quite a few coffee leaves on the ground, she paused. Was she imagining it, or did the coffee plants not look as healthy as they had a month or two ago? She examined several leaves that appeared discolored, spotted. Was this a disease, or insects? Alicia moved slowly. She had noticed discoloration a few days ago but on just a few bushes. Now many plants seemed affected. The green cherries, as if anxious to be harvested, were quickly turning red. She collected a few leaves to show Jorge. They looked almost burned around the edges. The *ceniza?* But it was no longer hot by the time the winds carried it way over here.

She had resumed her trek back toward the house when the jeep appeared on the dirt road.

Jorge leaned out the window looking cross. "Where have you been?" he asked.

"I decided to walk out and have a look at the coffee. Look at this." She presented the discolored leaves.

The partial deception was out of her mouth without thinking as soon as she saw his furrowed brow, his stony face. It had rolled out so smoothly, so unexpectedly, she'd startled herself. She prided herself on her honesty. It was not a lie exactly, she told herself, but an omission to avoid haranguing. Jorge seemed in no mood to tolerate her "eccentricity."

He got out of the vehicle to inspect the crop more closely. He was distracted from quizzing her. She realized she still had the orchids in her hand. She wanted to show him, but that would mean fessing up. She placed them gingerly behind the seat.

"Puta!" Jorge swore after examining the damaged leaves.

He looked around at the other bushes taking in the number of ripening cherries, the yellow leaves on the ground.

"I think we may have to harvest sooner then we planned," Alicia said.

He gave her a look that said it was not her decision, but replied slowly, *"Tal vez.* I'll try to get hold of Papi."

Jorge wasn't in a hurry. He didn't drive into Escondido to use the phone until the following day and then he couldn't get through.

"I guess we'll wait," he told Alicia. "We were going to organize it in a few weeks anyway when Papi comes."

———

They were standing in the fields again the following morning with Paco. There were plenty of coffee cherries, but they were ripening more quickly than usual. A plant under stress will go to seed rapidly if it senses its health is threatened. It is nature's way of re-seeding and preserving the species even if the plant dies. Alicia implored Jorge to start picking the beans.

"If we wait another two weeks we might lose part of the crop," she fretted.

Some of the ripened cherries were already shriveled. Finally Paco, turning his hat in his hands, spoke respectfully to Jorge, "*Patrón*, it looks to me...that is to say...the fruit will start rotting if they are not harvested soon."

"*Sí, sí,*" Jorge waved a vague hand in the air. It was still the dry season and he did not see the rush.

"Send a cable if you can't get through by phone," Alicia urged.

Jorge scowled. "I'm not going to send a cable! Let me handle this, would you?" Alicia was stepping into his territory, he thought furiously. It was one thing when he'd been on crutches last year, when he needed help, but now she would not back off. She was always giving him advice, telling him what to do, as if he had no clue. In fact, he had already changed his mind and decided to go into the village to call Felipe. He drove off without a word.

After Jorge left, Alicia told Paco, "Start rounding up the workers."

He was surprised that doña Alicia was giving the orders but knew she was right. A hard rain would knock the fruit off the bushes, and even without rain, the red cherries would be mushy within a few days at the rate they were ripening. He hoped don Jorge would not chew him out.

The pickers arrived early in the morning two days later, some with their own baskets over their arms or tied over their backs, a few with pails balanced on their heads. The men, and many of the women, wore dark felt hats.

If Jorge was surprised by how quickly Paco had assembled the workers, he said not a word. They fanned out among the rows of coffee plants. Alicia and Jorge joined them, much to the laborers' surprise. Although Alicia had joined in harvests before just for fun, now it was a more serious matter.

"Look out for the snakes," a stocky female worker cautioned her.

She was not kidding. The green snakes that were sometimes found among the bushes were small, but poisonous — the bane of coffee pickers. They worked fast, since they were paid by the basket, but not so fast that they became careless.

Late in the morning Paco paused to inspect the cherries piling up as each basket was unloaded onto the cement pad. Unlike past harvests when the cherries were bright red and plump, some of these were shriveled. They formed meager piles compared to previous pickings and the workers had thrown in some that were half-orange with specks of green to compensate.

———————

The following afternoon Pepe and don Felipe arrived to help with the arrangements to deliver the beans to the coffee buyers. They were wearing fresh white shirts. By contrast, Alicia and Jorge — collapsed with fatigue in their chairs — badly needed showers. They were both covered in red bites from the tiny coffee bugs.

They sat at the table with Pepe and Marta, mostly wordless and somber. Jorge examined his dirty fingernails as if they belonged to someone else. The collar, back and underarms of his shirt were stained with perspiration. Alicia's clothes were also grimy, her hair unkempt. But worse, far worse, was that the volcano was again churning ash into the atmosphere, darkening the skies and silently falling on the workers and the plants, covering everything gray.

Finally Pepe said, "In all these years nothing like this has ever happened. It's the worst harvest we've ever had."

Claudia had a fit when she learned of Jorge and Alicia working the fields, and Felipe was none too pleased either.

"We had to...we needed all the help we could get," Jorge said wearily.

"My family working like peons," Felipe cried. "And Alicia! I would rather we suffer poverty than subject you to manual labor. No! No more!"

Chapter 12
CENIZA

Felipe scanned the sky hoping for patches of blue—or even rain that was not gritty. When the ceniza started falling months ago he came almost every week. At first he walked the fields and then came back to the house and slumped in a chair, but the next day he went out again. Lately he came to Las Nubes less and less and mostly sat around, or wandered about aimlessly.

This had not only been the family jewel—a place of beauty, a retreat—but the source of income by which he supported the family in upper-middle class fashion. At his age, Felipe didn't have a back-up career. He looked frail and blurry, lost in his clothes, a mere watercolor of his former self. Gone were the banter, the laughter and the lighthearted family interaction.

Peter arrived in early March and stayed silently in the background. Alicia found him packing two days later.

"Not a very good time for you is it?" he straightened a moment and looked at her.

"You don't have to go," she said, meaning it.

"Ahh...you have a houseful," he leaned over the bed and tossed a T-shirt into his duffel bag. Alicia resisted the temptation to fold it. "Besides I can't stay long this time."

She didn't believe him. Even the children sensed the gloom and were quiet.

———

Felipe sat stirring his coffee, even though there was nothing to blend, since he drank it black. As he stirred, he stared into the cup as if looking for something.

"Sing us a song, Papi." Jorge handed him his guitar, urging him to make things more like they were before. Felipe shrugged and shook his gray head, but then took the instrument when Jorge insisted on planting it in his lap.

He strummed a few chords and they tried to recapture happier days in the sound. They'd enjoyed sitting on the veranda, laughing and singing. Felipe had seasoned the mood at Las Nubes with his music — either playing his guitar, or Mozart's *Eine kleine Nachtmusik* and Vivaldi's *Four Seasons* on the old record player, lending an air of Old World culture and dignity. The love songs he'd crooned when he was feeling tender or playful nudged his listeners to be romantic, and his flamenco rhythms stirred up passion, dancing, singing — savoring life.

Felipe stopped, "I never thought...." But he didn't finish. He sat with his head lowered over the strings as if listening, trying to choose the most poignant tune of all. When he found it, the guitar rendered his emotion. He sang a lament so moving that tears formed in Jorge's eyes. The sound reminded Alicia of the litany primitive people wail at funerals. They were in mourning and this was their dirge.

The stars gleamed along the east side of the heavens as if nothing unusual was happening. To the west the crescent moon was invisible, shrouded by the ash cloud.

Jorge and Alicia lay awake in bed that night hearing the music echo in their ears. She took his hand, played with his fingers.

"Where is your ring?"

"Umm...I took it off." She could tell he didn't know where he left it.

"Last time I saw it was on the hall table," she said.

"So if you know, why did you ask me then?"

"That was weeks ago. I wondered why you took it off. I was afraid it might get lost."

They stared at the black nothingness of the ceiling until sleep took possession of them and they slipped exhausted into darkness.

Felipe went back to Bogotá, but Pepe showed up the last week in May to discuss the financial situation.

Alicia was surprised, but glad that Marta was with him — Las Nubes was hardly a pleasure trip anymore.

Marta shook her head and heaved a sigh, "It looks terrible! Can the finca recover from this?"

Dark circles underscored her eyes, suggesting she had worried as much as the rest of them. But the life Pepe and Marta led did not depend on the coffee. He had a separate career as a banker, and was financially secure

A pensive Pepe strummed his lips with three fingers. "If it stops soon…maybe," he answered, his voice trailing off. "Or else…I don't know what we can do."

"I know what I'm going to do," Jorge said. "I'm going to move back to Bogotá." He raised his eyebrows and spread his palms out at right angles to his arms, as if to say this was the logical course of action.

"Well," Pepe replied, "If you *want* to. You can always drive back on weekends."

Alicia breathed. Pepe studied her face, which she kept impassive so no one could gauge the turmoil in her head. Jorge did not respond to his brother.

Later, when they were alone, Alicia told him, her voice firm, "I'm not leaving."

"Yes, you are."

"No."

"Look outside," Jorge said. "This isn't a coffee finca anymore, this is…a disaster."

The volcano pumped out volumes of dark clouds filled with ash — usually in insidious silence, but sometimes prefaced by faint booming in the distance.

"Even if the volcano did stop tomorrow, the soil is buried, and the plants are damaged," he continued.

"You don't know that."

He turned away without responding. Jorge was depressed. She knew he missed the city. He didn't need the problems of this grim landscape. His jaw was set, his face carved in stone.

Sometimes she caught him staring at her with vacant eyes. It was startling to see the same brown eyes that were once so soft, now cold and hard. In the course of that blighted year he'd grown distant, a self-absorbed stranger. There was no arguing with him or with her either. She turned away, then back. "Don't give up, Jorge...don't go. Please," she said softly and heard the desperation in her own voice.

Alicia went downstairs to ponder their fate in solitude, but found Marta. Her sister-in-law was slouched against the wall, staring out the window, her eyes bright with tears.

"Marta! We'll be OK."

Marta bit her lip. Tears clung to the dark lashes of her lovely eyes and then one spilled over the edge. Her eyebrows reminded Alicia of butterfly antennae, so graceful and fine.

"*Ay!* Forgive me Alicia, this is a bad time for you."

"What? What is it?"

"*Estoy embarazada.*"

"Again?" Alicia blurted without thinking, then went to Marta and put her arm around her as if to shelter her.

"I'm sorry." She wasn't sure if she was sorry that Marta was unhappily pregnant or if she was apologizing for her outburst. Both.

"I love the children...but four!" Marta whispered. "By the time I'm thirty I'll be old and fat and have nine or ten!" She was only twenty-five.

"But...do you use birth control?" Alicia was hesitant to ask, knowing that many Colombians take Church doctrine seriously.

Marta pulled back and stopped dabbing at her eyes which had widened as if stunned, "No.... Do you?"

"Of course," Alicia replied. She never once forgot a pill. The thought occurred to her she might not need them if Jorge was moving out. "Have I offended you?"

"No.... Well, maybe it's alright for you...you're not really Catholic. But I'd go straight to hell!" In fact, Alicia had to convert for the priest to perform the marriage ceremony. She'd been willing enough at the time.

They sat there, two dejected women holding hands, their knees touching. Marta wore a straight skirt and stockings, as if she was still in Bogotá. Alicia couldn't help but notice her ankles looked large and puffy.

"Don't tell anyone, uh?" Marta said...and in the next breath, "What will you do?"

Alicia shook her head, "I don't want to live in Bogotá."

"*Ay, mi'ja!* It is not so bad."

"I'd feel stifled in a big city. They are so noisy and chaotic. Too many people," she replied.

After all the moves every few years throughout her childhood, she hoped she would never have to move again. She could not imagine living in Bogotá anymore. The noisy buses kept her awake at night. She would hate it.

When the rest of the house had gone to bed, Alicia went out to sit on the veranda. A moon the color of flan was just starting to wane, casting a faint light over the landscape. In the semi-darkness the ugly ceniza was hidden, but there remained a sense that all was not normal.

She caught sight of the orchids she'd found in the jungle and placed in the fork of a jacaranda tree where they were visible, even in the dim light. With all the recent turmoil, she'd forgotten about them. The plant had survived its ordeal and apparently rooted in its new home—now new buds were blooming. She raised her face to the moon and stretched out her arms to its glow. She had never belonged anywhere before. At Las Nubes she'd found her place in the world, but it was under siege.

———

A few days later Jorge prepared to leave with Pepe and Marta. The tension in the house lay on the surface like a drop of water on a waxy leaf. Alicia sensed that Pepe and Marta were mildly disapproving—both of her staying and of Jorge leaving. She heard Pepe reasoning with his brother in low urgent tones, then the house became quiet.

"Papi is going away for a while," Jorge told George, who was nestled on his mother's hip.

"Por qué, Papi?"

Jorge kissed him and patted his head, then kissed Alicia on the cheek—more like a friend than a lover. Marta observed forlornly.

Alicia walked out to the road and watched them disappear. George waved goodbye by clenching and opening his chubby fist. He did not understand, and Alicia gave him a hug and a weary smile. The car became a small cloud of dust and was gone, but still Alicia stood there, her posture slumped, hugging her son. The ever-present yellow dog looked up at her.

"Old Yeller," she said and gave him a pat. The dog wagged his tail.

"O'yella," George said in that little voice that never failed to make her smile.

Humberto waited on the veranda, one leg and both arms wrapped around a post.

"Will you take George to your mami and play with him in the kitchen?" she asked, setting George down at the door.

Humberto nodded, took George's hand and helped him toddle inside.

"Let's play, George."

She went upstairs and stretched out on the bed. She could think of nothing else she had to do. After a while, George came looking for her, his usual smiling face serious for once.

"You tired, huh, Mama?"

"Yes I am sweetheart, very tired."

Her son gazed at her, taking in her expressionless face, her slack body.

"You sick, Mama?" he asked, his eyes big, his head nodding.

"No, I'm not sick, Georgie," she said in a flat voice, "Go see what Humberto is up to."

He studied the bedspread somberly a while longer before growing bored, incapable of understanding adult problems, and left to find his playmate.

She would have stayed there staring at the ceiling until the shadows grew long, but she knew Carmen would come looking for her soon, and also ask if she was sick. Reluctantly, she swung one leg and then the other over the side of the bed and got up. It seemed to take an inordinate amount of effort to stand up, put one foot in front of the other and walk downstairs.

Jorge's wedding ring lay on the coffee table. She picked it up and put it in her pocket. Later she would drop it into her little jewelry box for safekeeping. Her fingers trailed along the fern-green wall as she made her way to the door. She walked out into the gray world, along the rows of spindly coffee plants.

Jorge's absence left her with a profound sense of loss. A panicky, fluttering and constricting sensation somewhere in her chest made it difficult to breathe at times. She could see how someone might die of a broken heart, for what she felt was almost physical.

Would he come back? Only time would tell.... Should she stay? Yes — that was one decision she was comfortable with despite any opposition she might encounter.

It wasn't as if she couldn't manage the finca without him, she told herself. She had for most of the last year. It wasn't as if she'd rent to pay. She could even go to the bank now and get money for gas and food. Thank God Claudia suggested to Felipe that Alicia be able to access the account when Jorge was laid up with his broken leg. It made things much easier. She would be frugal, but would not have to ask the family for money.

So, what was this insecurity? He had not left her destitute, but the feeling was much the same. Failure. Fear. Loss. Grief. Guilt.

Looking back she could see they had been drifting apart for a long time. She traced it back to the accident—his head injury. They'd never really quarreled much before that. It frustrated her that no one else in the family acknowledged that.

Reminders of Jorge were everywhere—a razor in the bathroom, shirts in the closet, his boots on the front porch. Each such encounter pierced her core.

Alicia poured coffee into her green glazed cup. "I'm just going to have cereal and coffee," she told Carmen. She sat in the breakfast nook with George.

On the second day she marched back into the kitchen with her plate. Carmen swallowed her bread quickly as she looked up, "What do you need?"

"This is silly...we might as well eat together," Alicia said. "Come with me."

"No, No. We are fine!"

So Alicia brought George in his high chair and plopped herself down next to Carmen at the small wooden table. The table where they prepared meals, where Carmen ate, and where Paco joined her for a *cafecito*.

"*Hola*, George!" Humberto laughed.

"*Hola*, Berto!" George chortled. He couldn't say Humberto yet, and this would lead to the older child being tagged with the nickname. The boys thought this was a good joke, great fun invading each other's territory.

"And at lunch you will have to come eat with us!" Alicia told Humberto trying to join in their fun.

The boys looked at each other with glee. Carmen looked uncomfortable. The rest of the family would not approve, but Alicia could only smile at the children's small pleasures.

The first few days without Jorge were the worst, or so Alicia thought until the weekend came and Carmen went away to visit her man.

"*Mi hombre*," she called him proudly. Humberto's father, who drove one of those gaily painted buses they called *chivas*.

Saturday night Alicia felt overwhelmed, almost frightened by an existential aloneness that she had never felt before. Like a newborn experiencing the chaos of life, emerging for the first time to noise and light. Except that there were no welcoming arms, or comforting words. She had trouble sleeping — the sounds of the forest amplified until she put a pillow over her head. Crickets and frogs and other unknown calls made a deafening, unbearable racket.

Finally she shut all the windows and the outside shutters too. As she reached out for one shutter, a bat or something flew off, causing her to cry out. It was so dark she could not see her hand in front of her face and yet she imagined she could see someone standing by the closet. She stared at the figure for what seemed like hours, waiting to see if it moved. In the light of dawn it turned out to be a shirt she'd hung on the top of the door.

George yawned and then smiled when she trudged in wearily to get him out of his crib. She felt a tightness in her own smile, artificiality which had not been there before. At least he was a reason to get out of bed in the morning.

After dusk on Sunday night, Carmen returned lugging the slumbering Humberto up the gravel drive. Alicia was so glad to see her she almost flew off the porch rocker to greet them.

They exchanged pleasantries a moment. Carmen, knowing something had not been right since the day he left, asked tactfully, "*Y don Jorge?* When is he coming home?"

Alicia stared at her and then looked down, trying to control her mouth from trembling, trying not to cry.

"But doña Alicia, what's the matter?" Carmen, of course, had a pretty good idea, but no one had told her.

"He's...gone," she managed to whisper, the word choking in the back of her throat, not wanting to come out.

Carmen put her hand on Alicia's shoulder. The sympathetic face was more than she could bear, and she burst into tears for the first time since he left. She heard herself sobbing, gulping for air as if she was drowning, grieving the loss as if she had been widowed. Carmen laid Humberto in the hammock and led Alicia to the bench.

"*Ay, mi doñita*. Don't cry," she wrapped one arm around Alicia and patted her with the other. Alicia leaned against Carmen's ample bosom and shoulder. She recollected a nanny comforting her like this as a child.

———

But it wasn't until ten days later that it truly hit Alicia that Jorge might not come back at all. She drove into Escondido and tried to call him, but couldn't get through to his parent's house. She called Marta instead.

"*Hola*," she said tonelessly, "*es Alicia*. How are you?"

"*Chica!* I'm ecstatic! You won't believe what has happened! I just got out of the hospital this morning!"

Alicia hesitated, failing to see that this was such a good thing. "Did you lose the baby?"

"It wasn't a baby," Marta's voice seemed to reprimand, then finished in triumph, "It was an ectopic pregnancy!"

"Oh...but isn't that dangerous?"

Alicia knew this meant the embryo had implanted in a fallopian tube instead of the uterus.

"Yes, I could have died! I've been in the hospital for days!" Marta sounded like she had won *la lotería*.

Alicia laughed awkwardly, not knowing what to say. "Well I'm glad you are home. Are you OK?" She couldn't very well congratulate her on losing the baby.

"Ah, I've been so sick. It hurt so bad! I have to stay in bed a few days. But I don't care, the doctor says I *must* go on birth control. I could die if I get pregnant again! I *have* to take the pill, Alicia!" she exclaimed.

Marta had almost died, but at least she would not have to confess the sin of birth control, because the doctor ordered it for her health.

Marta said, "Pepe plans to come at the end of the month."

"*Y Jorge?*" Alicia asked, "*como está*...is he coming back?"

"I don't know, Alicia. I don't know what he is going to do. But I'll come if it would cheer you up."

"I'd like that."

Marta hesitated. "He's sad, Alicia, but he...he thinks you will come back...when it gets bad enough."

Come back? Alicia thought. Back to what? His parent's house?

But it didn't get "bad enough." Ash might fall every few weeks, but the rain eventually cleared the air and brought promise. Carmen swept the house, Alicia squirted ceniza off the plants with water and remained hopeful that the coffee—and the finca— would survive.

Several weeks after Jorge left it occurred to Alicia that a burden had been lifted from her shoulders. With a mix of shame and relief she realized she would have never left him in the state he was in. Not only that, but how could she ever have left Las Nubes? He had done her a favor, she thought— feeling guiltier than before.

But she did not punish herself for long. Jorge had removed his wedding ring long before he left, she reminded herself. He had told her he wanted to go off by himself. She was doing the family a favor looking after the finca...nobody else seemed to want to.

She rocked George who had long since fallen asleep. But she did not get up to put him in bed. The weight and warmth of him was comforting against her chest and she was reluctant to let him go.

Chapter 13
CARMEN'S MAN

They rose with the sun each morning and had a light breakfast—home-grown papaya or *piña* with granola they made themselves. Carmen grated coconut, and Alicia mixed it with oats and a touch of oil and honey. Nuts or sesame seeds were added when the *tienda* in Escondido had them. Then the whole mixture was lightly toasted in the oven.

Occasionally, Alicia added items found during her explorations—like the time she found what looked and tasted very much like Brazil nuts, just lying on the rainforest floor. It looked like a cluster pod carelessly dropped by a monkey or some other arboreal dweller who had eaten one or two, then thrown the nut-laden twig away. But she had never been able to find the tree or more nuts.

Occasionally—mostly when it rained too hard for her to go out very long—Alicia made bread. Carmen found this skill very impressive. You are not supposed to bake bread when it rains, it doesn't rise as well. But Alicia did anyway. Today was only a bit misty and it would soon burn off.

"Buenos días, Carmen," Alicia said, coming downstairs with George on her hip.

"Buenos días," the ever-cheerful Carmen replied in singsong grinning at the toddler, tickling him with her finger to make him giggle. "Paco wants to know if you want the horses saddled this morning."

"Sí, por favor."

They had taken to riding instead of driving the jeep. It was so much easier. The horse could go up and down the muddy rows and she could leave him under a tree if she wanted to walk into the forest afterwards. Except now that the rainy season was back in full force she needed to be done by afternoon, when there was likely to be a cloudburst.

Alicia looked up at the gathering clouds. It was beginning to sprinkle and they were still in the fields.

"Regresemos a casa, Paco," she said, turning her horse back toward home. "It's starting to rain and Marta and Pepe will be here soon."

By the time they reached the house, her brother-in-law's jeep was parked in the driveway, the engine ticking as it cooled. The heavens opened up just as she dismounted and handed the reins to Paco.

Marta embraced her at the door. "We made it! I've been so worried about you."

"And I've been worried about you."

Alicia kissed Pepe's cheek too, *"Hola, Pepe."*

"We have your mail from Escondido," Marta said, handing it to her. In a lower voice she added,

"There's a letter from Peter," and raised her eyebrows teasingly.

If Pepe caught this, his face remained neutral. He said, "Things are looking better, no?"

"Yes," Alicia nodded, tossing the mail casually on the hall table, as if it was no more interesting today than the last time she picked it up. "We haven't had ceniza in weeks and the last eruption was mild...or else it drifted the other way."

The torrential rainfall should clean things up nicely to show Pepe, she thought. It was fortuitous. She didn't want to be told to give up.

As they chatted throughout the rainy afternoon, Alicia's mind wandered to the mail in the hall.

Carmen prepared an early supper since Marta and Pepe had not stopped for food along the way. Alicia was glad they retired early, even before Paco shut down the generator. She took her mail up to her room and flipped through it quickly, standing next to the low mahogany dresser. A couple of letters, a *Time* magazine courtesy of Peter — and only three weeks old.

She tossed them on the crackled wood surface and sat down to open his letter just as the generator went off. It was harder to read by the light of a gas lantern, but she always enjoyed hearing the rain and the quiet that ensued. Several pictures fell out of the envelope. Two were of the Indians, taken the day she'd gone in the helicopter with him, well over a year ago. A third was of Peter sitting on a rock, arms resting on a crossed leg. She smiled at his stance — he looked rugged...and attractive. There was no denying it.

Dear Alicia and Jorge,

Following a tributary of the upper Amazon, I met several Indians fishing in a pool this week. They swam with pointed sticks and speared a dozen fish. They invited me to a supper — served on large leaves. There are only 8 adults and a number of children in the whole village. They all dress alike (which is to say hardly at all).

The younger men and women were friendly, but I sensed a reserve bordering on coolness, perhaps even suspicion, from a few older adults. They also shared a brew which at the time I thought was alcoholic, but who knows what I imbibed. At any rate I enjoyed the experience and thought about sharing my grass, but I couldn't explain what it was to them and thought better of it.

I will be back in Bogotá in a few days and will mail this to you then. Hope I can come by the finca next month.

Enclosed find the pictures I took of the Indians.

Oh — I saw my first jaguar several weeks ago!

Peter

It was postmarked in July, only a few weeks ago.

She was jealous. She had lived in Colombia for years and never seen a jaguar. Tracks, yes, but not the animal. Of course Las Nubes was a bit high — jaguars preferred lower elevations.

She thought it best not to show Pepe and Marta the letter because of his reference to marijuana. But then, would they think it was a private letter if she didn't share it? She sighed, then shrugged. The envelope had been addressed to herself and Jorge. She would show them the photos — without mentioning she and Peter were together when they were taken.

She propped them up by her mirror and began to unbutton her shirt.

An animal cry caused her to freeze with her hands still to her chest. She moved closer to the window and cocked her head. The rain had stopped...and there was the noise again. But it seemed to be coming from the hall. She opened the door to listen.

"Pepe! Ay Dios...Pepe!" she heard Marta exclaim in a voice that under different circumstances might have been mistaken for pain or anguish. Alicia realized it was neither.

Lower, huskier, but equally as fervent, Pepe replied, *"Marta! Mi amor!"* with a passion Alicia would not have attributed to the quiet banker. Still waters run deep, she thought with a smile as she tiptoed back into her room.

But closing the door only muted the sounds of lovemaking and now the progressively insistent thumping of a headboard against the far wall overtook their lusty cries. She leaned her head back against the doorframe, touching the soft skin of her neck. When the noises from the bedroom next to hers ceased, she took a deep breath, finished undressing and slipped between the sheets.

Finally, the household slumbered. Pepe and Marta stayed two days.

———————

"Not a good day for the horses," Paco said.

She didn't ask what he meant by this because since it was not raining, she divined it was code for "my son is here, and he has never ridden in a jeep." But Paco would never admit that was what he was getting at, any more than Alicia would put him on the spot.

"OK," she said.

"*Doñita...*" Paco bit off the end of the word as he realized he had started to use her nickname and his face colored. The workers called her "*la doñita,*" the little mistress, alluding to her age. It was applied half in fun, half in affection, but never to her face. He was deeply embarrassed and hoped she had not heard. If Alicia had, she ignored it.

Paco pretended he had merely been clearing his throat. "*Perdón. Doña Alicia,*" he began again, as they walked around to the front of the house, "you could teach me how to drive. I know how...a little."

He stared at his shoes thinking that he would not blame her if she never did, after his lack of respect. And, he had set a bad example in front of Miguel, his eldest son. Maybe neither of them had noticed. He scattered the chickens out of the way, "Move it!"

The hostile cock who crowed at dawn most mornings — but also at intervals throughout the day — eyed Paco and *buck-bucked* angrily. He was a colorful bird with a large ruffled comb, handsome and haughty. They kept the kids away from him for he was known to spread his wings and peck if annoyed.

"Well maybe not today," she answered, reasoning that it would not be a good time for a driving lesson with a youngster in the car.

She noticed Paco no longer scurried to open the car door before she could get it. She took it to be a good sign that he was accepting her as someone capable. She remembered a professor at the University of Virginia had once introduced her as "This is Alicia Collier and she can hold her own with any man in the department."

He had meant it as a compliment, of course, because more women than men were likely to drop out when they came to physics and calculus requirements. Perhaps he hoped it would encourage more female students to follow her example. It had not bothered her, as it might have a staunch feminist. She was raised on sexism and knew how to deal with it—or at least stomach it.

"And why isn't this young man in school?" she said smiling at Miguel.

"Ah! It is hardly worth going, the school is so bad. Half the time we let him help us...he's getting big enough to work now." Miguel was all of nine. By "us" Alicia took him to mean his father, his mother and perhaps his grandparents.

Paco gripped his eldest son's arm and helped him into the jeep.

"But Paco, you want him to read and write," she protested.

"I can read and write better than my children and I only went for two years. There are thirty *estudiantes* at that school, only one teacher and hardly any books."

"The teacher is no good," Miguel piped up.

"Manners!" his father growled gently. A teacher is generally the most respected person in town—save for the mayor or a doctor, but Escondido was too

small, too poor and too far away to have either on a
regular basis.

"Well...education is important."

"It's not just that we want Miguel to work, doña
Alicia. It really is a waste of his time...if you could see
this school you would understand."

"Maybe I should go talk to the teacher. After all,
George may be attending that school someday."

This pronouncement left Paco momentarily
speechless. A Carvallo going to the village school?

"*Pero...señora*, you can send him to a fine school in
Bogotá."

Yes, but she might not want to, she thought—not
until he was a bit older.

That was how Alicia Carvallo happened to
appear at the schoolhouse in Escondido. It was three
o'clock in the afternoon when she parked on the
muddy road. Most of the children were gone, but two
barefoot boys walking home turned around to see
what she was up to. Their pants were faded to gray
from many washings.

"*Hola*," she greeted them.

Alicia's smile vanished when she got a good look at
the schoolhouse. She had driven by it many times
without realizing what it was. The one-room building
sat on an eroded slope. Red paint was peeling off the
corrugated aluminum roof. Generations of children had
carved their names and written graffiti on its plaster
walls. One of four small windows was boarded up.
Evidently a shutter was missing and the opening could
not be closed. None of the window openings were
encased in glass. The thick wooden door was riddled
with worm borings attesting to its age, and the bottom

corner was rough and worn. Stepping in, she saw that the walls had never been painted. It was a dingy, dark room with a littered, dirty floor. The state did not have the money to pay a janitor.

Señora Ramirez, bent over a desk shuffling papers into a pile, looked up in surprise. Parents never came; no one ever came, except a regional supervisor who showed up once a year to make sure she was actually teaching. Now, out of nowhere, a light-haired woman—obviously a foreigner—walks in. What could she want?

"*Si?* Are you lost?" she asked, neither rude nor polite. The teacher was thin and stern looking.

"Señora Ramirez...I am Alicia de Carvallo. I've come to see your school."

Ah.... Appraising the young American who married into the coffee finca, she stood to shake hands and then swept her arm around the small space as if to say, "This is it."

"And the desks? There are only...what? A dozen? Excuse me, but I heard you have thirty students."

Señora Ramirez shrugged. "Thirty-four, if they ever came at the same time. Usually I have three or four children without desks. But they share."

She had long ago given up on providing a good education to so many children of different ages and abilities, particularly when they missed so much school that there was no continuity. It was an impossible task, so she just focused on teaching the students who showed up regularly. These tended to be the brightest and those whose parents could pay the minimal fee for books and paper.

There were not even extra chairs. Alicia could picture half the kids kneeling next to a desk to share a book or sprawled out trying to write on the dirty floor.

"It must be hard to teach under those conditions. I...hope I don't seem presumptuous, but I'd like to help. Perhaps we could at least get some new books and supplies."

This woman was mistaken if she thought Colombia was as rich as her country, and could afford luxuries for rural kids who would just grow up to pick coffee on her finca anyway. The teacher was perplexed by the offer of help, but could think of no reason to discourage the señora Carvallo. As long as she didn't make more work for her.

That night Alicia wrote three letters. Two were addressed to the Peace Corps—one to an office in Bogotá and the other to the Washington, D.C., headquarters. The third was to the regional superintendent of national schools. She explained the conditions and requested textbooks, desks and a second teacher, or teacher's aide.

———

Late afternoon was usually a good time to shower, when the water from the tank was warm from the sun. Alicia was just rinsing off when the bathroom door burst open as if from an explosion. For a split second she thought guerrillas or bandits were storming the finca. But it was Carmen who pulled the shower curtain aside, screaming. She cried, carrying on hysterically and clutching herself as if in pain.

Alicia's throat constricted as she grabbed her arm. "Is it the children?" she asked, chilled.

Carmen shook her head with a wail that tore the air, *"Mi hombre!"*

Alicia turned off the water as Carmen fell heavily against the tiled wall and then slid to the floor, collapsing in a pathetic, quivering pile, her arms draped uselessly at her sides. Through the open door the two little boys stared wide-eyed and open-mouthed at the sobbing Carmen and the naked Alicia. The yellow dog, which had never before been in the house, stood between the boys watching like a stunned third child—his mouth open and panting. Realizing something was amiss he had followed them inside and up the stairs.

Alicia wrapped herself in a cotton robe and coaxed Carmen up, along the length of the hall and onto the bed.

"*¿Qué paso?* What's happened? Tell me!"

"Mi hombre! Mi hombre! El papá de Humberto!"

The tale came out in gasping starts and stops as Alicia tried to comfort Carmen.

Her man had been killed when his bus was stopped by guerillas. He apparently said something in defense of one of his passengers and was shot in the head. Carmen rocked her body back and forth in unabated grief, wailing unintelligibly. It was a primeval sound, a frightening lamentation.

"My son's father!"

The boys were frightened now and starting to sniffle. Alicia reached an arm out to them, the other firmly around Carmen. Humberto climbed on the bed and curled up next his mother, throwing an arm around her and laying his head on her bosom. He didn't understand what it meant for his father to be dead, but his mother's anguish was enough to make him cry as well.

All four were on the bed now and George began to stroke Humberto, saying, "Gosh! Carmen's really sad, huh Mama?"

"Yes, darling." Even the yellow dog put his head on the bedspread with a mournful look.

Later, Carmen retreated to her room where she stayed in bed, refusing food.

"Come on Carmen, you have to eat sometime," Alicia coaxed the following day.

"No. I don't want anything." She mumbled something about her man's dead body and wanting to throw up.

Alicia had never been in Carmen's quarters before—a lean-to next to the main house. In dismay, she noticed ceniza sifting through the cracks under the sagging ceiling, and a tin can placed under a leak where water dripped during heavy rain.

"*Uy uy*, Carmen. I want you to move into the house."

"*Por qué*? And where? There isn't enough room."

"Don't be silly there are two empty rooms," Alicia said.

"*No, no*. Those are for don Felipe, don Pepe y don Peetro."

"They don't live here...we do. There is still a spare room for when they come. Humberto can sleep with George. This bed is too small for both of you." It was a narrow cot—not even a twin size. Listening to these plans, Humberto opened his mouth in delight and smiled at George, who imitated his expression, and clapped his hands. The boys jumped up and down in the doorway, chattering excitedly.

"Come on, get up...please?" Alicia begged.

Carmen rolled over and stared at the wall.

"What about the funeral? It must be today," Alicia pressed in desperation.

Carmen pinched her lips together before replying, "He is...was... married to another. We are *la segunda casa.*"

The second family. Practically an institution, *la segunda casa* was the mistress and the children she bore a man outside his legal marriage.

"I would like Humberto to go to his father's funeral, but...out of respect for...the widow..." her voice trailed off and she started crying anew.

She chose to spare the widow the burden of her presence.

"Humberto will not have a father to take care of him now, and I will never again have *mi hombre,*" she shook her head and wailed into her pillow.

The bewildered boys watched this strong woman, whom they had only known as happy and smiling, fall apart. Alicia understood what Carmen was saying—that she was past her prime and might never again have any *hombre* in a long-term relationship, but this was not the time to argue.

"Come on boys. Come help me in the kitchen," Alicia said, not knowing which was better—staying with Carmen or keeping the boys out of the way.

Alicia took care of the house, the cooking, the children and the garden. The boys helped her weed, although they had to be watched carefully, especially George, who in his zeal was likely to pull up the parsley and smaller lettuces as well.

Carmen stayed in bed for days, despondent, getting up only when Alicia started to move her belongings into the main house.

"I was looking at your roof, and the ceniza is so thick I think it is dangerous." The ceniza had blown off the steeply pitched main house and accumulated over the attachment that was Carmen's bedroom in a pile two-feet thick.

Carmen moped around the house, but at least she was on her feet. Her eyes remained red and swollen. Alicia rubbed her shoulder or sometimes gave her a hug as they passed each other. There was nothing she could do or say, really, and they both knew it. Carmen resumed her duties, but without her laugh the house seemed gloomy, especially on days when the falling ceniza enshrouded them.

Humberto and George were the only ones who could bring on a wan smile. Alicia worked that to her advantage.

"You have to go on with your life for the children," Alicia said.

"Now we are both without our men," was Carmen's reply. "Two women with children."

After a few days the boys turned their interest to other things — as children will do — helpless to change the situation and unable to suppress their own little worlds. Eventually Carmen stopped crying, and gradually her smiles returned—albeit less frequently. The gold-toothed grin was seldom seen.

———

Carmen and Alicia continued to teach each other to cook. Alicia showed Carmen how to bake and prepare a few American dishes. Carmen, an excellent cook, taught her employer to make a few staple meals she could put together easily. Carmen was amazed that Alicia did not know how to make something as simple as *empanadas*—a kind of popover filled with meat or cheese—or that eggs must be cooked slowly or they turn rubbery, and that *plátano*—plantain— must be so ripe that the peel turns black before it is sweet and tender enough for slicing and frying. How could a girl grow up without absorbing these things?

But Carmen thought Alicia was talented for she could bake, and make foreign dishes with exotic flavors the likes of which Carmen had never tasted: scrumptious pies, cookies, spaghetti, and stir-fry which Carmen called *comida china*.

And Alicia did unusual things—like chopping up vegetables and adding them to eggs so that the resulting scramble had more mushrooms, spinach and onions or chilies than egg. Carmen would never have thought such a concoction could be so tasty. Success made Alicia bold, attempting new recipes like East Indian mulligatawny stew. She phoned Marta and asked her to find spices to make a curry and have Pepe bring them next time he came. Her growing spice collection intrigued and astounded Carmen.

Chapter 14
THE IGUANA

The water had a funny smell when Alicia showered one afternoon in late November. She went downstairs with a towel wrapped turban-style around her wet head.

"Carmen, are you boiling our drinking water for five minutes? Because the water smells bad."

"Yes, of course."

"I wouldn't drink it unboiled if I were you," Alicia tilted her head. "At least don't let Berto drink it."

Carmen smiled noncommittally. She and Paco had never bothered with boiling their water. They had survived their childhoods and must be immune to all the microbes that sickened the city folks, but since she had to boil water anyway she gave it to Humberto instead of opening the tap. She cocked her head to one side, to the sound of gravel crunching under tires. "Listen. We have visitors."

"Papi!" cried George running to the door, where his father lifted him in the air.

This was the first time they had seen him since September. His third visit since he had left over five months ago. On the phone the first couple of weeks, she had urged him to return, but now Alicia was aware of her mixed feelings; although George's happiness made her feel warm and glad.

In the recesses of her mind came an unformed thought—maybe Jorge would solve the water problem and take some of the burden of the finca from her shoulders. At the same moment she realized how opportunistic this was. So this is how it is, she thought. This is how I am, how I feel? She was glad he could not read her mind.

"Hi," she greeted him with a small smile.

George was nestled on his hip. "Guess what Papi?"

"What Georgie?"

"Me an' Berto found a red and green frog!"

"Yeah?" Jorge asked, widened his eyes and opened his mouth for effect, and then turned to her. "How are you?"

"I'm OK...You?"

They were polite to each other, this new strained formality. They kissed cheeks, George still hanging on his father.

On his last visit, Jorge seemed pent up with sexual tension. Alicia had made an effort to ignite the spark to reunite with George's father. They made love, but their former heat had turned to mere embers. It surprised her, after all the passion they once felt, that she had to compel herself. That was when she realized it was not possible to rekindle their marriage. They were both emotional afterwards.

Although it seemed no one agreed with her, he was not the same Jorge she'd married. No doubt the family blamed his change in personality on their separation, but he had become querulous, sullen and difficult before that. Their troubles began after the accident, even before the ceniza. She felt she had to make allowances for him, that he could not help himself, but this did not endear him to her. Now he was back. After all they had shared she wanted to be close friends.

"Friends, Alicia? *Friends?*" Her suggestion clearly offended him.

He was morose and hurt; she sad and guilty. She was relieved when he left. She had come to the realization that she was better off alone. Alicia did not want a reunion on his terms. The hard truth was she did not think she wanted him back on any terms.

How had that happened? Hadn't she promised to love him in sickness and in health? If he had not left, would she eventually have had the nerve — or the heart — to leave him?

Alicia studied the wedding ring on her hand a moment before slipping it off and dropping it next to his in the small jewelry box in the drawer. A box she rarely looked at — she had little need for jewelry here. Her hand looked curiously naked without the gold band, a pale indentation marked the place where the sun had not tanned her finger. She closed the drawer.

He had not checked out the water.

———

"Paco, we need to get a ladder and clean out the gutters."

"I did that just a few days ago. They were full of ceniza." Indeed there were piles of wet ash all the way around the house where it had been removed from the gutter and plopped to the earth. Like a miniature gray moat of sand surrounding their home.

"Well something is not right...the water is smelly and it even looks dirty." There were tiny bits of black slime in the sink.

"Maybe we need to clean the tank," Paco said.

She hated to chlorinate their rainwater, but asked him to use bleach. He pulled the ladder out and mounted it. It was an old paint-spattered thing someone had made by hand years ago.

"Watch out," he called down to Alicia as he removed the tin top of the water tank. She jumped aside as a load of ceniza slid off and plummeted to the ground.

"Well?"

"It does smell a bit. We will have to drain it and clean it out." Which meant no water at all today — or tomorrow if it didn't rain. Normally this was only done once every year or two. It might take days to refill the reservoir.

"*Está bien,*" she told him. "We can get water from the stream." She preferred it under the circumstances.

"Ceniza probably got into the tank. I'll ask Mario to help me."

"That's fine," Alicia said.

Paco and Mario spent half of the next day scrubbing the tank. Alicia was both glad and horrified that they did. They found the remains of a large iguana, which had somehow got into the tank and died. The blackened, slimy particles they'd been bathing in were decomposing iguana flesh.

Later that day she came running to the back of the house at the sound of a loud crash. She wondered if the roof had caved in.

"*Ay Dios!*" cried Carmen. "They've fallen through the roof."

The kitchen was still intact, so they ran out the back door. Dust was settling out of Carmen's old room.

"Are you all right?" Alicia called as she backed up to see where the men were. She could hear them exclaiming to one another.

"*Sí señora!*" Mario grinned down at her.

"We were sweeping *el techo*, piling ceniza onto Carmen's room. We were going to clean it next, *cuando...bam! Se cayó!*" Paco explained.

The roof over the lean-to collapsed under the weight of the ash. The accumulation exceeded the strength of the zinc—like the proverbial straw that broke the camel's back. And just as the volcanic outpouring of ceniza appeared to be waning. She was afraid to be overly optimistic and say it had stopped.

"You see! I moved you out of there just in time!" Alicia told Carmen who nodded as she crossed herself, closing her open mouth.

Jorge came and went over the months. She was always uncomfortable during his brief stays, although glad for George's sake. Sometimes he halfheartedly nagged her to move to Bogotá. It became a ritual argument for them. His seemed to think that even though they were separated, they could reunite any time.

Sometimes they didn't see him for a month or two, then he came twice in the space of two weeks. But Jorge always became bored and left after a couple of days, so his stays were brief.

He had indeed bought a *moto* to tour South America, but from what she could gather he only made it to Peru and Ecuador before turning around.

Once he took George with him for what was to be two weeks. There was something unsettling about her son waving goodbye with a big smile. He had never been apart from her for more than a day since he came home from the hospital. To her great relief, Jorge brought him back after just one week. No explanation. She didn't need one.

It was Pepe who came regularly to check on the finca. The rest of the Carvallos became infrequent visitors to the farm, although Alicia wished they would come back. She missed the whole family, but that tie had apparently been broken. That year, right after Christmas, don Felipe survived a heart attack at age sixty-one. Alicia never saw him again.

She and Carmen spent hours in the kitchen chatting and working while the little boys played at their feet. Clothes pins became doll-people — sometimes a whole village. Humberto's favorite game was to reenact the ceniza crisis. All of the clothes pin people ran around moaning about the dirt and how the coffee was ruined.

"Quick, we have to pick it!"

"Quick" parroted George.

The women measured ingredients, preparing to make bread. Carmen was skeptical when Alicia told her unrefined flour was more nutritious than white flour.

"How can that be when it costs less?"

"When they take out the brown, they take out vitamins, and that extra procedure costs money."

This made some sense, but still skeptical, Carmen asked, "Then why do they do it?"

Alicia shrugged. "You've got me! I guess because people will pay more for the way white looks."

"Just as well we are almost out of the white flour."

"Really? It must be somewhere. I thought I just bought some."

Carmen showed her the sack with only a cup left in the bottom. Alicia shrugged at the mystery.

They both found baking bread a satisfying, creative endeavor — and it distracted Alicia when ash fall or rain kept her indoors. The garden would rebound whenever there were good weeks but it had lost its luster.

"Don Jorge isn't coming back, *eh?*" Carmen asked.

Alicia shook her head. Their marriage was truly over.

The women took turns kneading the dough, for it was physical work to mix the ingredients and give it the right texture. Alicia leaned into the dough, sinking her hands in. As it became sticky she added a little more flour. Kneading, pulling it towards her, folding it over, turning it and starting over again and again until the dough was satiny and soft. The process became a smooth, meditative rhythm that could not be hurried or interrupted.

"Y donde está don Peetro?"

"No se," Alicia replied but she often wondered herself.

"Es un buen hombre." Carmen had picked up on the chemistry between them. Did he fit into the picture of her future? Alicia didn't know, nothing had been spoken. He might not even know she and Jorge were separated. It had been months since the letter, which she hesitated to answer until she knew what to say about Jorge. At any rate, it seemed prudent for there to be a time gap.

After mixing the simplest ingredients, they showed the children the magic of the dough rising under the thin cloth on the wooden table and allowed them to punch it down. This never failed to delight them, but they were cautioned not to disturb the dough during the two hours it was expanding.

Next the women shaped loaves, filled buttered pans and covered them again for their second rising. If the dough did not rise enough it would be overly moist and heavy. Once, they experimented with one of the pans to see how long the dough rose without collapsing—but collapse it did, leaving them with a hard loaf Carmen fed to the chickens. They tried again, letting it rise not quite as long. This produced a big loaf, but full of coarse air bubbles and with a yeasty flavor. After only a few attempts, they perfected their method and the smell of fresh bread brought anyone within olfactory range to the door begging for a warm slice.

But Paco and Carmen were the only full-time Las Nubes workers now. The others had always been seasonal laborers, except for Mario.

"We have to let him go Alicia," Pepe finally told her, "Our cash flow is minimal. We're dipping into savings now."

"I understand. I just feel bad about it. And the ceniza has all but stopped."

"But production is still down. I'll try to find him something...somewhere."

Mario could still work part-time, as needed, she thought.

"Can we give him a months' notice?"

Pepe cocked his head as if in regret, and grimaced, "Two weeks." He was wearing his usual snowy white, long-sleeved shirt.

She realized Pepe had not thought to give Mario even that much notice, and was glad she'd intervened.

"Another thing," Alicia said. "With the grass buried under ceniza, Morenito doesn't have enough to eat. I had to buy him extra grain."

"Your horse may have to go too."

"I need him around the farm." And she was fond of the horse. "I'll try to graze him elsewhere."

As the purse strings tightened, they ate less meat. Alicia tried to convince Carmen it was healthier to fill up on vegetables, fruits and grain instead of meat.

But Carmen drew the line there. Her own mother had always scrimped to buy her children meat two or three times a week so that they would grow strong. Look at how healthy rich children are! People needed meat, especially beef, but she did not press her point since money was the issue. Alicia and George ate the same meals as Carmen and Humberto.

And after all, they killed and roasted a chicken every week. The next day the women would turn the leftovers into chicken stew. Sometimes Alicia would treat them to beef, either ground or cheap cuts requiring extra liquid and more cooking to render them tender. She did not want to kill off all the chickens, their source of eggs. And she worried that some of the chickens were looking scrawny. Those got eaten first.

"It's the ceniza they are eating," said Carmen "We are feeding them the same as always."

In exchange for credit, they took their produce and bread to the González family who owned the little store in town. The shop owners then sold it to the only eatery in town, Soda Maria.

"Señora, I will buy all the bread you can bake," Señor González told her.

So they began baking every other day. They started at dawn and it would take the whole morning. Alicia delivered the rolls and loaves in the afternoon. Only their time and the capacity of the stove limited them. On those days not much else got done, but then with coffee production down there was less work anyway.

If only the chickens would produce more eggs they could sell those for credit too. The yolks were still luscious and orange-colored in spite of the ceniza—not like the small yellowy ones found elsewhere.

If only she could produce more vegetables, but their yield was down. The dark skies and the thick blanket of gray were taking a toll there too. And Sr. González wanted the difficult veggies, like the temperamental tomatoes which were also delectable to bugs. But Alicia intended to plant more.

There was one thing she possessed—two actually—that she could sell. The gold wedding bands. She felt a bit guilty, but Jorge thought he had lost his and wasn't her ring hers to sell? She resolved to take them to a jeweler next time she was in Bogotá or another big town, but she had no plans for a long drive right now.

Chapter 15
PETER

Peter turned off the engine and bounded up the front steps only to find the front door locked. When no one responded to his knocks, he cupped his hands around his eyes and peered into the windows overlooking the front porch. There was a thin film of dark volcanic dust on the window sills. He had never encountered the door locked, much less an empty house. Could she have moved out because of the ceniza?

"Alicia?" he called and waited another moment before making his way around the hibiscus to the side of the house. The chickens were still there, scratching the sparse grass and bobbing their heads back and forth. They clucked nervously and scattered as he approached. The rooster stood tall and crowed, but not too impressively; his feathers no longer seemed full and shiny. Peter ran into a lone worker raking leaves and ceniza.

"Buenos días," Peter nodded, "Do you know where Alicia and Carmen are?"

The man smiled sheepishly, revealing a broken front tooth, but shrugged and shook his head. Did this mean he didn't understand or didn't know?

Mario's two-week notice was over, but Alicia had him come at least once a week, until he found something else. *"No se,"* he said leaning on his rake, and then said something else of which Peter only caught Paco's name.

"Sí! Paco...donde...?" Where is he? Peter asked as Mario pursed his lips and used his chin to signify the direction of the coffee bushes.

"Paco!" he called. "They are looking for you!"

Peter walked in the direction Mario indicated and Paco appeared from behind a heliconia. He grinned shyly, his machete hanging from his belt.

"Buenos días," Peter said smiling back.

"Como está, señor?" Paco replied, touching the brim of his hat.

He made Peter understand that the women were in Escondido. Peter tried to remember if he had seen a jeep in the village. He might have driven right by it. Paco opened the back door for him to bring in his things.

Half an hour later Peter heard the jeep and went to the window. He watched her get out, long legs first. She was wearing a skirt—short, but not like the minis they were wearing in the States now. He did not remember ever seeing her in a skirt. He watched them help the children out and unload two woven bags full of groceries. The children were so much bigger. He would not have recognized George—walking and talking now.

"*Está Peetro.* I'll get them, you go in," Carmen told her.

"No, it's OK," Alicia said, her eyes scanning the front porch, the door.

Peter waited until she came inside. She paused. There he was. She would have recognized his stance in the dark. The relaxed way he stood, the way he turned his head. They stood at opposite ends of the hall. She touched one hand to her chest.

Alicia felt an urge to run to him, and at the same time felt rooted to the spot. Momentarily speechless, she felt happy, excited and nervous all at once. Peter had not been here for almost a year and she had begun to wonder if she would see him again. The hiatus was perhaps a good thing. But now that he was here, she knew she had been waiting for him.

"Long time no see," she joked as they always did, moving toward him.

"Too long," he said. "I wrote."

"Yes." Unspoken was the fact that she had not written back. She had started a letter over a month ago and recently resolved to finish it. Did he know about Jorge? He strode to her and they embraced. She clung to him and he stroked her hair. He moved his head back and looked into her eyes, their multi-hued shades of blue and green.

"You OK?"

She nodded. He knew.

"They've kept me busy," Peter said. "Sent me all over South America. I had a chance to come visit in September or October, but I ran into Jorge and...he

213

discouraged me. I knew it was a bad time...for the finca, but...it took me awhile to figure things out, and then I thought maybe I should give you a little time."

She thought he was eminently wise. It would have added to the confusion and complications if Peter had shown up right after Jorge left.

They kissed...a slow, warm and gentle merging. Alicia heaved a sigh as if she had been holding her breath for a long time. She wanted to hold him forever. He had a magnificent body and she was acutely aware of it under her hands and along the length of her body. He felt wondrous, comforting, intoxicating.

He took her hand and they went down to the porch. At first she could hardly speak, overcome with the sight of him sitting across from her. He sat as always — sprawled, comfortable, relaxed like a lounging jaguar. She marveled at the strong line of his jaw, wanted to touch the small hollow at the base of his throat.

"So. Can you stay for a while?"

Peter nodded, "I was worried about you...when you didn't answer my letter."

Slowly she unwound and told him about the ceniza, the iguana in the water tank, about Jorge leaving.

"So is having an iguana in your tank anything like having a tiger in your tank?" he kidded.

Alicia looked blank, "I don't get it."

"Never heard of that?" Peter smiled, realizing she was not up on American TV commercials. "It's...well, never mind, it's not worth it."

Alicia went on, telling him about Felipe's frail condition and her alienation from the family. "Mostly just Pepe comes now."

As he listened, Peter touched the corners of his parted lips with thumb and index finger — an endearing gesture of his she remembered...as well as his sensual mouth.

"I reckon you've got to expect Jorge's folks are going to side with him, right or wrong."

"But they know the facts. They blame me for not following him to their house in Bogotá. Or strapping George to the back of a motorcycle and touring the Pan American Highway."

More likely she would have been expected to wait with the Carvallos until he returned from his great adventure. Don Felipe had said "Your place is with your husband," and they all agreed. Even Marta had not upheld Alicia's desire to stay at the finca.

All I did was stay here, Alicia thought. I supported him — until he wanted to move to Bogotá.

"Is that what he's doing now...touring the highway?"

"I think he's back in Bogotá. Can you see us, with George wedged between us on a *moto*?"

In fact, Jorge had visited only a week ago to bring George a Christmas present. She thought that was a good thing because he would not be back while Peter was here. He would not be back for weeks.

Peter smiled. "So, what will you do?"

"Well, stay here as long as they let me. Try to make a go of the coffee. Keep doing what I always do."

A bird called from a nearby branch—a low hoot, almost like an owl.

"Look! It's a motmot...see his tail feathers?" she cried.

"A motmot....?"

They watched the bird with its elegant long tail, but when Alicia stood to get a closer look he flew off. She sat back down.

"What gets me is that I'm running the farm but I get no credit."

Peter laughed, "You're supporting them!"

She smiled, "I don't think they look at it that way. The finca didn't make much this year."

"Well look, I remember hearing somewhere, there are people who get things done...and people who take the credit."

Alicia could draw off the Carvallo account in Escondido but she didn't have the nerve to ask how much was in it. Felipe and Jorge indicated the crop was a catastrophe after the ceniza, however they were prone to exaggerate. Nonetheless she was frugal, spending only what she needed for food, supplies and gasoline. The salaries for Paco and Carmen were now the biggest expense.

Peter gazed at her and then said, "You could go home."

"Home..." she echoed, "Where do you think my home is?" Alicia smiled.

"Don't you have a state that you are from?"

"Not really."

"Family?"

"Of course I have a family, but they are, ah...mad at me, over my marriage. I don't think they'd appreciate me and George moving in with them."

In fact she had not yet written her parents about Jorge. Living with them—even moving to Virginia was out of the question. Peter lifted his eyebrows and cocked his head, half in jest, half-questioning, "You feel you made your bed, eh? And now...?"

"My mother writes occasionally...even my brother has written a couple of times." She thought that was remarkable for a younger brother.

Peter nodded, absorbing the information, pushing out one cheek slightly with his tongue. "Where are they from?"

"My Dad was from the Midwest and my mother is from Virginia. But we only spent vacations there and I always felt..." she paused, "like a stranger. You know? I looked right, I sounded right, but I didn't feel like I fit in. I knew nothing about popular culture or what to buy at the store or the latest rock stars. It seemed unreal to me...artificial."

"I can understand that," he said.

"It's very strange because I've always been good at assimilating with different cultures," Alicia mused. Living in different countries as a child, she had to learn to blend in or stand out and be left out. "But in the States, where others expect me to be so...*American*...it just isn't *me*."

"Well, in many ways you seem as much a Latina as American...it's the little things, like the way you use your hands when you talk, and you tend to stand closer than most Americans do."

"I do?"

"Yeah, all Latinos do. I found myself stepping back when I first came here, but they would just step forward into the vacated space. Pretty soon I was backing up across the room!" he chuckled.

"I used to have trouble with men when I went to college...they thought I was flirting when I was just being friendly! Maybe that was part of it."

Peter laughed, "That could be...I liked it of course," he smiled mischievously. "But Colombians do flirt more and are friendlier. And then there are subtler things, attitudes."

"Like...?"

"Hmm. Let's see. Something about the interaction between men and women...more acceptance of the differences."

What other choice was there, she thought.

"And Colombians just seem to enjoy life to the hilt," he added.

Alicia nodded, "I appreciate my life. It's tough right now, but I love being here. The sounds, the people, the beauty, even the smells. I never had a place to belong to before."

There were mornings she would wake up to the pink glow of sunrise, with the pearly mists evaporating from the trees, the cock crowing and the birds singing. Except for the ceniza, it was so idyllic that she had to wonder, how can I be so lucky? Las Nubes seemed to be her destiny. She was a natural here.

Later, after the sun set, the generator shut down and they could no longer see each other clearly, he moved his chair next to hers and they held hands. They listened to the nocturnal wooing of insects and other creatures. A warm, moist breeze caressed them, bringing with it the fragrance of citrus blossoms. The sky was clear and the stars were coming out one by one, dotting the heavens like crystals.

"Has it always been so beautiful here?" Peter said.

She nodded, thinking, even more so tonight. Their senses were acute.

He stood and leaned over her, both arms on her chair, creating an intimate space.

"Let's go to bed," he said.

He led her past her own room, to the one that had become his. A smaller bed, but she understood why he did not want to share the room that had been hers and Jorge's.

With the door closed behind them, they leaned into one another, finally free to allow themselves to feel and savor their bodies' messages, long suppressed.

"I've waited...*years* for you," he murmured.

She nodded, speechless and happy—a happiness that was almost a relief. They undressed and felt each other's skin for the first time. He traced her flank with one hand, exploring.

"I didn't know there was anyone like you in the world," Alicia said.

Peter chuckled. "You're the unusual one! The woman who lived all over the world and speaks multiple languages..."

"Only two, really."

"...who lives in the jungles of South America," he continued with a playful grin and then more seriously, "and who is...so lovely." He shook his head slowly with a small smile and a look of wonder in his eyes. She smiled back, glad he thought so.

She marveled at the smooth curve of his chest muscles, enjoying the feel of his body, so different from her own...the straighter line from waist to hip...the swell of his biceps...the hair on his forearms, in the cleft of his chest and nestled in the soft skin of his armpits...the contrast of hard bulges and vulnerable hollows.

Peter's body was different from Jorge's. More compact and muscled from work. His skin was almost as pale as her own except his forearms, brown from daily exposure to the sun, his face and back lightly tanned.

They made love slowly at first, almost tentative in their explorations. Her fingers followed the line of his collarbone. Alicia wanted to trace every line, every feature.

They kissed and the current that began hours earlier grew, flowing fast like rapids on a river. Alicia heard his breath catch. Or was it her own? They were bombarded by sensations, caught in a torrent surging toward a great waterfall. They were the only people in a universe where time was infinite.

"Why don't you take me into the jungle?" Peter asked over breakfast.

"I want to go too!" chimed George.

Yesterday was baking and marketing day so today was her day for the rain forest and the finca.

"Maybe not this time," his mother answered. Then to Peter she said, "I usually take my time. I stop to draw or take notes...you might get bored. But, I guess I don't have to...take notes, I mean."

"Don't worry. I won't get bored."

First, they toured the farm taking George with them. When they got out of the jeep Peter carried him on his back, George grinning broadly.

"Giddy-up!" he exclaimed, nudging with his knees.

Peter obliged by trotting awhile then turning and trotting back.

"You may have created an unwanted precedent," Alicia warned, purposely choosing her words so that little ears could not follow.

Peter put him down and jabbed at the gray ceniza with the toe of his boot. He eyed the coffee bushes, noting the loss of leaves and said, "The coffee has suffered, hasn't it?"

"Yes but it's much better now. All of the bushes were covered with ash before. It is waning...don't you think?"

"Your observations are as valid as my opinion. Geologists really just don't know when it might be over...or start again. I read in the paper that they think some of the coffee farms are suffering from acid rain."

"Acid rain?"

"Yeah, from the volcano...the sulfur."

I'll be damned, Alicia thought, that explains the burned-looking leaves.

"Hey, I've got an idea," Peter said, digging into his pocket. He pulled out a small piece of metal and bent over, touching it to the ceniza. "George, look at this...it's magic!"

Tiny black minerals jumped toward the magnet, forming short strands as they clung to each other.

"Wow!" Alicia said.

"Wow!" George parroted.

"It's magnetite," Peter explained, prodding the black grains.

"How did you happen to have that your pocket?" Alicia asked laughing.

"Trick of the trade my dear, trick of the trade," he joked. "Geologists often carry them."

Paco took George back to the house when they were done. He went willingly as Paco lifted him into the saddle with him.

"You didn't find gold or anything near us, did you Peter?"

He stopped a moment and shook his head before they went on.

"Would you really have reported it?" she asked.

Peter pulled on his lower lip, considering her question. "It would have been tough, knowing you might've been unhappy, but...that's my job."

Alicia didn't reply, but her face was stony.

"So why are we having this discussion now?" he asked. "Do you see me as a raper of the land?" He rushed on before she could respond. "Did it ever occur to you that you are in the same spot? Your workers are paid a pittance compared to the profit coffee brings in Europe and the States."

"We pay them as much as we can and still turn a profit," she replied, feeling lame.

"My company would say something similar...we pay an environmental and social tax."

"But it doesn't seem to trickle down to the people," she insisted, pointing the way to a steep stream, cascading over rocks. "Doesn't that bother you?"

"Yes it bothers me! And we should pay twice as much for metals, gasoline, plastic...and coffee!" There was heat in his voice now too. "And this was once a tract of virgin rainforest."

That stung. She stared at him. "That's hardly fair," she said coolly, but had to acknowledge the point.

"Let's not fight, Alicia," he said softly. "We are cogs in the wheel of global problems. We just do what we can do."

"Locals should benefit more," she said.

"Companies could be taxed more, but the politicians control the money."

"Companies could invest directly in the region," she countered, but put a hand on his chest signaling a truce.

They climbed a few arduous feet to a trail Alicia had once tried to blaze. It was tough going. The vegetation was thick and where it wasn't muddy, it was steep and rocky.

"I haven't been up this creek much...at least not very far."

"I can see why. You're one hardy woman, Alicia."

"Here," she said, smiling, as she handed him the machete. "You can be machete man and clear us a trail."

"Hmm. I hope you are not taking unfair advantage of my masculinity." He tested the machete on a hanging vine.

"Of course I am! It will give you something to do. But you won't need it much at first."

Half an hour later a bird flew by with a flash of yellow tail and landed in a tree.

"We should have brought the binoculars," Peter said.

"It's pretty close. See it on that lower branch?" she pointed.

"Good eye. Do you know what it is?"

She stared at it, trying to recall. It was a large bird, reddish-brown and black, its long spatulate tail bright yellow with a black streak down the middle. As they watched, the bird made a loud gurgling call, spread its wings, and suddenly swung around the branch to hang upside down and flare out his tail feathers.

"Oh! Now I know what it is!" Alicia exclaimed in delight, just as Peter laughed loudly and the startled bird flew off in another flash of color.

"It's an *oropendola*. If we find its nest we might see others. Look for a long hanging basket!" They scanned the surrounding trees and when the bird trilled again Peter spotted him.

"There," he pointed. "And there's the nest. Look, there's another one." There were several nests about four feet long that looked like hanging baskets of moss. An *oropendola* watched from the limb of the tree and a second one clung to a nest, with what looked like a long string hanging from its beak.

"Neat birds," said Peter. "What's with the gymnastics?"

"It's a male mating ritual...pretty unique, actually. It's how they got their name, 'golden pendulum,'" she said. "This is so cool...we can come back and find them again since they are right on the trail."

"Are you going to sketch them?"

"I can try but I doubt they will pose for me." It was no good drawing from memory. She couldn't take her eye off of whatever she was sketching without breaking the spell.

Alicia pulled out her sketchbook. The one building the nest looked to be the most likely candidate. She tried to sketch quickly and wished she were closer.

"Those birds are so lucky. I wish I had their view of the canopy," she whispered.

"Yeah," he agreed. "Look, I'm going ahead to trail blaze some more."

"OK." She was already going into her drawing trance.

The sketch wasn't turning out as good as she wanted, because the bird she was working on flew in and out of her nest.

"Hey, Alicia. I found something!" The bird hopped into its nest at the sound of Peter's voice. She had no idea how long he had been gone. More than ten minutes?

"A trail!"

"Really?" she said doubtfully.

The only trails around here were either hers or animal trails. They'd made good progress with Peter clearing the way for them—farther than she could have come alone although hard to say how far. She followed him through the narrow aisle he had cut in the undergrowth along the steeply flowing stream for perhaps ten minutes.

"Here!" He pointed at a footpath crossing the stream.

"It does look like a trail. It must be an animal track," she said.

"It's a trail all right. It's been used. Look at this." He showed her an old machete cut on a woody stem.

"I guess it's a trail the Indians maintain. Seems like a long way from anywhere even for them. I've never run into anyone."

"Either that or someone is growing or processing cocaine on your land!" he joked, "Is this still Carvallo land?"

"I don't think so. I don't really know where the boundary is though." They had walked for a while, she thought, surely they were beyond the property line.

Deciding to head back, they passed the *oropendolas* and paused briefly to glimpse one, half-hidden in a suspended nest. Like a child in a swing.

"How long can you stay Peter?" This had been on her mind.

"They owe me a lot of overtime. I've hardly had a day off in over eight weeks. I have at least two weeks off."

She was so excited she threw herself at him and hugged him.

"I guess it's OK if I stay awhile!" Peter laughed.

"You can stay forever." That was a bit forward, she thought, but there it was, she had blurted out exactly what she meant.

During those two weeks they explored the countryside as their relationship blossomed.

"There is something I have to ask before you go," Alicia said. She had hoped he would bring it up, but here it was their last day together.

"Yeah?"

"There's no girlfriend back home?"

"No. Not really."

"What does that mean?"

"Well, I've been with other people too. I like to think my feelings for one person don't affect the way I feel about someone else."

"Well, it would affect me. I'm not into those open relationships people like to have these days. I don't want to be 'another person' to you," she retorted.

He put his arms around her, "You're not. You know that. Don't get all riled up on me."

She wanted them to be exclusive, Alicia fumed.

He looked at her pensively. "On the subject of other relationships, I think I should tell you something."

"What?" She furrowed her brows.

He exhaled. "I've seen Jorge with someone else."

"Irene," she nodded, "his old girlfriend. Marta told me."

Marta had said to her, "You'd better do something about this, Alicia, before it's too late." But she'd felt only the slightest twinge of jealousy...quickly followed by a mix of relief and regret.

"Good," Peter said. "I guess we don't need to feel guilty on that account then." He stroked her cheek. They were still entwined and stayed that way a moment until the two little boys came bursting in on them. It only occurred to her after he left that he had not asked if she was getting a divorce. She would have to bide her time with Jorge. If she asked now it would only antagonize him. But if he was getting serious about Irene...maybe not.

Chapter 16
THE JAGUAR

Paco rode his horse in the early morning mist. There had been one thing after another the last few years at Las Nubes. He wished they could settle back down to their routine of the old days. His life, over all, was easier, happier than most workers because of his position at the finca, but still, the strain of calamities weighed heavily on him.

The volcano, don Jorge's accident and then his leaving the doñita, don Felipe's heart attack.... Mario's layoff had been most unsettling and he was glad it was don Pepe who broke the bad news to his co-worker. Carmen had not been the same since her man was murdered. All of Escondido had been abuzz for weeks with talk of it. People were afraid to take the buses now.

He felt the warmth of the sun coming up over the horizon behind him. On his way to the shady tree by the house, where he usually tied up his horse, he spotted a dark stain on the courtyard. He stopped, curious at first, and then dismounted hurriedly. Even before he knelt to touch it, he spotted the remains of the hen. A limp, bloody corpse surrounded by feathers, its head at an angle. It was like stumbling upon a murder. But could one chicken produce all the blood splattered on the stones? No, there were large red drops all the way to the door.

Two women and two children living out here all alone, he thought in horror.

"Carmen!" Paco panted as he ran to the house, *"Están bien? Qué paso?"*

As she told him the shocking story he exclaimed, *"Mi alma!"* My soul!

They had gone to bed that night, as usual, but sometime after midnight Carmen was awakened by frightening sounds. She bolted upright in bed and listened for half a second before she was on her feet, running down the hallway. Those were not the ordinary calls of nocturnal creatures. There was a ferocious fight going on in the courtyard and it sounded for all the world like the bark of the yellow dog.

She ran up behind Alicia who was approaching the back door, flashlight in hand. Peering out the window, they saw chaotic flashes of movement near the fountain. A snarling jaguar was attacking the dog.

"Dios mío!" exclaimed Carmen, her hands at her mouth.

"Carmen!" Alicia whispered urgently, "Get a gun, get something!" There was a .22 locked in the closet of Felipe's old room.

Humberto toddled up sleepily rubbing one cheek, "*Qué pasa?*"

"Stay here Humberto!" Carmen commanded as she ran.

There was no time to find the key and run upstairs for the rifle. She grabbed a broom and a heavy skillet from the kitchen. By that time the jaguar had the dog pinned down on the ground.

"Be careful," they gasped simultaneously as Alicia snatched the cast iron frying pan.

She ran outside bellowing like a warrior "*YAAAA!*" and hurled the makeshift weapon at the jaguar. Carmen prayed it would hit its mark, and not the poor dog.

"*Fuera!*" Get out! Carmen yelled as fiercely as she knew how, running behind Alicia and brandishing the broom over her head.

The skillet hit the large cat's hindquarters and bounced off, clattering against the stone tiles. Startled, the predator turned on its heels and ran off into the night. Juanita, the monkey, chattered hysterically from her perch. Both women exhaled loudly and Carmen realized she had been holding her breath.

"Do you think he's gone?" Alicia asked as she crept toward the injured dog. "They are so dangerous."

Carmen nodded, panting, "They can kill a man. That beast could do the two of us and the dog a lot of damage." Alicia glanced up and saw Carmen lowering the broom.

"*A broom!*" she exclaimed with an edgy laugh. "You were going to fight it with a broom!" Carmen did not look amused.

The dog tried to stand and whined sharply. It looked at Alicia pathetically and crawled a few inches towards her. He seemed grateful, trusting, as Alicia knelt and stroked him. Her hand came back wet with blood.

Juanita was still screeching, pacing and bouncing on a limb just above them.

"*Silencio!*" Carmen yelled and the monkey lowered its volume. She turned toward the house and spotted Humberto, his eyes as big as coconuts. She hugged him close and told him to stay put.

Alicia started off with the flashlight to find some disinfectant when she heard Carmen scream, "*Ayyy!!*"

Her heart leapt and she pivoted swiftly, but it wasn't the jaguar returning — the chattering monkey had jumped onto Carmen's shoulder.

"*Maldito mono!*" she swore.

"I'll hold her, Mami...she's scared of the jaguar!" Humberto said. As he reached for the monkey, she stretched one scrawny little arm toward him, keeping the other firmly gripped around Carmen's neck.

That dog may have saved the little monkey's life, Alicia thought as she riffled through her medicine cabinet. Alcohol was no good — too harsh on raw flesh. She had hydrogen peroxide somewhere. There it was. She grabbed some cotton balls and the brown bottle and ran back downstairs.

They laid Old Yeller on the kitchen table, panting and trembling from fear and pain. By lantern light they saw the dog had numerous bite wounds and a gaping gash several inches long near the neck.

"Oh God. He needs stitches," Alicia stated.

"*Ay. Pobre perro*...we may have to put him out of his misery," said Carmen. What would the doñita do? Drive dangerous roads for hours in the dark to a veterinarian? It was unthinkable to do that—for a dog.

"It must be almost dawn, Paco will be here soon and can take care of it." Carmen told her.

"What can Paco do? I need you to find me a needle and thread...actually, bring me the whole sewing kit...oh, and check on Georgie, would you?"

Carmen stood rooted for a moment, astounded. Needle and thread? Had doña Alicia gone crazy? "The dog will bite you!"

"Let me worry about that Carmen. Hurry, *por favor!*"

When Carmen returned with the kit, she saw that Alicia had poured peroxide over the wounds and it bubbled pink on the dog's bloodied flesh like an alchemist's brew.

He whimpered a bit and Alicia made a mental note to buy iodine. She dabbed the wounds carefully, examined each one and trimmed away the fur.

"Well, this one is going to need quite a few stitches to hold it together." She chose a thin nylon thread she doubted had ever been used before and the smallest needle she could find. Facing the dog as she would a child, her hands on both sides of his head, she said, "Old Yeller I have to do this....It's going to be OK."

Amazingly the dog allowed her to work on him for fifteen minutes with only muted growls and whimpers. She stopped and caressed him twice when he yelped.

"You are a brave, brave dog," Alicia told him and meant it. "A jaguar-fighting hound." From now on, she vowed, the dog would sleep inside.

They folded a soft blanket on the floor for him to rest on, and he fell asleep right away. Humberto was back in bed, George had slept through the entire event, and both women were exhausted, but still pumped on adrenaline.

Alicia went out and unchained Juanita so she could escape if the jaguar ever returned. "I've been meaning to do this for a long time anyway," she told the monkey.

"Well, you've seen your jaguar now," Carmen said, "I hope we never see another."

"You know maybe it wasn't a jaguar. I think it might have been a puma...this high up in the mountains. Did you notice if it had spots?"

Carmen rolled her eyes, "Puma, jaguar...what's the difference?"

"Pumas are just as fierce, but don't have the spots. And ocelots are smaller."

Carmen had never heard the word puma. Everyone calls all the wild cats "jaguars," be they spotted, small or large. She shrugged, "I think it was a jaguar. Whatever it was, I hope we never see another."

Paco stared at the injured hound as Carmen finished recounting the story. Old Yeller lay on the floor where Alicia had made a pallet for him. The dog had rarely known such comfort and attention. He lay still and appeared to be listening to the conversation, as if he knew it was about him.

"I guess the jaguar was looking for...food? The chickens...maybe the monkey?" Paco said, "You will have to be careful about leaving the doors closed and make sure the hen house is secure."

Carmen nodded. "Alicia thinks the animals the jaguar ate moved away from the ceniza to find food."

Paco frowned, "The ceniza hardly falls now."

"Yes, but it covers the ground and plants still."

After a moment she continued. "Paco, she *talked* to the dog...in English...face-to-face, like you would a human. I think she explained the situation to him and the dog understood and agreed!"

Berto squatted in front of the dog and demonstrated, "O'Yela, it OK," he imitated Alicia.

"Listen! Now your son is speaking foreign!" Paco laughed.

"Yes," she grinned. "He is learning *inglés* from the doñita and Georgito." George was awake now and stood with a finger in his mouth trying to absorb the story.

"Yela?...*Olla*...is that what she calls him?" Paco asked. "What a funny name for a dog. Why do you suppose she calls him Cooking Pot?"

Carmen shook her head and continued stirring a pan with oats and honey for their granola. "It must mean something in English."

"Not *'olla,'*" Humberto quietly corrected the grown-ups, *"es O-Ye-la"* he said, trying to refine his pronunciation and imitate doña Alicia's.

"But a dumb dog understood...and he let her sew him?" Paco grimaced over his coffee and shook his head in disbelief.

"*Si!* The dog knew she was helping him and let her stick the needle right in his flesh," Carmen tightened her arms and shoulders in a shudder, "and La doñita stitched him up like a *doctora* in surgery!"

Humberto interjected excitedly, "And the jaguar snarled...like this!" He made a ferocious face, lifted his hands into little claws and made attacking noises for George's benefit. "And the dog growled, like this: *Grrr, GRR!*"

"Keep your voice down, doña Alicia went back to sleep," Carmen told her son.

"I wanted to see them fight!" George said, "Why didn't you wake me up?" The two grown-ups laughed heartily at this.

———

Rumors got around that doña Alicia was a *doctora*. Soon people were dropping by the finca for medical help. It was useless for Alicia to try to explain that she had no medical training or urge them to go to the doctor. Dr. Benevides was in the next town and only stopped by Escondido once a week.

All they knew and cared about was that she knew what to do. Paregoric would ease stomach cramps, and soothe a teething baby when rubbed on the gums. If a child had a very high fever she would bathe it in cool water and the fever would drop.

Humberto had diarrhea and Carmen knew to give him bland foods, but Alicia also urged him to drink lots of boiled water with a bit of sugar and salt stirred in. "Children get dehydrated when they have diarrhea."

Whatever that means, thought Carmen. What she said was, "I was going to boil him a potato, but we seem to be out."

"How could that be?" Alicia said. "We harvested a huge sack of them."

"I thought maybe you gave some away. I'll make some rice."

Carmen came back a moment later. "Alicia! The rice looks low too."

Alicia knew they had plenty of rice. She bought it by five- or ten-pound sacks. "Where are you storing everything?"

"In the storage closet next to my old room."

"I better take a look," Alicia said, and went out the back door, Carmen and the two children in tow.

"I don't understand," she said, inspecting their supplies. "Do you think someone's been in here?"

"Mami, look what I found," George piped up. He held out a small wooden carving. Alicia squatted to take it and passed her hand over the crude sculpture of an animal. "Why...it's a jaguar!"

"Can I keep it Mami?" said George. "Is it *our* jaguar?"

"It's like a phantom leaving an offering," Carmen said, looking spooked.

"Someone must be hungry and leaving behind a payment," Alicia said, looking up at Carmen.

"Hmmh! Some payment. Who wants an old carving like the *indios* make?"

"That's it Carmen!" Alicia stood up. "With all the ceniza, the Indians must be having a hard time with their crops...and hunting."

Carmen sighed. "Paco could put a lock on the door but they might come in through the roof." The Indians were so stealthy, she thought. This would not happen if the yellow dog still slept outside where a guard dog belonged.

"No, we won't do that," Alicia said. "We can afford a few cups of rice now and then for a hungry family."

Carmen half smiled, half shrugged as if she half approved. "As long as they don't start stealing chickens or the clothes off the line—"

They were interrupted by a call from the front of the house. A woman scuffled up the porch steps holding her right arm out at an angle. *"Me caí,"* she said.

"You fell?" Alicia brushed her hands on her jeans and examined the swollen limb. The woman winced in pain.

"See this bump *señora*?"

The skin was intact, but a hard, swollen knot protruded from her forearm.

"I think your arm is broken...it must be very painful. You need a doctor," Alicia told her.

*"Ahh, sí...*it hurts, but I trust you *doña*. You fix it," the woman smiled feebly but nodded confidently. She cradled the fractured forearm as tenderly as if it

were a baby. It was an arm muscled by physical labor. She might still be no more than forty, but she was aged by hard work, her face lined by the sun. Her bare feet were splayed and callused. She wore the standard dark felt hat and was dressed entirely in black, indicating she was in mourning for a family member. Perhaps she was a widow.

"No, no. I have no training for this. You must go to the doctor." Alicia told her and then asked, "When did it happen?"

"This morning, *señora*. I fell getting out of my brother-in-law's oxcart."

This morning. The fracture needed to be set right away or it would heal crooked. She sighed and bundled the woman into the jeep to go see Dr. Benevides.

It took all afternoon to drive the patient over the dusty roads, assist the doctor in plastering the arm, and then take her home. Home being a barely visible trail off the main road.

"May God pay you because I cannot," the woman said as she got out. The new cast shone like a white light against her black clothing. She nodded her head and disappeared within seconds.

So, in addition to nursing, if there was an accident or a person was seriously ill, Alicia and her jeep turned into an ambulance. The locals knew she had a soft heart as well as a soft touch and it was easier to walk thirty minutes or more to Las Nubes, or send someone to fetch Alicia, than to spend half of the day on the bus. Plus, when the doñita was with you, Dr. Benevides took care of you right away.

The doctor was a kindly, older man with a bit of a paunch over which he folded his hands while he listened to his patient's complaints. He regularly agreed to accept vegetables, chickens or services in return for his ministrations. Alicia felt guilty when she brought in people who had nothing to offer by way of fees. Occasionally, if she tried to help pay an indigent patient's bill, the doctor whispered, "No charge this time."

The main determining factor seemed to be if the patient or their parents wrung their hands in distress over how they would ever come up with the money, but secondary determinations were unknown to her. Often it was in the case of a child. Other times, she had to figure he liked the patient or knew they would reciprocate when their circumstances improved. Who knew, maybe it was just the whim of the day.

She liked Dr. Benevides. They were something of a team. He trusted her enough now to supply her with antibiotics and a few other medications for emergencies. At times she had coffee with him and his wife, Gabriela. They were become neighborly — even if they were 90 minutes away and only saw each other once a month or so.

"Come again," Gabriela told her early on. "It's nice to have another woman to talk to."

But at the end of that year, 1974, Gabriela had something else to tell her.

"Alicia I know you don't have any family here to advise you, so I hope you don't mind me saying this, because...people are starting to talk. About the *americano*. The culture here...women are not as independent as in your country. Colombians are more conservative."

"I know..." Alicia said looking down at the jeep keys in her hand, "but Jorge won't give me a divorce." Not that it would make a difference. A divorced woman was a fallen woman, just like the one who lived in sin with a man. If she lived in Bogotá the repercussions would be unbearable.

Gabriela put a small hand on her arm. "I understand, but the Carvallo family might not."

Alicia thanked the woman for her concern. She did not think the Carvallos would go so far as to kick her out. She was too far away to embarrass them much—out of sight out of mind.

Every few months Carmen or Alicia would notice beans, rice or some other staple food missing from storage shed. Usually something was left in its place as payment: a woven bracelet, yucca wrapped in banana leaves—which they were afraid to eat—and most recently a tanned animal skin belonging to a small cat of some sort. Most likely an ocelot Alicia thought. After the first incident the women were more careful about locking the house up at night. But no valuables ever went missing, just the foodstuff.

"They take the cheapest food imaginable," Alicia told Peter who had just arrived from Bogotá with a cooler full of steaks and other goodies. Whenever he did this they felt like they were celebrating.

Peter admired the animal skin so she placed it on the floor on his side of the bed.

"Did you bring me and Berto chocolates?" George asked, hands behind his back.

With a flourish and a grin Peter whipped out two small chocolate bars. "There's more where that came from," he whispered to Alicia.

Chocolate was surprisingly hard to come by in Escondido, considering Colombia was a cacao producing country. Alicia sometimes wondered if they should try to grow their own.

Chapter 17
THE PURPLE SCHOOL
1975

The volcano had ceased pumping out the destructive ceniza, the rainy season had tapered off and another year began. Alicia learned the eruptions had indeed contributed to acid rain and that was how the coffee leaves had been burned. But for now the volcano had reverted to smoking picturesquely in the distance.

Peter came for a few days here, a week or two there.

In March Paco found Alicia poking around the old shed next to the stable.

"I thought I saw some paint in here."

"Paint? What do you want painted?"

"The school Paco, the school!"

He was astounded. The government ran the schools, not the people...not even the Carvallos—but you never knew what this señora would do.

"There is not enough paint for the school."

"Looks like there are half a dozen cans here to me."

"But none of them are full and they are all different colors...pink, blue."

Not enough of one color, but there was a full can of white and they could mix the rest.

"Who is going to paint the school *doña*?"

"You are...and the other parents. You can supervise."

Paco would do anything to please Alicia now that she let him drive the jeep. And what did it matter if she wanted him to paint the school or work at Las Nubes? He was paid either way.

"Doña Alicia is trying to get new books and supplies...maybe even a second teacher. We just have to paint the walls and fix it up a bit," Paco told the parents and any other adult who would listen.

But the natives of Escondido were unfamiliar with the concept of working for the cooperative good of the town; most of them lived hand-to-mouth and had nothing to give to others. Paco had to badger them and promise a good lunch—to be cooked by Carmen. Alicia planned to put in a few hours herself.

On a Saturday three weeks later five people showed up. Not many, but enough. It had taken that long for Paco and his wife, Emilia, to talk people into working without pay on their day off. The women scrubbed walls and floors and the men sanded and prepared the surfaces. They had wanted to slap the paint on without any prepping, arguing that it would cover up any dirt or defects, but Paco insisted that it be done properly. Alicia was pleased to have a man oversee the male volunteers. They had stared at her when she arrived.

"*Buenos días,*" she said with a smile, and they shuffled their feet and mumbled back a greeting. She was used to being stared at merely for her fair complexion, but knew this time it was because they could not believe she was going to work with them, like a man. For the first hour, men and women alike rushed over to assist whenever she went to lift a bucket.

"No, let me do it señora"... "*Permítame...*"

She decided her presence was stifling camaraderie and shortly after noon, Alicia went home. By mid-afternoon they were all impressed with their handiwork and stood back to admire it. The interior boasted four freshly painted walls in a pale shade of lilac—the color being the result of mixing blue, pink and white paint. There should be enough left to paint the exterior the following week, if the rainy season held off. One of the men promised to bring a cousin who was a carpenter to repair the broken shutters.

Between the weather and a local festival, it didn't happen the next week. After their initial burst of enthusiasm, it was harder to get people to show up. Two weeks later the outside was yet to be painted, but Alicia was used to the slow pace of the country. She could be patient—or at least persistent.

The Colombian superintendent of schools wrote thanking her for her interest, but regretted that funding was not available for an additional teacher. They would, however, send desks for each child officially enrolled. Alicia realized that meant they would somehow have to get each occasional drop-in student to officially enroll. She filled out the forms herself, as the parents might themselves be illiterate or just not prioritize the matter.

Then Alicia had a reply from the Peace Corps. They would send someone out from the Bogotá office to have a look. Alicia extracted a promise from Peter to drop by their office when he was in Bogotá and remind them about Escondido. Peter just shook his head — she never ceased to amaze him.

She became more involved in the school and dropped by for a couple of hours each week to help children who had fallen behind. That allowed Señora Ramirez to teach the rest of her pupils, and she grudgingly admitted this was easier for her and better for the students. The school children were charmed by George and lavished him with attention, which he relished.

It had been a year since Paco and Alicia had first spoken about the school, and now it had an assistant teacher named Lynn Olson, new desks, new books and a check for pencils, chalk and miscellaneous supplies.

Miss Olson was a twenty-two year old Peace Corps worker who had majored in Spanish. It didn't take her long to realize that studying the language was not the same as speaking it all day, every day — much less teaching in Spanish. Regardless, she managed to teach arithmetic and a little social studies, and added music to the curriculum—while Sra. Ramirez handled everything else.

Sra. Ramirez, it turned out, was not so bad after all. She was actually in good humor these days. Whereas her job seemed hopeless before, now it was a cheerful environment with desks and books for everyone. Enrollment increased and she found she needed Lynn Olson more than ever—even if her language skills were deficient. The perk was the children were learning English—an increasingly useful skill even out in the country. The little school in Escondido was on its way to becoming the finest in the province.

Shortly after the American teacher arrived, Paco organized a work party to complete the exterior paint. They had waited for a break in the wet weather but it did not come until July. He insisted Alicia attend the unveiling—which meant she had better bring food.

"Of course I will," she said, pleased to be included. Carmen prepared *empanadas*—her flavorful meat pastries—and Alicia baked cookies.

Alicia helped George out of the jeep and stood beaming at the little building as he ran on ahead of her. The school was magnificent, she thought. Even its unusual color—which matched the lavender interior—fit in fine among neighboring homes painted blue, turquoise, pink or white. The new shutters were a contrasting bright white, and someone had raked the grounds and planted a vine with magenta flowers next to the entry gate. There were even potted plants next to the door.

The door was draped with what looked like a worn tablecloth...part of the decoration, she figured. As they entered the yard she heard someone say, *"Aqui viene la doñita."*

She was used to the moniker. If it had originated as a joke, it was now an affectionate nickname.

"Here she comes!" another person repeated urgently.

There was scurrying as she approached, and the frayed cloth over the doorway was ceremoniously pulled down. And then there was clapping.

A hand-painted sign on the door read: *"Escuela Alicia de Carvallo"* in ornate black script.

"Oh my gosh!" Alicia blurted in English, surprised by the tribute. She put a hand over her open mouth and looked away as tears filled her eyes. People milled around her grinning and patting her shoulders. For a minimum investment of time and virtually no money, Escondido had a fine school and she was revered by the local populace.

"You'll be coming to this school in February Berto," Carmen told him proudly. He was not yet six years old.

Alicia and Peter sat on the veranda — the site of all the comings and goings over the years.

"When do you think you'll be back?" she asked.

"Can't say for sure."

Alicia sighed. It was the nature of their relationship. He always going, she living without him most of the time, like a ship captain's wife. But they were used to their solitary habits — the spaces in their togetherness countered by the closeness of their relationship. When he was here they tended to put their own things aside and spend hours together. And he would spend the Christmas holidays with them next month.

"I need to get going," Peter said, "what are you doing today?"

"The usual. Making the rounds and then I think I'll go into the cloud forest."

"I want to go, Mami," George said as he watched her kiss Peter goodbye.

She was over feeling guilty about leaving George behind on her rain forest days. She tried taking him with her when he was a toddler and found herself afraid to put him down, even as she worried about carrying him in her arms while she trekked over treacherous creek rocks and tree roots. He squirmed the whole time and wanted down to explore.

George was a surprisingly rambunctious boy — surprising because she and her brother had been such quiet children and she expected her children, most children actually, would be the same.

Thomas and I were a couple of mice, she thought. Seen but not heard — in a word: repressed. But George was animated, full of energy and inquisitiveness... definitely a "Curious George."

When he learned to crawl, he would scramble over the edge of the fountain and into the shallow pool whenever they turned their backs. Invariably, he could find a caustic cleaning chemical or sharp object within moments of a cupboard being left open.

"*Que niño mas travieso!*" What a mischievous little boy, Carmen would exclaim. And George would giggle at their exasperation and Humberto's delight in his antics.

She'd decided to drain the fountain for a year to make sure he didn't drown in it. It was full of ceniza anyway. When Paco turned it back on, he filled only a few inches in the bottom, which meant that instead of cascading and burbling, it trickled and dribbled.

More recently, George spent hours playing with leaf-cutter ants, following their wide path through the yard and the finca to find their home. Alicia wondered how long the trail had been there— decades? How many generations of ants had used and maintained it?

George tried to remove a bit of leaf from their backs and substitute it with something else for them to bear; see how much of a load a poor ant could carry. Then he tried to divert their well-trodden trail and caused a panic within the colony, although the ants were not fooled by any man-made track. He kept at it until several bites left welts on his arms and legs. Alicia applied a paste of baking soda to take out the sting.

The last time Alicia took George into the rainforest her usual three-to-five-hour escapade was shortened to less than an hour. And Carmen admonished her, pointing to red bug bites he had come back with, although George was oblivious them.

He would soon be four and she ventured with him as far as the trogon hangout. It was one of two places she could rely on to hold his interest—the other being the tadpole pond.

She liked the trogons, as they invariably stayed close to the laurel trees where she could find them. The *oropendolas* she'd found with Peter had been dependable only that one season and then had abandoned their nests and moved on.

"You have to hold my hand if you come with me, Georgie, okay?" Otherwise he would stumble into trouble. It meant she could not sketch or take many notes.

George nodded solemnly.

"Now," she said, "We have to be quiet and look very hard for them because they are almost the same color as the trees."

They stared onto the trees in silence for several minutes.

"You're being very good George," she whispered to him. He leaned against her and she put a hand on his thin shoulder. A loud resonant call drew her eyes to one, but she waited to let George find it on his own. They crouched and listened.

"Oh, hear that?"

"There he is!" George cried, pointing to a striking bird, glistening in metallic green colors trimmed with scarlet.

After a while they spotted another one. Probably his mate.

"Aren't they beautiful?' Alicia whispered, as much in awe as her son.

"How come the birds only like these trees Mami?"

"Because laurel fruit is their favorite food." Or perhaps their only food source, she thought. She read once that the rare resplendent quetzals, another type of trogan, relied on the laurel fruit to the extent that if the crop had a bad year the quetzal population would plummet.

"Tomorrow I want Berto to come," George said.

"Berto's in school tomorrow. Maybe Saturday."

———

Carmen was sweeping the porch when she looked up to see a wiry man carrying a child through the gate. She held the broom against her sturdy shoulder and put up her other arm to shield her eyes from the glare of the late afternoon sun. Something about the man's hurried gait told her there was trouble even before they came close enough for her to see little boy's blood-caked leg.

"Come in," she said, holding open the door and pointing toward the kitchen. "I'll find the señora."

Near the back door, Alicia dismounted from her horse and lifted George down.

"A boy is hurt — it looks urgent," Carmen told her, taking George's hand. He quickly disentangled himself and ran inside to see the visitors.

Alicia washed her hands at the sink and looked at the nasty slice in the child's leg. He had swung a machete on a banana stalk and it had come down on his thigh. She cleaned off the blood and dirt and saw that the thin leg needed several stitches. The red muscle was just exposed, but fortunately not cut. The boy looked to be all of ten. She thought she recognized him from the school.

"He needs to see Dr. Benevides. You should have taken him straight in."

"But *señora*," the father said, "Dr. Benevides will have gone already."

"Well, we will have to find him at home." As soon as she said it, she wondered if he and his wife were back from visiting relatives in Bogotá.

The father twisted his hat in his hands, "Doña Alicia, the doctor does not live in Escondido. He lives far away...who knows where...but you can stitch him up like you did *el perro*."

Hands on her hips, Alicia looked at the man aghast. She wanted to say, "Your son is not a dog!" but not in front of the child. She shook her head slowly.

"What is your name?" she asked the boy, putting a hand on his back.

"*Andrés, señora*," the father answered, pursing his lips. "He is careless. He is small but brave." He shrugged.

"You've carved a notch in yourself, Andrés," she told the boy.

"*Sí señora*." Andrés pressed his lips together.

"*Por qué?*" Why, asked George in all earnestness, causing the boy to smile.

She was not about to sew up a human being—much less a child. She shook her head again and blew out a cheek. The cut was about an inch long.

"Let me see you move your leg."

The boy complied. Luckily the cut was not close to the knee, or anywhere near tendons, and the muscle appeared intact. But if they waited until morning when they might find a doctor, the wound would scab and refuse to close, at best—more likely it would get infected.

Alicia cleaned the wound with iodine as gently as she could. The boy grimaced a bit but was a good sport. Maybe a butterfly bandage would do. At least it would close the gaping wound, reduce the chance of infection and hopefully minimize scarring. Under the circumstances, it was her only option.

She cut several narrow strips of tape and clipped a notch in the center of each, like a bow tie. With her fingers, she carefully joined the edges of skin together.

"Carmen, put the first piece of tape on here... *gracias*. OK, now this end."

In the middle of all of this, Peter walked in with Humberto.

"What are you doing back here?" she grinned in surprise, for it had only been a few hours since he left. "What happened?"

"The road is blocked at Leon, so I turned around. Found Berto walking home."

"Oh Berto, I forgot about you!" Alicia bit her lip, looking at Carmen. "I am so sorry!"

Carmen had not forgotten about her son, but this little boy's emergency took precedence. Humberto could walk home from school. She had walked everywhere for years.

"What's going on here? An operation?" Peter asked jovially.

"Yep," said George, sounding grown-up and very American.

Alicia pulled the remaining bit of skin together and put the last bandage in place. It formed a nice clean seam. The trick was not to get it wet or allow it to come off until the skin grew back together.

"Why don't you leave your son here and come back for him tomorrow. It will be best if he doesn't walk until then," Alicia told the father.

This was partly true, she wanted to keep an eye on him, but mostly she wanted to make sure his leg was kept clean. His home no doubt had a dirt floor, no running water and he would be expected to do his chores.

"*Si no es mucha molestia señora*...that sounds like a good idea."

"No trouble," Alicia reassured the man. "Come back in the morning. Andres will still need to go to the doctor for a tetanus shot." Even as she said it, she knew by his casual, dismissive nod he probably would not take him in. She found it hard to persuade people of the importance of preventive and recuperative care.

"Impressive repair job," said Peter as he bent over, his hands on his knees, to examine the closed line of the boy's wound. He stood and ruffled Andrés' hair.

"I hope Dr. Benevides will approve. He still needs a tetanus shot though," Alicia told Peter, but looked at Andrés.

"Why don't we take him tomorrow?" Peter suggested and she nodded gratefully.

"So, was there a landslide?"

"Yeah. I might have been able to get over it, but it seemed a little dicey and then some men told me the guerillas had triggered it with explosives."

"Oh dear." Lately, she was hearing more and more about guerillas and drug lords.

"I didn't want to mess with them, if that was true," he laughed. "So you have me for a couple more days."

"We'll put the boys in one room and they can have a slumber party."

"A party!" echoed George grinning at Andrés and Humberto.

"That one is going to have a bath first." Carmen declared, looking at the urchin.

"Only a sponge bath, Carmen. He can't get the leg wet!" Alicia cautioned her.

Andrés had never seen a bath tub before—or for that matter a bathroom. At dinner he sat at the table in awe—of the food, the setting, the clean tile floor, the large table with carved wooden chairs. There was a tablecloth and paper napkins, salt and pepper shakers made of glass, and the two Americans speaking their strange-sounding language. Later he slept in a real bed with clean white sheets, a soft pillow and warm woolen blankets.

The next day, after breakfast, Andrés told Carmen, "I think I should stay awhile. My leg hurts very much." And to prove it he limped and winced for her.

"*Ah, si?*" replied Carmen with only the faintest twitch of a smile as she and Alicia cleared the plates from the table.

Alicia walked around the wet cafetal with Pepe on his next visit. The thin clouds were starting to lift and weak sunlight shone through.

"See, the coffee really is doing a lot better since last time you were here."

Pepe's visits had dwindled from almost every month to every few months, to once or twice a year. No one ever said they trusted her to run the finca, but she thought Pepe would show up more often if he didn't.

Don Felipe had died the previous year and Alicia was saddened that she and George were not able to attend the funeral since it was customary to bury the deceased within 24 to 36 hours. Word had not reached her until the day after the funeral when Antonio González borrowed his brother's jeep to drive from Escondido to tell her.

"I wish Papi could have seen this," Pepe replied. "It has recovered more than I thought possible a few years ago."

"Me too Pepe. Me too," she paused a moment. "I've been thinking that maybe we should go into the specialized coffee market. You know? The gourmet coffee market in Europe?"

Pepe pursed his lips. He had all but written off the finca income until the last couple of years. He had his job, but the long-term savings the rest of the Carvallos relied on were seriously diminished.

"Las Nubes is good coffee, but you have to breed the plants for gourmet coffee..." his voice trailed off and then resumed, "You can't have any green berries mixed in, and the pickers throw way too many unripe berries in as it is..."

This was true. The workers just wanted to fill their baskets as quickly as possible and get paid.

"We could do it," Alicia interrupted. "We might have to pay them a bit more."

"But then where is the profit?"

"The coffee would fetch a higher price," she persisted.

Pepe smoothed his mustache and cocked his head while he thought—a pose that so reminded her of his brother that Alicia felt a nostalgic pang. He put his hand on the small of her back as they walked back. A small thing, but she was glad for it. It showed some empathy or even affection, like in the old days.

"Well Alicia, I will give you the name of a Dutchman who called me..." he blew out his cheeks trying to remember "...a year ago. Before Papi's...his last heart attack. The man was interested in something like this, but we told him the troubles we had with the ceniza."

"Does he speak Spanish or English?"

"English. So you could deal with him better than I. His Spanish is worse than my English!" Pepe smiled. "There is something else you should know. Have you heard of the Black Frost?"

"Not a disease?" Alicia said in fear. Not another blow to the coffee.

"No, no. Brazil had a terrible freeze a few months ago that killed half of their coffee plants and ruined their crop. It means demand is not only way up for Colombian coffee, but the Brazilians are planting *robustica* instead of *arabica*."

Of the basic two types, Las Nubes grew the higher quality *arabica*.

"Because *robustica* grows faster?"

"Exactly. So the demand for our *arabica* may go up even higher," Pepe grinned. "We should be in good shape for next year's harvest."

Alicia was sorry for Brazil. She didn't want to make money on someone's misfortune, but ...*Dios!* It's time for us to have some luck, she thought.

She wrote to Holland and even sent pictures of the coffee. The Dutchman replied that he was interested, but he might not be back in Colombia for a few months. She crossed her fingers that he would come, and wrote again a month later to remind him. Patience and persistence are the companions of determination, she reminded herself.

Chapter 18
THE COFFEE CONNOISSEUR

Sr. González handed Alicia the mail in his little store. In spite of the sunny day, it was dim inside and she carried it to the window to read. There was a letter from Peter, but for once she opened another one first. A letter from Holland, postmarked two weeks ago.

"*Buenas noticias?*" Good news? González asked her.

"*Si! Muy buenas!*" she smiled, "*Necesito usar su teléfono, por favor.*"

She called Pepe at his office and told him, Willem van der Lande was coming to Las Nubes.

"I have *buenas noticias tambien*, Alicia. Green coffee broke a dollar a pound yesterday!"

Alicia stopped twirling a strand of hair. "Good grief! Has it ever been that high?"

Smiling behind his desk Pepe put his tongue in his cheek and shook his head. "No."

Consumers were hoarding coffee worldwide, driving up the prices faster.

———————

Mr. van der Lande was looking for the *arabica* that grew in the cloud forest and wanted to cross breed it for special blends. He was a tall, pleasant middle-aged man. He called the *robustica* coffee grown down slope "decent cheap coffee" but not what he was looking for.

The Dutch, she learned, are heavy coffee consumers. Six or seven cups a day van der Lande told her.

"Of course I'm not limiting myself to Holland. The United States is the big specialty market, and the rest of Europe."

It would take five years for new plants to mature and he wanted to take out the older and less vigorous bushes.

"I guess I don't have a problem with that," Alicia told him. Some new stock was a good idea. After all, some of the plants were near the end of their lifespan when the ceniza hit and others never recovered. And the timing was right. Their next harvest would bring in more money than they had made in years, so they could afford to sacrifice some plants while waiting for the new ones to grow.

He admired the trees growing amidst the bushes on the cafetal. Shade-grown coffee.

"What is that one?" he asked.

"The one with the pink blossoms? That's a *roble*...one of my favorites."

"And the ones with the red flowers?"

"Fuego del bosque."

"Flame of the forest. I could see those from the air, flying into Bogotá... Most everyone else grows coffee in a mono-culture and it is more susceptible to insects."

"And disease too," Alicia added.

"Oh yes. Just like bananas. When Standard Fruit planted thousands of acres in bananas, a disease that loved bananas moved in and wreaked havoc. Of course the natural check and balance system was destroyed when the rainforest was plowed in for the crop."

"And now they are spraying and dusting for disease and insects, but it has not recovered," she shook her head.

"We don't want insecticides or pesticides of any kind here," Van de Lande said.

"Well, we haven't used any for some years." Not in the years I've been here, thought Alicia. "And they were rarely used in the past, because they were not really needed."

"This supports the theory that the trees attract birds and the birds take care of the insects."

Alicia showed him the outbuilding where the Carvallos had once processed their own coffee beans — the concrete pads for drying, the fermentation bins. Paco had cleaned everything up nicely for their visitor.

"Watch your head!" she cautioned as he nearly walked into an old beam. The doorways were not constructed for someone over six feet tall. "This is where we pour the cherries into the chute."

Van der Lande took off his hat—exposing a bare head he wisely protected from sunburn—so he could see better overhead. Then he bent down and squinted. "We may want to keep some of this. Some people like the old-fashioned methods," he said.

"Yes I like what I see," he said as they walked back. "What I'm really wanting also is a place to process the coffee. Would you be willing to let me build it here?"

Alicia looked around trying to imagine where to put another building and how big it might be. "We'll have to think on that one."

They climbed the steps to the porch and Carmen brought them coffee. She would have dearly loved to eavesdrop on the conversation but it was all in English anyway, so she went back to the kitchen to speculate with Paco. She'd just have to wait until the visitor left—she knew Alicia would share the news.

It was the first time Alicia had served home-grown coffee and worried if it passed muster. She watched Willem van der Lande savor it. First he looked in the cup—discreetly, but she noticed. Next, he sipped it with his eyes closed, then inhaled the steamy aroma. She thought she detected a faint smile. Then the Dutchman nodded with approval.

He would buy the coffee, but the extra income from the processing would belong to him the first year. The next year they would split it and after that it would belong to Las Nubes.

"I'll have to ask the family. Is there a catch?" The decision was not really hers. It was an attractive offer although she did not like the idea of another building on the property.

"A *catch*?"

She explained the idiom and he laughed. "You are very straightforward señora Carvallo! To be candid, one does not expect that in Latin America. The 'catch' is you must promise to sell only to me...unless we agree there is a surplus. But the price will always be a fair one we will agree on and it will be above the going rate for most *arabica*."

They shook hands as he got into his rented jeep.

"I think we will enjoy doing business together, Mrs. Carvallo."

"I think so too, Mr. van der Lande," Alicia grinned.

Pepe loved the investor's proposal for a processing plant. Even if the finca had a bad year, they could still process beans from other farms. He had no trouble dumping the old buyer, Rogelio Camacho, even if his father might turn in his grave. Business was business and Camacho had shown no loyalty to them when times were tough. Jorge had always had misgivings about him.

Alicia discussed her own strategy with Paco. They had to convince the workers to leave the green cherries on the bush and harvest only the ripe ones.

"I think it will work if we pay them more. That way we all win...we make more money, and so do they," she said.

"The problem, doña, is that the first crop is heavy, so they make less money as the year progresses. It is harder to get workers to come back for the next harvest when they must pick more and more red cherries just so they can fill their baskets."

"I've thought about that. Maybe we can give them a bonus for coming back for subsequent harvests."

Unheard of—of course it had to work if the pickers made a bit more money than at the other fincas.

———————

The weather had turned quite hot, with hardly a cloud in the sky. It was the hottest July Alicia could remember. It was a Saturday and the women lolled around the breakfast table with the boys.

"*Que calor!*" Carmen said. "I can hardly work in this heat."

She had been on her hands and knees yesterday polishing the wood floors with a coconut husk. Alicia worked outside in the morning, but after lunch collapsed in the hammock trying to catch a breeze. She rested there half the afternoon reading and napping, unable to get anything done in the sultry weather.

"Well, take it easy today. You worked too hard yesterday. You made me feel guilty. You lie in the hammock today!" Alicia said.

"It is even hotter in Escondido, Mami," Humberto told his mother. "George and I were falling asleep at our desks yesterday."

"Yeah! It was really, really hot!" George chimed.

"Do you want to go up in the cloud forest with me?" Alicia asked the boys. "It will be cooler—or you can put your feet in the stream."

"*Sí!*" said Humberto. "Do you want to come, Mami?"

"*Ha! Dios guarde!*" Carmen said, "I'm not going to expose myself to snakes!"

"Carmen, in all these years I've seen very few snakes here and one of them was in our own back yard!" Alicia retorted.

But Carmen opted to stay and enjoy the quiet house she seldom had to herself. Maybe she *would* relax in the hammock and sip lemonade.

"Alicia!" she called after them. She had long ago dropped the "doña," unless she was speaking of Alicia to Humberto.

"*¿Qué?*" asked Alicia turning around.

"You can take us all out for ice cream when you get back!"

Alicia chuckled and took George's hand, as was her habit — although he often pulled away to explore. She had taken the boys into the rain forest on numerous short excursions, but when he was younger he was likely to skin a knee or sit down on an ant trail. Now that he was starting kindergarten it was more enjoyable. And Carmen had given in to allowing Berto to come along too.

"Look at the funny little fish!" exclaimed the older boy. His English had become so fluent that he sometimes helped Mr. Harper, who had replaced Miss Olson at school. Alicia liked speaking English with the two of them even though the boys usually fell back into Spanish when she was not addressing them directly.

The three of them squatted on their haunches for a better look.

"Oh! Those are tadpoles...baby frogs."

They were swimming in a miniature pond next to the stream.

"They don't look like frogs to me," Humberto said quietly, not wishing to contradict George's mother.

"Look, there is one starting to grow little legs," she pointed. "The mother frog lays her eggs and they start out as tiny fish in the water then grow into tadpoles."

"How do they breathe in the water?"

"They have gills, just like fish, and their skin breathes too...it absorbs oxygen."

"Oxi-gin," George repeated.

"Their skin breathes?" Humberto made a droll face at this preposterous statement and the boys looked at each other and cracked up.

"Tadpoles can only live in water, but when they turn into frogs they can be in water or on land," Alicia explained, smiling — she was quite used to their antics.

"How do they turn into frogs? " Humberto asked.

"They lose their gills and develop lungs and legs. It's a big word: metamorphosis. Let's come back tomorrow with a jar and we can raise a few in the fountain."

"Cool!" said George. A word he had picked up from Peter.

"Can we take them to school to show the other children?" Berto asked.

"What a good idea!" Alicia said as she brushed her son's hair off his forehead.

"Yeah!" George agreed, jumping up and down, nearly knocking her over.

On Monday, Berto stood in front of thirty children of all ages, as George walked around with a jar of tadpoles.

"Amphibians are sort of in between land and water animals," the seven-year-old said with authority. "They start out in the water but then they change and live part of the time on the land." He took a gulp of air before going on. "The tadpoles look like fish and they eat algae and plants."

Hardly a child knew that tadpoles became frogs.

"See that one? He already has little legs," George showed a little girl whose mouth widened in delight.

That week the rest of the tadpoles grew legs. A few died and Alicia discreetly discarded them. By the following week, the remaining ones miraculously turned into little gray-green frogs.

Humberto and George were champions when the school went to a nearby creek to release the little frogs into their habitat.

Shortly after Willem van der Lande's first visit to the farm in 1976, a little more than a year ago, ground coffee skyrocketed to $2.55 a pound. Now it was selling for over $3.00 a pound

But just as Alicia was envisioning the finca making them all rich, Colombia — and Brazil — raised taxes to take advantage of the high prices. Growers, like the Carvallos and sellers, like Van der Lande would not see their income triple with the price.

"What's going to happen is the small farmers who cannot pay their debts from the previous years will start growing marijuana or coca instead," Pepe warned.

"How much is the government taking?" Alicia asked blowing on her *café tinto*. She still used her favorite green mug.

"We'll only get a third of the global price."

"A third! That's robbery."

"I heard men are even smuggling coffee across the border."

Even so, the good news far outweighed the bad in Alicia's mind. Pepe was angry at the government's greed, but still happy with the profit they had turned the last two years.

"Anyway, you don't need to worry about money. Make any repairs you need...buy something for yourself!" he said.

"Thanks, Pepe. Oh...and I hired Mario back." She failed to mention that happened almost a year ago.

"Of course, of course."

———

The new machines arrived from Brazil in November, just as they finished construction of the new shed. Van der Lande showed Alicia and Paco where the overripe cherries would be separated by flotation.

"The dense red fruits sink. The older cherries float and we skim them off...they can be sold as cheap coffee, but it is probably more trouble than it is worth. Better to just add them to your mulch pile along with the other organic refuse. I want you to keep up the mulching...or increase it. We may still have a few green cherries mixed with the red, but hopefully not many."

Next the cherries went into a rotating drum with scrapers which removed the red peel, and trapped the green fruits. The shiny new separator was twice the size of their old one. The older machine, with its rusting gears, looked like the quaint antique it had become.

"You will need someone to clean out the green cherries often, Paco."

"*Sí señor*," Paco said, clearly impressed with the operation, "and then we soak the peeled cherries here to remove the rest of the pulp?" he pointed to two fermentation vats.

"Yes," said Van der Lande. "And then to the drying machines!" He opened his arms and grinned. This was his *piece de resistance*: two huge rotating drums fired by wood.

"We used to leave them in the sun for ten days, but what a problem when it rained!" said Paco.

But Willem was not done yet.

"First we take the parchment hull off then we sort by size, because if you roast different sizes the small ones will burn."

"Ah," said Alicia. She had not thought of that. They had never done their own roasting. The sorter shook the beans through different sized screens and the roaster, hardly bigger than a breadbox, was a drum that rotated over a gas flame.

He noticed her looking at the big drying drum and back to the tiny roaster.

"Well, this is just a sample roaster for us to test the final coffee...it's called cupping...you know? Now here's where you have to increase your labor costs," pointing to the roaster and an assembly belt. "You will need several people to pick out any inferior beans by hand. It is a good job for women or older people who can't work in the fields."

"My wife can do it! And my grandmother too," Paco offered.

"Your wife has a job. And your grandmother is too old to work at all!" cried Alicia. But I might do it, she thought. It was easier than bending over to pick coffee hour after hour.

At the next harvest Alicia and Paco's wife, Emilia, sat at the assembly belt and picked out the overly dark beans. Emilia was a tiny, quiet woman whose fingers moved like a speed typist's. Heat radiated from the drying drum and with the humid air, Alicia's blouse stuck to her damp shoulder blades.

Willem van der Lande personally taught Paco how to gauge the roasting of the final beans. It was a time-consuming art, done by hand. The color and condition of the beans were checked every few minutes, and near the end, every few seconds. The final product was aromatic, shiny dark brown coffee beans. Willem encouraged Paco, Emilia and Alicia to chew a few of the crunchy beans.

"*Delicioso*," they all agreed. Heavy taxes were not going to squash their celebration.

"This should do well, very well indeed," said Van der Lande grinning broadly. "Let's make coffee!"

Over the next few years visitors to the finca were more frequent. A coffee expert from Brazil stopped by to see the operation, another from a farm in Antioquia to the north. One day a Dr. Walkman from the Smithsonian Institute drove into the finca. He was studying the effects of acid rain from volcanic eruptions on crops, and was fascinated by Alicia's detailed notes and her observations as she guided him on a walk through the cloud forest.

That visit led to the Universidad de Los Andes taking an interest. Even *profesor* Talavera contacted her, making no mention of their miscommunication years ago when she thought he was going to hire her. She gladly put his students up for a night and showed them around.

PART III

DELIVERANCE

1983-1985

Chapter 19
THE DEAL

Jorge lit another cigarette, leaning back in his chair. The smoke curled slowly towards her in the damp air and Alicia fanned it away.

"I wish you wouldn't smoke in the house. You hardly ever used to smoke."

"Alicia, it is time to think about George coming to Bogotá for school. He's ten years old already." George would be eleven next month. Did Jorge know that?

"The school here is perfectly adequate for now," Alicia replied.

"No, it is not. A public school? He's studying with illiterate *campesinos*."

"They are not illiterate anymore...remember? The Peace Corps stepped in. We have two teachers for just thirty kids, and all the latest text books and supplies. And me. I help at least once a week."

She did not mention that the Peace Corps had pulled out of Colombia for safety concerns and Bill Harper was staying on—temporarily without pay.

The smoke billowed on an invisible current of air then spiraled upwards before Jorge put his cigarette out and flicked the butt out the open window into the wet garden.

"Maybe someday I should take him to the States for high school," she broached the subject gingerly. "How would you feel about that?"

"Are you thinking about moving to New Mexico?" There was an edge to his voice and a mocking tone. "I thought you were a *colombiana* now?"

Alicia shrugged. Peter had suggested she bring the subject up to see what Jorge's reaction might be.

She had at least toyed with the idea, but Jorge could stop her in her tracks. She could not legally take George out of the country without his permission.

"Maybe...someday. Or maybe Virginia. If we are concerned about his safety and education." She had no intention of going to Virginia. It was a silly thing to say.

He stared at her. "We're still married, you know." A muscle clinched in his jaw making his face hard.

"Really, Jorge...."

This seemed ludicrous. They were both in long term relationships. She had not thought of them as married for nine years now. When she'd brought up the idea of divorce years ago it had fallen on deaf ears. No public scandal. Or did he just want to keep her from being free to marry Peter? This issue lay buried — until now. It was time.

She went on, "Well that's something else we should talk about. We should get a divorce. You're living with Irene and — "

They heard a jeep pull up. It was Paco bringing the boys home from school.

Jorge interrupted and got up abruptly. "Not with my son you are not."

George burst in crying, "Papi!"

Jorge smiled at his son and his whole demeanor changed. George was his soft spot, although he only saw him three or four times a year. He might forget his son's birthday, but he usually arrived with a present when he did visit.

Sometimes she doubted if they ever would have married if she had not become pregnant. Then she would flash back to the Jorge she'd loved and married — her first love. It was like remembering someone else.

But there he was — older, only a bit of a paunch, the chocolate hair laced with gray. Still an appealing man. He would turn his head to the side when listening to someone, especially George, in the old attentive gesture that never failed to touch her. And would she have gone back to the States — married a Virginian? It was useless to speculate; unthinkable that George would not be in her life.

Jorge would maintain they might still be together if she had come back to Bogotá with him. This was not true of course. Their marriage would never have survived in Bogotá. But if he had stayed at Las Nubes? Possibly, if things had not changed. Their first two years here had been magical. He had brought her here, but it was fate that kept her here. This was her place in the world. She was content with her life. More than just content. She loved it.

Then, there was Peter. She had hid their relationship for the first year, and then, two years after the fact, Jorge had ranted and raved at her. But he must have known all along. Marta knew, of course, and therefore Pepe knew, but Jorge never mentioned Peter's name. And so Alicia avoided referring to him, although the boys innocently did so a few times.

Jorge blamed Peter—and her infidelity—for their break-up, but that was not the truth. She would have stayed at Las Nubes with or without Peter. However, she was convinced she and Peter were fated to their unusual relationship. Jorge never broached the subject of his relationship with Irene, either.

By good fortune, the two men's visits had coincided only once, in the early years. Jorge had seen the extra jeep and mounted the steps with a stony face. Once the quintessential gentleman, he had been insufferably rude. Peter met him at the door and leaned against it, barefoot and in a T-shirt.

"Hi Jorge," he'd said lightly.

"What are you doing here?" Jorge asked in a rancorous tone.

He turned his head to the side, "Visiting Alicia."

"You shouldn't be here when I'm not here."

From behind Peter, Alicia said, "I can see anyone I like, Jorge."

"I could kick..." He was going to say that he could kick her out too, but bit back the words at the sight of George.

That was years ago. Peter and Alicia had just waited him out, keeping a low profile for a couple of days until he left. They spent most of that day in the rain forest and the next with Diego and Gabriela Benevides.

———

The rainy season dragged on in 1984 and the respite of *veranillo* seemed too short. The conversation about George's schooling had been over a year ago. Now Jorge and Alicia made a deal. Irene was pregnant and Jorge was going to marry her — so now he needed a divorce — quickly.

A divorce would not change Alicia's life after living as a single woman for over a decade. She felt more married to Peter than to Jorge, anyway. Yet she was surprised to feel a twinge of regret.

George was to go to the international school in Bogotá — the same one Alicia had attended, and his father agreed to "consider" high school in the states. She did not think she wanted to leave the country, but the option needed to be aired.

For one thing, the instability grew worse with each passing year. The drug cartels exceeded the violence of the guerillas and bandits. Cocaine ruled, and drug lord Pablo Escobar was feared throughout the country. Many Colombians who could afford it opted to leave.

Marta and her kids never left Bogotá anymore, so Alicia only saw her on rare trips to the capital. They stayed in touch mostly by letters. Alicia sometimes called from the public phone in Escondido, but if Marta was not in there was no way for her to call back. Recently though, Marta was in more often than not.

"It has gotten to where I'm afraid to go out. I never drive anymore and neither does doña Claudia."

"And Claudia used to love to drive her Cadillac!" Alicia exclaimed.

"Not anymore. Not even in Bogotá," Marta disclosed. "I know I've advised you to leave the finca before, but now you really must—you should leave Colombia if you get a chance."

Marta had read her unformed thoughts. Pepe and Jorge also thought anarchy reigned. There was less incentive for small owners to grow coffee or other crops when an incredible amount of money could be made in cultivating coca.

Willem van der Lande had urged Alicia to get a phone connected, but they were miles from the nearest line. Anyway, Alicia wanted electricity before the phone and that was an expensive and difficult endeavor. Pepe said he would help her, but never got around to it. He only thought about it on his annual visit to check on things. He left the running of the farm to her and took care of financial matters from Bogotá.

"I agree with Mr. Van der Lande though, you should get a ham radio at least," he said.

"I hate those things, "Alicia replied and they had left it at that until Peter came home. How would a phone or ham radio make them safer?

"But I don't *want* to live in Bogotá," George protested, "I just like to visit there."

"It's so much more exciting there. You'll meet lots of new friends and learn about the world," Alicia said, feeling somewhat lame. It was the right thing to send him, but she had a hard time justifying it to him when he knew his mother didn't even like the city.

"But why don't you come? We could live with *Tio* and *Tia Marta*." To George, Pepe was simply *"Tio"* – Uncle.

"I think Papi wants you to live with him and Abuela Claudia. It's his turn. And someone has to mind the finca."

As Alicia said this she realized George would be living with Irene. She wasn't sure if George's lack of response was petulance or resignation.

He left at the start of the school year and Alicia missed him keenly. On the verge of adolescence, he was in some ways dearer to her now than he had been at six — certainly more so than during his terrible twos. He had calmed down a bit and was a capable student. He would do well with more of a challenge, but she had no doubt he had a solid grounding in the basics that would serve him well. She saw the sort of man he would be: kind, intelligent and funny.

The day-long drives to visit him in Bogotá were grueling. Not just the length of the trip, but the tension—worrying about roadblocks and the potential of being kidnapped. She had denied the dangers for years, insulated as they were at Las Nubes. Now, she made the trip once or twice a month, and Jorge—or sometimes Pepe—brought George home once a month for a long weekend. Marta no longer came to the finca with Pepe, and Claudia had been back to see George just once in the last decade.

Alicia didn't know which was worse—the long drive or worrying about George the day he was due. It was impossible to work or relax after the hour when she expected him. She would find herself walking out to the veranda, watching for the dust that signaled a car on the road.

Humberto was bored without George, his constant companion since they were toddlers. They got along as if there was no two-and-a-half year gap between them. Humberto had been like an older brother, encouraging him as he learned to walk, showing him how to feed the chickens and collect the eggs, helping with his homework. And George looked up to Berto, and helped him with his English.

"Remember how George used to hold up his arms to you even after he had learned to walk? And you were scarcely bigger than he was, but you used to carry him all over?" Carmen asked.

The women smiled at the lonely adolescent and he nodded. The table seemed incomplete with just the three of them. Except when Peter came. He always enlivened them, filled them out.

And Humberto enjoyed speaking English to Peter. He always tried to speak English to doña Alicia but she would usually answer him in Spanish if his mother was there, and of course she invariably was. But when don Peter came, the conversation was of necessity mostly in English and Humberto could show off a little. Not that he dominated the conversation.

He let the grownups do most of the talking but listened intently and showed an aptitude on topics of little interest to most teenagers by interjecting a comment here and there. Alicia tried to translate some of it for Carmen's benefit, but it was hard to keep up in a fast moving discussion. Carmen didn't mind being left out she just beamed at her son. On the other hand, she'd become unreserved with Peter and made him repeat half of what she said to him in Spanish.

"*Mas papas?*" More potatoes? And she would hold on to the dish of *papas criollas* until she was satisfied with the reply.

"*Mas papas, por favor,*" he'd said grinning. "We're running a regular language school here."

The dog barked enthusiastically at something in the yard one Friday evening—he rarely got excited at his age anymore. Alicia looked out the window and saw Peter driving up after months of absence. His company had sent him prospecting in Africa. She flew down the stairs. Old Yeller was yapping and wagging his tail, glad to see him and scolding him for his long absence all at once.

"I didn't think you would come until tomorrow!" she cried.

The stars were just starting to appear in the twilight. They hugged each other and walked arm and arm up the porch steps. Still a romantic couple after over a decade together.

"I got away early. They owe me so much overtime."

That was the saving grace of his job. He was away for weeks at a time, but when he came to the finca he could stay for at least a week and usually more. This time he had three whole, splendid weeks.

He was leaning back in a kitchen chair watching the women prepare the evening meal, his legs stretched out. He had once tried to help, but Carmen would never allow it when she was in the kitchen.

"The company is pulling out," Peter told Alicia. "We have two more months."

Alicia had just taken a pinch of herbs to season the stew. She stopped and stared at him, her hand poised above the pot for a moment before the seasonings fell from her fingers. She was so stunned she didn't know how to reply. Carmen looked at her questioningly but had little inkling of the scene unfolding in English between the two Americans.

Alicia's outward calm belied her inner panic. How could he sit there so relaxed and drop this bombshell on her? He had mentioned the possibility a year ago or more but she'd filed it in the back of her mind, impotent as she was to do anything about it. She would cross that bridge when they got to it.

Now suddenly they were at the bridge, and it seemed to span a vast chasm. She patted her hands on a dish towel and went to stand next to him. He traced her arm with the back of his fingers, his face expressionless, and stood up.

Alicia glanced at Carmen, but didn't need to say a word. Her bare feet were already planted in front of the stove and she flipped her hand to indicate she had charge of the dinner. She knew Alicia would tell her what was going on soon enough.

Peter and Alicia walked outside to the veranda where they had the majority of their conversations. The yellow dog padded silently behind and dropped to the floor between them.

"Why are they leaving?" she asked, although she had a pretty good idea. The political situation had been bad enough, with guerillas and drugs making it so much worse in recent years.

"The cost of doing business in Colombia has gotten too high. And one of the geologists was kidnapped while I was gone."

"Who?" she asked wide-eyed. She hardly knew any of the geologists, but recognized all their names from his stories.

"John. They were able to ransom him back but he was pretty shaken up and the company has been in an uproar. John promised his wife not to return here, but I don't think the company would let him anyway. So he's going to Africa too."

"How long did the guerrillas keep him?" She had heard such horror stories.

"Three months. He's OK, but I guess it cost them a fortune."

"John's family?"

Peter nodded, "I imagine the company put up most of the money, but not all."

"What will you do?" she managed. What will *we* do? she thought.

"Go back to New Mexico, Africa...wherever they send me."

Alicia's mind searched for a solution. "Stay," she whispered. She knew it was useless...a wish rather than a request that he give up the work he loved. He looked at her and his eyes told her they both knew that.

They were quiet a long time, thinking, before Peter said, "So...will you come with me?"

"To New Mexico?" She looked out at her surroundings, verdant even after dusk, and listened to the evening sounds. Could she swap all this for that? For anything? "Isn't it hot and dry there?"

He nodded in reply. "We've talked about it before. It can be nice there, real pretty. Especially in the spring. Or at high elevations. We don't have to live in town. And the desert is neat too."

She grabbed his hand and held on to it. She loved him for hoping, perhaps assuming, they would stay together but still asking. Her mind worked in double time. This was the only real home she'd ever had. The finca was doing so well now. And what about George? Once Peter had implied she should go with him even if Jorge didn't let George go.

His eyes held hers as he gripped her hand. She had never seen him look so intense, his voice so earnest. "It's just too violent here...it was bad ten years ago, but now it's crazy, Alicia."

"I won't go without George."

Peter nodded gravely, "I guess that depends on Jorge." He withdrew his hand and smoothed his mustache with his thumb. Eventually Carmen ventured out to see if they were going to eat.

Alicia nodded, "We're coming."

She agonized over the decision and he became impatient with her. "You have to come Alicia. Don't be so damn stubborn."

When Peter left right after Christmas the issue was still unresolved, so they said goodbye under strained circumstances, not knowing when they would see each other again.

The house felt lonesome with both of the men in her life gone. On a whim, Alicia decided to go into Escondido to call George. She drove slowly over the water-filled potholes by the town square, trying not to splash mud on pedestrians. As she got out of the jeep a villager called out to her, *"Hola doña Alicia!"*

"Hola!" she called back. A wrinkled man hunched over his cane smiled under his gray mustache and touched the brim of his hat. *"Buenas tardes, doñita,"* he sang in a croaky voice as he hobbled by. He was a relative of Emilia's.

After almost fifteen years she knew everyone in town at least by sight. She could gossip with the woman behind the counter of the little store. There was a feeling of community she had come to cherish. She'd lived here most of her life now.

Alicia was surprised when Claudia answered the phone—although she shouldn't have been—it was

Claudia's house after all. But it had been awhile since she had heard the familiar voice.

"Abuelita died last night."

"Oh!" she was stunned, momentarily speechless, "Wh... when is the funeral?"

"Tomorrow. She liked you...you know. Once she got to know you."

She could imagine Claudia nodding her head.

"I'll be there." Alicia paused. "Claudia, I'm so sorry I wasn't there for don Felipe's funeral. You know I loved him."

"You weren't? I was in such a state, Alicia, I didn't even notice."

They chatted a moment about George before hanging up. He wasn't home but she would see him tomorrow. Talking to Claudia had been like old times—as if there had been no intervening years or problems. But how different things were: Felipe and Abuelita dead, George in Bogotá, Jorge with Irene, Peter—who knew where Peter was.

———

While she was in Bogotá she discussed her quandary with Jorge. He and Irene had a newborn daughter, just a few days old. She wondered how Abuelita had reacted to the pregnancy.

"What's her name?"

"Magdalena."

"I've always liked that name," she said, wondering if Jorge remembered it was what she'd suggested as a girl's name when she was pregnant with George. Now George had a sister.

After the funeral Alicia visited Claudia with Marta and Pepe, knowing Irene was there with Jorge.

"Are you sure you want to go?" Pepe had asked.

"Sure."

"Claudia was worried over how you would feel about Irene, but we have to accept her now that they are married," Marta confided. "Do you understand? You know we still love you."

Irene...her old rival. But they were all civil — more than that — cordial. It broke the ice and Alicia was amazed to think they might all get along like the family they'd once been.

Jorge was surprisingly sympathetic with Alicia over her dilemma with Peter and considered the situation without animosity.

"I would want George to spend his summers with me," he said.

"Of course," Alicia replied, astonished that he was so cooperative. Perhaps they were they finally going to be friends after all.

But she still wasn't sure what to do. George had just started high school. Their life was here...but Peter's was elsewhere. He might never return to Colombia. And if she followed him? Her thoughts turned to a sorrowful Cuban exile song about leaving your heart and life behind in the land you loved....

> *Cuando salí de Cuba,*
> *deje mi vida, deje mi amor.*
> *Cuando salí de Cuba,*
> *deje enterrado mi corazón.*

Chapter 20
LOST IN PARADISE

The heavy rains had let up, yet not enough for it to feel like the dry season. A month had passed since Peter left, and Alicia was still debating what to do. Life did not seem altered at this point—after all, Peter had always been gone more than home. It was as if she were still expecting him to pull up in front of the veranda any day now.

Maybe he would be able to return two or three times a year, and would that be so different from what they'd always had? She could even visit him occasionally. It would do her good to take a trip. Get out in the world.

Alicia picked a profusion of sweet peas—shades of purple, red, pink, and white—to fill the dining room with their fragrance. The day was so beautiful it made her heart swell. She brushed her hair back off her face with a forearm, and turned to Paco.

"I'm going into town for groceries today, Paco. We won't go out to the fields until later."

He adjusted his hat. *"Está bien,"* he said, but hesitated, looking off. He had always been such a soft-spoken, understated man, she'd learned to sense the unsaid.

"What?" she asked, inhaling the flowers' heavenly scent.

Paco smiled slightly. "I could drive," he offered.

Carmen was picking oranges around the corner of the house, but overheard and chimed in, "I'll go too and watch the children."

George was home for a long weekend. The children were almost twelve and fifteen now, hardly in need of supervision, but the image of the four of them laughing in the jeep came to Alicia. A trip into Escondido would be fun—why not let Paco take them? Also, with everyone else occupied, she could steal off into the rainforest on her own excursion for a few hours.

"Paco, you drive Carmen." To Carmen she said, "I'll give you a shopping list and you can take the boys on a *paseo.*"

Paco gave her an uncharacteristic grin.

"Un paseo, George!"—an outing—shouted Humberto, who jokingly began marching around singing as if he were still ten. *"Un paseo a Escondido!"*

The boys were restless without much to do. Alicia laughed at the silliness. She was still getting used to Berto's voice, which had changed to a deep tenor in the last year.

"Good grief! You'd think I suggested a party rather than a trip for groceries."

"But don't write down a list...just tell me," Carmen responded.

"I've already written it. Milk, butter, bread, potatoes..." she said absently, thinking ahead to what she needed to do before she could leave. Get some water, her notebook....

Carmen stared at the paper Alicia handed her, repeating Alicia's words, *"leche, mantequilla, pan, papas...*anything else?"

"It's all there," Alicia inclined her head to indicate the list and began walking away.

"Well, just tell me," Carmen insisted, counting the items as she followed her. "There are eleven items...that is only four."

I should have written it better Alicia thought, a bit exasperated—she had written it for herself at the time. "You can't read my handwriting?"

"No, but if you would just tell me each one..." Carmen apologized.

By her sheepish response, Alicia suddenly realized Carmen could not read at all.

"Did you never go to school?" she asked gently. How was it she didn't realized this when George and Berto were learning to read? All these years and she just assumed Carmen knew how to read. How well she'd hidden it from her.

"Only a year or so, my parents needed me to take care of my little brother. But I can remember everything!"

So common—working parents leaving the care of younger siblings to a girl who should have been in school. Alicia made a mental note to try to rectify this, then read the list aloud slowly as Carmen repeated each item. Berto or George could read it of course, but she might not want to ask them.

"I have it!" Carmen said and Alicia pretended it was no big deal.

As she headed out the old yellow dog followed her to the edge of the clearing, as was his habit.

"Go home now," she told him, pointing in the direction of the house, as was her habit.

He raised his ears to show he was listening, and watched her disappear into the underbrush. After the jaguar-puma incident—after the dog had become a pet—he would follow for twenty feet and then bark at her when she did this. Going into the jungle where creatures like the big cats live seemed folly to Old Yeller, and a dog barks to warn those he loves.

But he'd given up barking and accepted that she would disappear and at some point, she would emerge. Some days he would lie down in the shade and rest his head on his front paws to wait for her, but he knew from experience it could be a very long time. And sometimes she did not come out from the same place she went in.

One time, dusk had fallen, the workers had gone home and he was beginning to worry about her—and besides, it was time for his dinner. Next thing he knew she was calling his name from the direction of the house. When he trotted in, Alicia smiled and petted him.

But Carmen scolded him a bit as she pointed at the flies buzzing around his food. "Where have you been?"

So this time, after he lost sight of Alicia, he sniffed a coffee bush which was apparently unmarked by his scent and lifted his leg for a leisurely pee. Then he went back to see if the boys were playing outside, only to discover they were all gone. He ambled around to the front and sure enough the jeep had gone. Old Yeller dropped from all fours simultaneously, collapsing to the ground dejectedly in the shade of the jacaranda tree. His bones ached as he waited for someone to come home.

———

Alicia walked carefully through the foliage, inhaling the rich, fragrant air. The perfume of the forest was an unlikely potpourri, mixing aromatic organic decay with a bouquet of freshness. She felt reinvigorated and refreshed every time she stepped into these sublime "Green Mansions" as naturalist W. H. Hudson had poetically entitled this tropical scenery.

It was, Alicia never failed to notice, a resplendent display ranging in size from diminutive perfection to the august majesty of the trees—eloquent beyond words.

She startled a small poison dart frog, black with neon green stripes. The Indians applied the poison from the frog's skin to their blowgun darts to bring down small prey. By the time she opened her notebook to sketch him, he was gone. She wrote instead: *Dendrobates auratus.*

A golden beam of light falling through some window in the upper tree limbs drew her toward it, like finding the end of the rainbow. Instead of a pot of gold, however, she came face to face with an unkempt, awkward looking creature—a sloth. He was maybe thirty inches long, with a cute pug face and three-inch claws. She froze, staring at him. So many neotropical mammals are nocturnal, she was always astonished to see one.

A sloth lives in the trees but this one crawled at a snail's pace on the ground through the understory. He appeared unthreatening and easy to catch, but she knew sloths could attack if provoked. Why did this sloth seem so helpless? Then it occurred to her that with their long claws curving under their paws sloths cannot walk properly on the ground.

"You OK?" she addressed him softly.

He hesitated, looking over his shoulder at her almost placidly. His neck was extremely flexible, turning well over ninety degrees to keep her in his line of sight.

"Who's observing who, eh?"

She got out her notebook, matching the sloth's protracted progress like a tai chi dancer, and began to draw. Although the animal made a good subject—in that it did not run away and allowed her to sit within ten feet—she found it hard to capture his peculiar looks. His coarse hair grew in an odd fashion, towards the spine, and it had a greenish, algal tinge—his camouflage.

As she moved around to get a better angle, a disagreeable odor reached her nostrils. She had read that some sloths descend from their canopy about once a week to defecate. No one knows why they bother, they could fertilize from on high without the assiduous effort it takes to climb down and up again.

When the sloth reached the large roots that buttressed the nearest tree, his movements turned graceful now as he began to use his long claws as hooks. It had taken him perhaps five minutes to cover the six feet to the trunk of the tree.

"Ah. You do much better in the trees!'" she observed.

It was half an hour before the sloth reached a height where she could no longer see him. I'm getting a stiff neck, she thought as she started to get up, realizing it was time to be heading back home.

Alicia heard a creaking sound and turned in the direction of the noise. A crack and an alarming whoosh brought her to her feet and she had the sensation that the canopy was caving in.

In a sense it was. One of the colossal trees came smashing through the forest, taking out other trees as it fell. She ran amid a cacophony of chatter as birds took flight and frightened animals fled. Just as she heard the explosive sound of the violent crash, she felt the impact through the ground in the marrow of her bones.

Stopping in her tracks, she raised one hand to her heart, as if to still the agitated beating, and sucked in a deep breath of relief. Fear turned to excitement. Without hesitation she made her way through the thicket of green to the downed tree. She had to use her machete to get through, but she would finally have the rare chance to observe the canopy — from the ground.

She'd spent innumerable hours studying the jungle floor and shrub layer, but here was a cross-section of the rainforest from the roots and lianas through the middle branches and mysteries of the upper foliage. Each layer was a distinct habitat reflecting different microclimates, starting from the shaded wet bottom and ending in the strong sun, wind and rain of the treetops.

By this time of day it was normally shaded in the rainforest as the sun angled behind the mountains. But shafts of light streamed through the gap formed by the downed giant and the branches it sheared off other trees in its plunge. Alicia knew this light would give small trees a chance to grow and in ten or twenty years the break would close over as new trees become part of the canopy.

Some forty feet away she could barely discern the fat upturned roots of the end closest to her. She scrambled through debris and vegetation as she made her way to the prize, eager to clamber along the fallen trunk to what had once been the treetop. Jagged splinters of wood poked up among rotted limbs. She recoiled as a thick stem turned out to be a snake — green as grass — slithering smoothly away from her. Possibly an eyelash viper she thought, giving him a wide berth.

Good thing Carmen wasn't here. Snakes did not give Alicia the creeps, as spiders did, but they demanded respect. Poisonous or not, they can deliver a nasty bite.

If reaching the trunk was no mean feat, getting on top of it and navigating toward the canopy would be no easier. She stopped a moment to survey the situation. The trunk at this point was at least seven feet in diameter and well above her head. She would have to chop and climb through a snarl of vegetation to get on top of it.

She tucked her pants into her socks to keep out insects and other unwelcome intruders. She was wearing short sleeves and didn't want to put on her windbreaker in the warmth of the newly exposed sunshine. Steam rose from the wet foliage that minutes before had been in the protected shade. Thirsty, she took a sip of water from her canteen.

She had lost her pen. Damn, at such a crucial note-taking time. Ah, but there was an old pencil stub somewhere in the bottom of her canvas bag. She held it up triumphantly. And glory be!—there were the gloves she occasionally used.

Amazing, she thought, that everything didn't spill out when she'd scrambled away from the falling tree; there had been no time to close the bag and replace her notebook. She pinched each finger of the gloves before putting them on—spiders and other unpleasantries liked to take up residence in such dark cozy spaces.

The sloth was already forgotten.

Grabbing a broken branch to use as a ladder she began to climb the side of the trunk, pulling herself up with lianas. A woody vine broke free in her hand and a spray of wet debris and vermin rained onto her face and shoulders. Ants and insects of every description scurried away, disturbed from their daily lives. Grimacing she swatted them off her face, arms and clothes.

"Ay! Agh!" she cried as something clawy and sticky grabbed her. A praying mantis as big as her hand had wrapped it legs around her forearm. She pried it off, almost losing her balance.

Alicia reached the top drenched in perspiration. Waiting for her, lurking in a dark crevice, was a black spider the size of a medium crab.

"Oh!" she cried, spotting it within eight inches of her gloved hand. She jumped back — as did the spider — and fought to find secure footing.

Adrenaline coursed through her veins as she watched the creature in horror. He was indeed more like a crab, with a shell and pincers next to his mouth which waved menacingly. But to her surprise, he had only six legs instead of eight — which meant he couldn't be a spider at all, but an *amblypygid,* a whip scorpion, one of the creepiest creatures on earth. Not poisonous, but nonetheless ferocious-looking, they stalk their prey — anything from insects to small mice — skewer them and eat them alive.

Skirting around the hideous arthropod she began to question the wisdom of her venture. If she fell and injured herself no one would ever find her...but she was almost at the crown of upper branches.

Reaching her goal, she felt like Sir Edmund Hillary atop Mt. Everest, and raised both fists in triumph. Turning carefully she surveyed the trunk she had just traversed. The fallen tree was not quite horizontal, but at an angle because the branches were snagged on other tree boughs, holding the canopy high above the ground, invisible through the crush of vegetation below.

She made her way through the tangle of limbs, vines and ferns, spotting a bromeliad at chest level. It looked something like the top of a small pineapple, but with a depression in the middle, usually filled with rainwater.

Peering into it she was amazed to find two fat tadpoles floundering in the emptied bowl. She hoped they would survive to turn into tree frogs. Alicia also encountered numerous epiphytes, also called air plants because they do not require soil, including some orchids only slightly damaged by their 100-foot tumble.

She wrote hasty notes and had to pick and choose what she sketched, as there were too many wonders to document in one day. She cursed for not having brought the camera. Normally she was happier sketching—it fine-tuned her powers of observation, and often allowed details to show that a photo might shadow—but today a camera would have been more efficient.

She checked her watch and was shocked to see it was almost four o'clock. Carmen would be worried; Alicia was never out this late. Her head came up slowly as a realization sank in. It was not only late, but she was uncertain where she was.

It would be dark in less than two hours. She had been out all day and was unsure how much time she needed to get back. She had broken her own rule: stick with the streams. There was always plenty to see without straying from this network that led her back to the finca like an unraveled ball of twine.

But she had been distracted—first the sloth just a few feet from her safety line and then the falling of the forest giant. Alarmed, she turned to make her way back. She could explore the tree tomorrow—if she could find it again. Past the orchid, past the tadpoles, past the limbs festooned with greenery and back to the middle section of the tree.

She stood up, one hand shielding her eyes to retrace her path to the sloth's tree. It was impossible to discern, but she could find where she had climbed onto this tree and go from there. She noticed a long *oropendola* nest she had not seen earlier, but there was no time to more than glance at it now.

Oh! A coral anthurium — a lovely plant, only slightly crushed by the fall. Alicia could not resist touching it lightly as she passed. She needed to keep going.

She knew where she had climbed up the tree — near a broken limb and the whip scorpion. She had planned to climb down just before his crevice to avoid the scary creature, but now decided to retrace her steps as closely as possible.

There he was. No, there were two of them! She gasped, her muscles contracting as she cringed and skirted the horrible things. They were large enough to make scratching noises when they moved. She shuddered.

I'll probably have nightmares about them, she thought.

Alicia took one last look at the lay of the land — a boundless sea of green — and made a mental note of the direction she would take before climbing down to the ground. The clouds had come in. It was 4:30 P.M. and with knitted brow she quickened her pace in the direction of the sloth and his tree.

How far was it? One hundred feet? Two hundred? More? Her gait was so slow and circuitous through the dense vegetation it was easy to overestimate distances. Normally she would have taken note of unusual plants or something to help recognize her trail. Nothing looked familiar, but then she had practically run to the fallen tree without noting any features to use as trail markers.

If she over-shot her only landmark it would be difficult, but surely she would find the little stream she had walked away from to view the sloth. It was no more than a rivulet really, but she felt sure she would spot it.

After hacking through some two hundred feet of vegetation she was drenched in sweat. She stopped and looked around. In a different landscape it would make sense to scout left and right, but she didn't dare here for fear of becoming hopelessly lost. She decided to return to the fallen tree and change her angle.

Retreating, she wished she did have a ball of twine, or at least bread crumbs like Hansel and Gretel. She looked for machete cuts where she'd chopped at the dense vegetation, but it was difficult to see in the undergrowth and she soon lost the marks. This time, she bent twigs to help mark the way she'd come, the machete cuts were few and far between, and too clean to spot easily.

"You're such an idiot!" she berated herself.

She had never been in the rainforest this late in the day and it was getting dark even earlier than usual due to the clouds. If the sun had not yet disappeared behind the mountains it might as well have. Where was the fallen tree? Her heart beat quickly from exertion and anxiety. Stay calm she told herself, stay calm.

She squatted on her haunches a moment to think. Should she try circling to find the stream? Too risky. She had to locate the downed tree and start over. She could not see it through the forest, but it must be in this direction. She would climb back on it and get her bearings; figure out which direction she should take to find Las Nubes. Alicia walked very slowly, searching for the window of light in the canopy, but it was already too dark. It had disappeared.

How could she have been so careless? She had spent countless hours in this forest, knowing full well how easy it was to get lost. Step five feet off your path and nothing looks familiar.

By 6:00 P.M. it was fully dark. Alicia tripped every few feet over roots, vegetation or rocks she could not see. She ran into bushes and hanging vines that dangled like snakes. Her clothes and boots were sodden with sweat and cloud forest dew.

Alicia stood still a long while, unwilling to accept her fate. She could not continue to stumble around like this. Even if she had a ball of twine stretching back to the finca it would be dangerous to negotiate her way in the dark. Finally, she acknowledged that she was going to be spending the night in the jungle.

The longest, most wretched night of her life.

———————

The yellow dog sensed the tension in the household as night fell. Alicia was always back before dusk, usually even before Humberto came home, unless she packed the jeep. Then she might disappear for days at a time. Carmen rang the bell they used to call the workers in from the fields. But no one came because there were no workers picking coffee or doing anything else.

"I wish she had taken the horse and tied him up. At least then we would know where she went in," Carmen said. Close to dusk her voice had sounded irritated, then anxious. Now there was something else in it. Fear.

"I'll go looking for her," George declared, "I know where she goes."

"No!" the two grownups said in emphatic unison.

"I'll look some more. If you promise to stay here," Paco said.

"Don't you go getting lost. You have your family to think of too. Emilia will be worried about you soon."

"I won't go in the jungle, but I'll go up to my grandmother's. Maybe she ended up there and decided it was too late to come home."

Carmen nodded, chewing on her lip. Paco placed a comforting hand on her shoulder and whispered in her ear, "Don't panic. The boy is already distraught." Carmen patted his hand in acknowledgement.

George left as soon as Carmen was busy making dinner. The yellow dog followed him upstairs, where George grabbed the flashlight and whispered to Berto, "Don't come with me. Pretend I'm here!"

"*No vaya*, George!" Berto said, "Don't go in the rain forest."

"I won't. Just to the entrance of the streams. I'll be back in an hour!"

The dog viewed this urgent exchange and took off with the boy. He watched him go to the first creek and call his mother. They listened. Nothing but the wind in the trees and the sounds of the night. George went in a ways and Old Yeller barked anxiously until he returned.

"OK, OK."

They hurried to the second stream, then the third.

"Mami!" George called.

The dog cocked his head to listen, for he was the only one who knew this was indeed where Alicia hiked in this morning. He barked to tell George this, and even followed him in for twenty feet or so, but they both knew this was a bad idea in the dark. Only she was allowed to do this and now it appeared it was too dangerous even for her. The pair walked slowly, dejectedly, back to the house as it started to rain, the dog with his tail between his legs. George with a sick feeling in his stomach, wet hair plastered to his head.

The flashlight illuminated the raindrops. He fully expected Carmen to rant and rave at him and he didn't care. But she simply wiped her hands on her apron and embraced him. This brought on tears and he turned away. Tomorrow he would go up the streams with Berto. If worse came to worse he would have to call his father. Alicia might rather he call Peter, but Peter was gone. He didn't even know how to get hold of him.

Putting on her windbreaker and gloves, Alicia tucked them in carefully at the wrists and closed the wrist tabs to keep bugs from crawling up her sleeve.

It would also, she realized, keep in any insects had already found their way under her shirt. But she assured herself she would have a hot shower in the morning and get rid of them all.

She tucked her shirt in securely, cinched her belt and checked that her pants were tucked into her socks. Pulling the hood of the jacket around her head so that only her face was exposed, she wrapped her sketchbook with the plastic wrap from her morning snack to keep it dry. Her stomach felt empty, but that was the least of her worries as she hunkered down for the night. She saved the water in her canteen for morning.

Some of the forest sounds were familiar, if unidentifiable. What made that noise—an insect, a monkey? Funny how she could not tell a cricket from a mammal sometimes. And there were the rustling sounds of movement. They all seemed magnified. Alicia whistled a while to drown them out, then tried singing, but her voice sounded eerie and crazy. She decided she might attract the attention of predators rather than scare them off.

She shifted from one foot to the other, alternating with squatting on her haunches until her feet fell asleep. Finally she sat, hugging her knees. Time crawled—as did her skin. Itching, tingling. She would not think about the bugs or she would end up running, screaming like a banshee into a tree. Most of it was probably her imagination. She squeezed her eyes shut.

When she opened them a pair of large orbs was watching her. How long had they—it—been there? Shivering, sick with fear and discomfort, she stared back for what seemed like half an hour, both of them frozen. The creature could be a sloth, a coatimundi, a lemur...a jaguar. How long would it survey her?

A flying insect landed on her bare cheek and bit her, but she remained motionless. Finally she could stand the spying eyes no longer and she jumped up, flung out both arms, and yelled, "Hah!"

Whatever it was vanished instantly. She could hear the animal run, and imagined she heard other nocturnal beasts scatter as well.

Having stood up she realized how stiff her limbs were. She stretched, but jerked when her hand touched something slimy. Maybe it was just a wet vine or leaf.

Alicia was exhausted, but fear kept her too alert to sleep. Sleep would be a welcome way to get through the night. It was too dark to see her wristwatch, but she estimated it was around nine o'clock. She closed her eyes, but opened them wide a moment later as a vision of the whip scorpions came to her. She tried again. Any number of horrors could assault her — from slithering snakes to bats. She would prefer a jaguar to the whip scorpions, which was ridiculous, of course.

"*Kii, kii kii!*" something cried out, jangling her nerves. It was as if the whole jungle was laughing, stalking her. It rained lightly and water sprinkled on her from overhead leaves. She stuck out her tongue to catch some moisture. Beneath her clothes, she felt a little rivulet of water run down between her breasts. Miserable and frightened, she sat again, wrapped her arms around her knees and bowed her head, shivering in the chill of the night. She wished she were further downslope where it might be warmer.

Wait. Hadn't the fallen tree been in the rain forest—or at the edge of it? Was she now in the cloud forest? Had she walked up the hill without perceiving it? It had been so slow without a path to follow. The topography was undulating and she must have hiked more up than down and transitioned from rain forest to cloud forest. She should try to make her way downhill tomorrow.

After the rain, she gradually became aware of a dim illumination overhead—a nearly full moon wending its way through the trees. Straining her eyes, she could see her watch now. It wasn't even one o'clock yet, though it had seemed, and she had hoped, it would be closer to dawn. She was only halfway through this unbearable ordeal in the dark.

And what of tomorrow? What if she could not find her way out? She quickly shut out that intolerable idea. She would get through the night, and the thought of daylight made all things seem possible.

She became aware of a slow *whoosh, whoosh*. The forest was so full of strange noises, what was that rhythmic sound? She held her breath to hear better and it stopped—or changed. Finally, she realized it was the palpitation of her own pulse in her ear.

The need for sleep mingled with the need for vigilance. She felt delirious. She jerked into alertness, dimly aware of having escaped from snakes and cockroaches crawling on her. She'd been dreaming.

Alicia stumbled in the darkness a moment, fearful of what she'd touch as she put her hands out to catch herself. One of her fingers bent back painfully. What was worse — the self-torture of her mind or the dangers lurking in the night? It was pitch-black again, the moon obscured by clouds.

Suddenly, she felt a movement inside her shirt. Gasping, she tore off her windbreaker as something large and leggy ran across her chest. She ripped a button off of her shirt as she beat herself frenetically and let out a bellow, which ended more like a wail. She suppressed the urge to run, tear through the jungle, and scream at the top of her lungs. Clawing at her skin, she knocked off various unidentified bugs. She shook out her shirt and rebuttoned it before patting down her pants. Her clothes were so wet they clung to her.

She panted like a trapped animal, wanting to tear at her hair as well as her clothes. Her nerves were raw. She felt she would surely go insane before this night was over. Sitting back down she forced herself to take deep breaths and close her eyes. Driving the jungle monsters from her mind, she recited through clenched teeth a poem that came to her.

> *Out of the night that covers me,*
> *black as a pit from pole to pole,*
> *I thank whatever gods may be,*
> *for my unconquerable soul.*

How did it end?...

> *I am the master of my fate...*
> *...I am the captain of my soul...?*

She would not allow herself to hear the noises of the night or feel any creeper trespassing on her person. Mind over matter, she told herself. She would push away the reality of chill, wetness, hunger, insects and worse.

Reciting poetry was like meditating, self-hypnosis. She brought to mind another poem, Alexander Pope's *Ode To Solitude*. It was her favorite, although the title was ironic under the circumstances.

> *Happy the man, whose wish and care*
> *A few paternal acres bound,*
> *Content to breathe his native air,*
> *In his own ground...*
> *Thus let me live, unseen unknown,*
> *Thus unlamented let me die,*
> *Steal from the world, and not a stone,*
> *Tell where I lie.*

Chapter 21
PARADISE LOST?

Would it be possible to die here? *"Steal from the world, and not a stone tell where I lie?"*

Alicia brought her son's face into focus. Georgie's lovable face. She smiled, inhaling deeply to calm herself. She thought of him with Humberto under the tree while Carmen picked oranges. Carmen, with goodness written in the lines of her face. Peter. Alicia spent the hours concentrating on the people in her life, including Jorge.

She remembered something Peter said about her stubbornness. Jorge had said essentially the same thing. Was she really so headstrong? She had been intractable about moving to Bogotá...of course. But she had been right, hadn't she? In spite of the ceniza and Jorge's own obstinacy, it had been right. Not for their marriage, but it had worked out for the best. Nonetheless, she was suddenly contrite for her part in the break-up.

She didn't want to be inflexible with Peter. They had always been so independent, respectful of each other's choices, and had managed to make it work. Now one of them would have to make a sacrifice for the relationship—or sacrifice the relationship itself—and she understood it could not be Peter. He loved his work as she loved Las Nubes, but he had more to give up in some respects.

The finca had survived the volcano, although Peter said it could happen again at any time, and Willem had expressed his worries about doing business here too. Colombia had become an increasingly dangerous place. Only since George had gone to Bogotá had she understood the real perils. Bogotá was hardly safer than anywhere else in the country. The Carvallos just didn't want to admit it. They all ignored it—what choice did they have?

And none more than she, in her cocoon in the cloud forest, insulated from the reality of what was going on. Her love for Las Nubes had overshadowed everything and blinded her. After her nomadic childhood she had put down roots and obstinately clung to them, come what may. The irony was that her downfall wasn't due to the drug thugs or guerillas that everyone feared for her, it was her own carelessness.

Dawn came by infinitesimal degrees. The blackness around her transformed to dark shades of green, while above her, inky shadows faded to navy and then gradually to the pale gray of a cloudy sky.

Moisture had condensed inside the crystal face of her watch and she could not read the numerals, but she thought it must be after 5:00 A.M. Birds tweeted, monkeys called to each other. These were the sounds she knew. She stood and stretched with relief that the long ordeal in the darkness was over. She licked dew from leaves to save her meager water for later. She found a large, newborn leaf that had yet to unfurl. It grew upright and had captured enough water to almost quench her thirst.

Peeling off her shirt, she caught herself looking around out of social habit. I wish, she laughed grimly at herself, I wish there *was* someone to see me now!

Alicia was taken aback by the state of her flesh. She was covered with bites, reddish welts of varying sizes and a fair number of scratches. An ant and another small insect still roamed her torso. Annoyed, she picked them off methodically. Then she lowered her pants to pee and saw her legs looked almost as bad. Her neck itched intolerably, but she refrained from scratching with her filthy fingernails. She could feel a few bumps on her face too. If she'd had a mirror she would be shocked to see how grimy and blotchy it was. Her thick hair was sprinkled with dew and matted to her head.

Now she had to find her way home. She was daunted but having survived the worst, optimistic. How many hours had she spent winding her way deep inside the forest and out again? She looked around for a clue as to which way to head. In spite of walking through dusk, she knew she'd come from the right, and there to prove it was the last stem she had broken to designate her way.

There were no landmarks, but in spite of the cloud cover there was a faint luminescence where the sun was rising. East. It was almost ninety degrees from her path last night. East was a good direction to head. The finca would be east...or northeast, or southeast, of the cloud forest. She should come upon a stream and then even if she overshot Las Nubes, eventually find the road to Escondido. Eventually...because it might take a very long time to walk through the cloud forest into the tropical rainforest and to the road. But she would not think of that now.

Her rumbling stomach was a hollow cavern inside of her. It had been well over twenty-four hours since she'd had a light breakfast at home. She thought she was hungry yesterday afternoon when she still assumed she'd be home for dinner. But for the first time in her life she knew real hunger.

After a while she sensed she was not headed downhill, as she anticipated if she was bearing east. It must be a ripple in the topography. There was no longer any hint of the sun's location, but it was probably overhead anyway. She looked at her watch and could barely make out the time. 11:10. She was sorely disappointed she'd not encountered a creek. The streams near the finca were her lifelines, but she could follow any stream down to a river or a road. If she could find one.

Famished and weary, she kept a look out for fruit or nuts, remembering the tasty ones she had found once for their granola. That made her think of Carmen. What a loyal...friend, she realized — not an employee, but a true friend. Her best friend! She had never defined their relationship that way before. Carmen must be in a panic. But what could she do? It would be pointless for them to come looking for her in the forest. What would George be feeling?

In the afternoon she came across a freshly broken stem. Was it from today or yesterday? Had she doubled back on herself or did some animal snap this one? She sank down on an enormous root and felt the wet seep through her already damp jeans. She hung her head, her forearms lay limp over her knees.

Her hollow stomach ached, although she knew that a body could manage a long time without food. She had seen some crimson berries, but they had been so bitter upon sampling she thought they might well be poisonous. Red fruit often is in the tropics—the color a warning to predators not to eat them.

Contrary to what many think, the rainforest is not a cornucopia with bananas hanging off every branch. What she would give for a banana right now! About two tablespoons remained of her water and she drank it. She could find more.

Alicia cast her eyes up to the heavy cloud cover between the canopy branches. Was it cloudy down in the rainforest too? Probably. She could not endure another night. She could not do it.

What was George doing? Had Paco alerted authorities or called the Carvallos? It wouldn't help, so she hoped not. No one could find her in the dense immensity of the forest. Either she got herself out or…not.

Alicia thought again about her itinerant childhood and the nannies who raised her in four different countries. She was too young to remember the first in Persia and could hardly remember Ingrid in Germany, but the one in Peru had been her favorite. In retrospect, Conchita must have been only a teenager herself.

Alicia had not seen her younger brother, Thomas, in fourteen years. Since she had moved here. Conchita had called him Tomasito. It would be nice to talk to him again. Their parents had led busy lives. Striving to be well-behaved children in a formal household had bound the two siblings together. She had looked out for him and he had looked up to her. They had been close growing up, but had grown apart as teenagers and then Alicia had gone to college.

She had written him after George was born and he had replied that he was applying at universities. That was the last letter she had from him. Did he go to the University of Virginia? She imagined him as a teenager, but he could be married by now—no, her mother would have told her that. Surely she'd be invited to her brother's wedding. She should call Thomas, but didn't know how. She would write him. Someday she could go to his wedding.

Her parents would shake their heads if they could see her now. They would think this was a silly way to die. That she'd thrown her life away coming back to Colombia and getting pregnant and now brought this perdition on herself. An aborted life.

Who would miss her other than George? Really miss her, a year from now. Peter? George was the one who had a right to be angry with her. She felt a deep penetrating remorse.

My poor George, she thought. Who would love him like she did? Would Jorge take as good care of him? She honestly didn't think so. Jorge loved him, but would be distracted by his new family. For some reason she pictured her son as he was ten years ago. Little George with his chocolaty curls and sweet smile. And then she thought of Peter in the hospital ordering the nurses around the day George was born. That must have been when she fell in love with him.

A hummingbird hovered near a tiny flower and inserted its delicate beak into the funnel formed by the fused petals. Its wings whirred like a helicopter blade — so fast she could see and hear the motion but not the wings themselves. Her eyes closed.

Wouldn't it be nice if Peter could come rescue her in his helicopter? She imagined him wrapping her in a warm blanket and lying next to her while she slept for hours on end. Safe and warm with plenty to eat, she'd wake to the aroma of hot coffee.

She decided that if and when she got out of here, she would join Peter wherever he was. She had avoided making a choice because she wanted things the way they were, but that was not going to happen. She had vowed never to move again, never to leave the nest she'd feathered at Las Nubes. But by not making a conscious choice she was allowing things to happen without her. Happen to her, just so she could stay. She had tried to stop time with Jorge and now again with Peter. It would be a shallow life here without him. George was moving along in his life and she had to as well. It is the people that matter more in your life than the place.

Peter was gone and if she wanted him she had to go to him. It was simple, really. Why had she needed all those weeks to think about it? It was very clear. It felt so good to have made the decision. What would life be like in New Mexico? Totally different...unlike any place she had ever been. But it would be home because the three of them would be together. She began looking forward to it. She wished she could run to a phone right now and tell Peter. She smiled at the thought, and the energy of the notion ran through her. She sent it out in the world—a telepathic message for him to intercept.

She dozed and dreamed she was swimming in the warm Caribbean, slicing soundlessly through the aquamarine water. She somersaulted in the sea like a dolphin among colorful, tropical fish. Such a feeling of freedom. Like being a bird in flight—better perhaps.

She heard birds calling to each other. How noisy the forest could be! She listened to the sounds, her head resting on her knees. She imagined a palm seedling taking off, the sounds of plants growing. She opened her eyes and saw a gorgeously colored butterfly land near her, but it failed to delight her. She was numb to pain and pleasure.

A small troop of capuchin monkeys watched the strange prostrate woman and chattered to each other. An army of leaf cutter ants marched on a trail wider than a man's hand. Had they made this trail with their little feet over years and generations? Did they keep it mowed with their mandibles? Truly amazing. Staring, for a moment she forgot she was lost.

If this ant trail had been here earlier she would have noticed it. She was no longer sitting on the huge root, but on her haunches with arms folded on mud-caked knees, surrounded by a ferns, vines and mosses. When had she moved? How far had she walked?

I'm getting punch drunk, she thought, her mind foggy and dazed.

But she continued to stare, mesmerized by the ants carrying huge burdens of leaf-pieces. The afternoon was passing but she was hardly aware of it. Every ounce of energy depleted, she sat despondent and raised the canteen to her mouth before remembering it was empty. It hardly mattered now. Alicia kicked the canteen away as if it had betrayed her.

Somewhere in the distance, she heard a murmuring, like a crowd of people whispering. She got up quickly and followed the sound. For a moment she thought she must be near some workers or a party of people. Perhaps she had even come upon Escondido! Nonsense. Wishful thinking. It must be the wind up in the trees, she told herself, but the wind above was a mere breeze barely swaying the boughs. Just the usual creaking branches and jungle sounds.

"*Hola?*" she called. And then louder, "*HOLA!*"

Nothing. She closed her eyes to concentrate on her hearing, and the murmuring continued. She struggled through the vegetation, and there through the trees she spotted a small stream. Reinvigorated by excitement she rushed toward it.

A murmuring brook, she thought with glee as she cupped her hands and splashed her face. The notion of typhoid briefly crossed her mind from years of caution. Well, hopefully no one lived upstream to pollute the water...and she didn't care anyway. The stream tasted cool and delicious after the meager drops she'd had throughout the day, mostly from the drip tips of leaves. She was renewed by the hope of salvation and moved as quickly as possible. Within twenty minutes the stream was joined by another rivulet and she pushed onwards.

As shadows lengthened there was another bit of good fortune. Lying on a clump of damp moss was a twig laden with some sort of bruised fruit. Alicia tore open the discolored peel with her teeth to find a pale melon-colored flesh. The fruit showed signs of decay, but not in the least particular at the moment, she chewed every last stringy morsel off each seed.

She felt almost smug until she realized it would soon be dusk. She no longer had the machete Paco had given her, nor her notebook. She needed the machete, but somewhere in the recesses of her mind she felt the notebook was a greater loss, especially if she was leaving Las Nubes. She had never realized how dear it was to her. A fulfillment no one else ever saw or appreciated. The work in it was an accomplishment, a part of her. It would have been a comfort to take it out years hence and look at her drawings, her notes and remember each experience.

Ah well. Her first sketchbook was still at home. Home. She saw the house as it looked in the early evening, with the lights glowing from within, a warm, safe and cozy place. She had to get out of here.

Forcing herself up, Alicia continued along the creek, demanding stamina she did not feel, until darkness again began to encroach. The trees dripped in the heavy mist and the gray sky disappeared between the upper branches. It was only five o'clock but it was already getting dark under the trees.

Alicia sat in a daze for a long while, barely able to fathom spending another night in these deplorable conditions. She'd found something to eat, yet her stomach growled in the void inside of her. It had been a meager meal. She began to cry and then to sob for a long while until, completely drained, she fell asleep in a stupor. She woke once with bugs crawling on her and could feel more welts where she had been bitten. Her body shrieked with itching, but she went back to sleep from pure exhaustion.

The next day she dreamed someone brought her a cup — or gourd — of water and something to eat that tasted like bread fruit. It was part of the helicopter dream. She was back in the rainforest with Peter all those years ago, only instead of offering the Indians food, they were feeding her.

They stared at her — a curiosity — as she'd once watched them, and whispered among themselves. Some were dressed in loin cloths and leaned on blowguns, or carried bows. A short man patted her as if she were a child and taking her by the elbow, helped her stand.

There was another strange sound she had never heard — or couldn't place. She didn't care. She closed her eyes, anesthetized, and imagined herself on her great uncle's farm in Virginia. There were old wooden fences and tall grass with wildflowers…black-eyed Susans. There was a horse in the pasture and cows.

Cows! She had heard a cow moo and the sound of a bell. Her eyes flew open, but she was still in the cloud forest. It started raining hard and another ant colony scurried for shelter. Great drops pelted her. She felt someone give her a gentle nudge, but when she turned around all she could see through her tired, swollen eyes was the rain and the forest.

There it was again—a cow bell. If she had any energy she would have laughed, smiled at least, or cried, but there was nothing left. She stood drunkenly and began floundering in the direction the sound had come from. She tripped and lay trembling, sprawled against a slimy log. She waited, holding her breath, until she heard the bell tinkling again over the torrential rain.

Then she saw spindly new growth and knew she was at the edge of a familiar clearing. The cow belonged to Paco's grandmother. Roused by the thrill of deliverance she stumbled feverishly through the downpour, until just down the hill, she spied the wood cabin the old lady lived in. Alicia dropped to her knees and raised her face to the deluge, her arms dangled at her sides. Anyone who saw her with her eyes squeezed painfully shut and her mouth open might mistake the expression of gratitude and relief for anguish instead of jubilation. So extreme, so acute was her emotion. Tears mixed with raindrops on her face.

Alicia was not religious but her limp hand made the sign of the cross on her chest. She had lived long enough in Catholic countries to subconsciously absorb this gesture of gratitude and grace.

Eventually she staggered onto the step and almost collapsed again as Soledad Quiros, clasping her shawl with one hand, opened the door.

"*Madre de Dios!*" the woman crossed her own breast and reached for Alicia, "*Mi'ja*, they have been here looking for you!"

Weak though she was, she held onto George for dear life — embracing all of them — while the yellow dog tried to jump like a youthful pup for her attention. George, Carmen, Paco, Humberto — she loved them all dearly. Yes, you too Old Yeller, she thought.

Alicia just wanted to eat and sleep, but Carmen forced her into the bathtub and helped her bathe. Carmen was ten years older than she and, Alicia realized, sometimes a motherly figure to her. How strong she was, so healthy!

"*Mi doñita*," Carmen murmured squeezing her hand.

"You haven't called me that in a long time."

She was safe and clean now in her own bedroom. A pitcher of cool water stood on the bedside table.

"I want to tell you something I didn't really realize before," Alicia mumbled, clinging to Carmen's hand with both of her own.

"That you shouldn't be wandering around the jungle? I tried to tell you that!"

"No. Carmen, listen to me. I realize...that you're the best friend I've ever had."

Carmen smiled and patted her some more, making light of the declaration. But she was pleased. Pleased—and amused—because Alicia was so tired she seemed as if she had been drinking. Nonetheless she nodded slowly, deliberately, as if she had never thought of their relationship that way either. She stood up.

"Here's your notebook," Carmen said laying it on the bedside table.

Alicia blinked, confused, and a weak smile played on her face, "Where did you find it?"

"On the back porch by the storage shed, where you left it. Your machete too."

"That's not possible. I lost them yesterday."

"Well someone put them there. The paper is all wet though."

Alicia shook her head in vague wonder, "It was the Indians."

"What Indians?"

"The ones who made the trail Peter found. The ones who took our rice and potatoes." The Indians had not been a dream. Someone had given her food and water and probably led her to the clearing.

George was at the door, checking on her. Carmen glanced at him as if to say, she's not making any sense.

Someone had saved her life. Alicia took it as a sign to embrace her new life, as she had the old. She thought she was clinging to the present but it was the past she was trying to hold onto, and that was not possible. The past was gone. But it was a wonderful thing to move forward. People matter more than places.

"I'm so grateful...so happy," she murmured. Her eyes were closed and a faint smile on her lips as she drifted off into the bliss of sleep.

———————

No alien land in all the world has any deep, strong charm for me but that one, no other land could so longingly and so beseechingly haunt me, sleeping and waking, through half a lifetime, as that one has done. Other things leave me, but it abides...other things change, but it remains the same....in my nostrils still lives the breath of flowers that perished twenty years ago.

Mark Twain (on Hawaii)

EPILOGUE

Our lives changed radically. I went to high school — and university — in New Mexico. It was quite a culture shock after Las Nubes. I was hesitant to leave my country, and I'm sure my mother was too, but it was the right decision in the long run.

Peter has worked all over the world and Mami has followed him with her sketchbook. While he is out looking for precious metals in the rocks, she studies the flora and fauna in Africa or Honduras or wherever they are at the moment.

My parents were pleased when I was accepted at the University of Virginia for graduate school and my mother was ecstatic when I got a job at the Ronaer Agricultural Institute in Panama. I work on sustainable rain forest produce...bananas, coffee, cacao. Mami often visits me and spends her days happily roaming the rainforest.

On her first trip she presented me with the notebooks she compiled during our life at Las Nubes. They represent almost fifteen years of tropical research in Colombia and are also a work of art. I showed them to my boss, Dr. Matt Lerner, who was impressed and suggested they be published. I am doing this for her as a surprise — deleting her personal entries, as she is a private person. Her sketches and notes represent a valuable contribution to science, and I have a feeling they will be reproduced and yield a few royalties for her.

Matt and I suspected from her drawings and notes that the orchid she once found was previously undiscovered — as are most rain forest species, even today. It is now officially named *Cattelya aliciana*. Two colleagues want to study the sketches and notes to name other species hereto unknown, or if previously described by other workers, give their proper names and record such data as range and occurrence.

Papi has come to visit too and I like to return to Colombia, but Lucila, my wife, discourages me. The country has been at war with both the Marxist guerillas and left wing paramilitary for decades, but the violence since the 70's escalated with the drug trade.

In 1989 President Galan was assassinated and two presidential candidates killed. After a friend of tia Marta's was kidnapped and killed, she was afraid to leave the house for a while. In 2002, anti-corruption candidate Ingrid Betancourt was kidnapped by the FARC and rescued only after six years in captivity. Such threats have diminished significantly, but people are still cautious, especially in rural areas.

Nonetheless, there are hopeful signs of tranquility in recent years. In 2012 the Colombian congress approved the terms of a possible peace negotiation with guerrilla groups.

There is a new road to the finca and the all-day trip has been reduced to three or four hours. They have electricity now, and a telephone, though it is not the same without my mother and Carmen. The house seems empty — devoid of the vases once filled with fragrant flowers — and quiet with just Humberto and his wife, Patricia, living there.

The old garden is so overgrown only a trace of it remains. Here and there calla lilies poke up in the wild growth. The courtyard and veranda, once overflowing with fuchsias and ferns in Mami's many pots, are mostly empty or full of weeds.

They have one of those dogs one sees in Latin America, a tan-yellow, medium size mutt. Hardly a replacement for Old Yeller. He was my dog and it broke my heart to leave him, but he was old and practically crippled with arthritis by then.

Berto was like a brother to me and we remain close. He was one of the first in Escondido to finish high school and is the manager of Las Nubes, well paid for what Mami once did. He seems content and Carmen is proud of him, with good reason. It would be hard to find a competent manager to live there, so the family is lucky to have him. Miguel, Paco's son, works there too. He will be the foreman when his father retires, keeping the job in the family.

Carmen became the cook at the Restaurante Escondido — the one next to the González's store. The "Soda," as we used to call it, has become popular. People detour from the highway just to eat the specialties there — Carmen's "foreign" food. She has grown plump and gray, but is as sassy as ever. She still goes barefoot — to Berto's dismay.

Her comment years ago when Mami asked her if she wanted to come live in New Mexico was, "Then I would have to wear shoes!" Many *colombianos* would've jump at a chance to move to the States, but she enjoys her life, her friends and family and does not want to leave. She has consented to come for a visit. Meanwhile my mother writes her, but has to be content with Berto's replies.

Carmen learned how to read and write enough to get on in the world, but says she finds it tedious. They have a monthly date to talk on the phone and keep it religiously. They sound like a couple of girls laughing with each other.

The occasional scientist or gourmet coffee specialist still drop by the finca to learn about sustainable coffee growing. The coffee has rebounded with vigor from the ceniza years, but the business is always at the fickle mercy of politics, weather and the market.

My mother returned to Colombia just once, to visit Carmen. The change — which in truth was occurring while we lived there, although we were blissfully unaware — saddened her. She says a part of her heart remains there, but she wants to remember it the way it was. When we speak of our life there, she smiles faintly and gets a faraway look in her eyes.

George Carvallo Collier
San Luis, Panama
January 2013